HD JUN 2016

D0450762

The Committee

HD JUN 2016

The Committee

Terry E. Hill

www.urbanbooks.net

Urban Books, LLC
97 N18th Street
Wyandanch, NY 11798

The Committee Copyright © 2016 Terry E. Hill

All rights reserved. No part of this book may be reproduced in any form or by any means without prior consent of the Publisher, except brief quotes used in reviews.

ISBN 13: 978-1-62286-722-6
ISBN 10: 1-62286-722-X

First Mass Market Printing January 2016
Printed in the United States of America

10 9 8 7 6 5 4 3 2 1

This is a work of fiction. Any references or similarities to actual events, real people, living or dead, or to real locales are intended to give the novel a sense of reality. Any similarity in other names, characters, places, and incidents is entirely coincidental.

Distributed by Kensington Publishing Corp.
Submit Orders to:
Customer Service
400 Hahn Road
Westminster, MD 21157-4627
Phone: 1-800-733-3000
Fax: 1-800-659-2436

Chapter 1

It was well after midnight. Blue flames in gas lanterns throughout the French Quarter danced like children awake past their bedtime. Puffs of white fog crept down the lanes toward the icy embrace of Lake Pontchartrain. The steady, rhythmic clatter of horses' hooves on the cobblestone road and the scrape of wooden carriage wheels in their wake was all that could be heard.

The carriage came to a rolling halt in front of 543 Rue des Bourbon when the coachman pulled gently on the reins and uttered the command, "Whoa there, whoa!" further shattering the quiet of the night. The two neighing horses trotted anxiously in place until it became apparent they had reached their destination.

The coach sat still for moments while the fog formed a cloudy bed around the wagon wheels. When the door finally swung open, sugar baron Jean-Luc Fantoché extended his patent leather boot and emerged into the night. Dressed in formal evening attire from a night of dinner, theater, and libations at Victorian Lounge in the Columns Hotel, Fantoché was now more than ready for his final stop.

The home was the largest on the street. A short brick path covered with a trellis of dripping lavender wisteria led to the white antebellum mansion. The door opened slowly and Juliette Dacian Adelaide Dupree appeared in the threshold as Fantoché approached.

"You are late," she chided.

"Please forgive me, mon bel amour," he said removing his top hat and lifting her hand to his lips. "The play was longer than I anticipated. Please accept my sincerest apologies."

The couple entered the home filled with Rococo and Gothic Revival furnishings, finely woven Persian rugs, and a patchwork of oil paintings that gave it the distinct air of American aristocracy. Fantoché embraced Juliette passionately and kissed her lips. She quickly pried herself away from the clinging man and entered the parlor with him following close behind. Oil-burning lamps cast quivering shadows throughout the room, and a lone black candle flickered on an oak mantel above a fireplace. A silver chalice cradled the candle with an inscription at the base, "Dans cette flamme brûle le destin de l'homme." *In this flame burns the destiny of man.*

They were greeted by a loud, "Squawk!" from a blue and gold Macaw pacing anxiously from side to side on its perch in a cage at the far corner of the room.

"Quiet, Amadeus. It is only our master," Juliette said sarcastically.

"I've missed you so, ma chérie," he said placing gentle kisses on the nape of her neck. *"I could think of nothing more than your touch the entire day. Your intoxicating scent of lilac. The feel of your soft skin against my cheek."*

Juliette was unimpressed by his poetry. "Do you speak to your wife so affectionately," she asked mockingly, *"or are your empty words reserved for the mistress you come to at ungodly hours of the night?"*

"You are more than my mistress," he said continuing his journey of kisses. *"I love you and only you. She means nothing to me. Your kiss gives me reason to live.* Votre beauté nourrit mon âme."

Juliette was the illegitimate daughter of a French cotton baron and his thirteen-year-old slave. The mingling of French and African blood produced a beauty that was legendary in *New Orleans.* Her strawberry blond hair retained just enough nap to form naturally luxurious curls that cascaded like waterfalls over her shoulders and full breasts. Jade-green eyes devoured men's souls, and her skin shimmered like honey fresh from the hive. She was the exotic Creole jewel countless gentlemen of means and power longed to possess.

"Yes, but you love her money," she said with arms limp at her sides. "I am nothing more to you than your concubine," she goaded. "The whore you come to in the middle of the night and have your filthy way with."

"Please do not say such horrible things, mon amour," he replied painfully. "You are my world."

"Nonsense," she snapped, abruptly pushing him away. "I could be with any man I choose. Men wealthier and more handsome than you . . . and this is how you treat me. Like a common whore."

"I am your servant, Juliette," he said with pleading eyes. "What more will you have me do to prove my love. Shall I buy you more jewels? More gowns from Paris? A mansion more lavish than this? Tell me and I shall do it with joy and great pleasure."

Despite her young age of twenty-five, Juliette was a master of manipulation. She knew the shortest distance to a man's soul and once there, took complete control. For the last eight months, she accepted Fantoché's extravagant symbols of affection and feigned ecstasy when his hulking body pounded into her delicate flesh. She laughed at his feeble attempts at humor and praised his overly simplistic political ramblings. Not because she loved him, or even liked him, but because she had been charged with the seemingly impossible task of making Jean-Luc Fantoché the governor of Louisiana in the coming election of 1852.

Hattie Williams never dreamed she would still be alive today. Her life's motto had always been, "When the Lord decides to take me home, I'll be ready." However, He wasn't ready for her just yet.

The last year took a heavy toll on her once-sturdy body. Hattie saw her beloved pastor, Hezekiah Cleaveland, gunned down in the pulpit of her church. She wept at his graveside as they lowered the mahogany coffin into the ground. She also assisted in the home going of his wife, Samantha. The taking of a life would have destroyed a lesser woman, but her soul rested contently in a cradle of peace because she knew it was necessary in order to save other lives.

Hattie's once jet-black hair now gave way to a current of grey. Arthur, the name she affectionately gave the constant gnawing pain in her knee, slowed her once-imposing gait to an unsteady hobble. She stood in the center of her garden, surrounded by a six-foot pink brick fence, with the afternoon sun resting on her shoulders. A wooden cane in one hand and a wicker basket half filled with freshly picked tomatoes in the other. These days she couldn't walk the full distance from the garden to her back door without stopping to steady herself at least once.

This was her second pause on the walk from the back row of the garden to the house. She used moments like this to marvel at the bounty around her. Bursts of yellows, greens, reds, and whites surrounded her like spurts of colorful water from an underground spring. Squash of every variety, bell peppers, cauliflower, a rainbow of heirloom tomatoes, onions, and okra were the precious gifts the soil gave her this year.

Hattie stood with her rubber-soled boots planted firmly in the damp soil. Suddenly, she felt a gentle rumble beneath her feet. She thought it might have been the beginnings of a California earthquake, but quickly realized something more otherworldly was in the works.

The light-headed feeling she always had when God was about to tell her something slowly enveloped her body. She looked toward the house and saw the three-legged stool used when weeding standing at the foot of the steps. There was no way she'd be able to get to it in time. *Lord, couldn't you have waited till I got to my stool?* she thought as the ground continued the gentle quake. *I don't know how long I'm going to be able to stay on my feet.*

Hattie braced her hip against the cane and accepted she may have to stand in the center of the garden for a long time. She was ready, and the ground knew it. The intensity of the tremors steadily increased. Time slowed, and the clock stopped ticking. She was now in God's hands and on His schedule. "Tell me, Lord," she said out loud. Hattie saw her words form a ripple in the thick fog enveloping the entire yard. "I'm here, Lord. Tell me what you want me to . . ."

The ground quaked violently before the last word escaped her lips. She took a measured step backward to prevent herself from falling into the crevice forming only a few feet away. The front two rows of precious collard greens slid into the pit as the gaping hole grew wider. Next went an entire row of snap beans tied to wooden trellises with white string.

"Yea though I walk through the valley of the shadow of death, I will fear no evil," Hattie firmly recited, undaunted by the devastation to her garden and the danger to herself. "Thy rod and thy staff they comfort me." Hattie was now in full warrior mode. No hint of Arthur, and no sign of fear. She forgot the cane and basket in her hand. To her, they felt like the cold steel of a shield and sword. She was ready for whatever might leap from the pit.

The rumbling stopped, and the ground slowly steadied as suddenly as it started. Hattie stood only feet away from the cavernous hole. She looked down and only saw blackness. The snap beans and collard greens were gone. All that was left was the bottomless void. She stood poised at the edge knowing this was not the end. Something was stirring down there. She sensed it in her bones. Something evil and powerful. Something she would be required to do battle with.

Hattie stood beyond the reach of time. There was no before or after. There was only the now, and her senses were operating at their peak. She was prepared to see, hear, smell, and even touch whatever emerged from the black hole.

Then she saw them. A pair of glowing brown eyes appeared in the darkness as if they were switched on like a lightbulb. They looked directly at her. She didn't feel threatened. They looked at her with a silent plea. *Help me.*

The eyes slowly rose to the surface. Hattie squinted to see who they belonged to. There was something familiar. A gentleness she'd felt before. A kindness she had encountered in the not-so-distant past.

"Who are you?" Hattie said to the eyes as they crept closer. "What do you want from me?"

There was no response. Hattie pressed on. "In the name of Jesus, I command you to reveal yourself." Hattie gripped the cane and basket tighter. "Tell me why you're here."

Then she heard it. "Help me," came the weak reply to her command. "Please, help me." The words echoed in the hollow of the crater.

Hattie recognized the voice. She heard it again. "Please help me before they . . ." The voice trailed off, but the eyes continued rising.

"Before they *what?*" Hattie asked firmly.

A hand slowly sliced through the darkness and reached toward Hattie. She didn't move as the disembodied eyes and hand continued rising. Hattie was ready to reach down to the hand, but first she insisted on confirming to whom it belonged.

"I will help you because God sent you to me for a reason, but first you have to tell me who you are. Say your name!"

The eyes and hand were almost level to the ground when Hattie finally saw the face. It was Gideon Truman. "Gideon, is that you?" Hattie called out.

"Help me, Hattie." The plea became urgent as if he were being chased. "Help me, please," came again as she scrambled to the edge of the hole, "before they . . ."

Hattie dropped the basket and reached forward. "Give me your hand, baby," she said, bending to the edge of the abyss. "I've got you, Gideon. Just give me your hand."

Gideon's fingertips were only inches from Hattie's open palm. She stretched further and struggled to keep her balance with the cane. Then, suddenly, a massive howl erupted from the depths of the pit. The earth began to shake again. Hattie's feet slipped on the edge as the dirt gave way beneath her.

"Help me. Please help me. It's here. Don't let it take me," came Gideon's frantic plea.

"You're almost out, baby," Hattie said as she neared the limit of her reach. "Take my hand. You can do it."

The terrifying wails from the bottom of the pit continued as the two struggled to make contact.

"I can't reach you!" Gideon cried out.

"Yes, you can. Just a little further."

Hattie overestimated the strength of her knee and lost her balance. She tittered on the edge with no thought for her own safety. "Just another inch. You can make it."

Their hands finally met. Hattie grabbed Gideon with a grip strong enough to transform a lump of coal into a diamond. She planted her heels into the ground and struggled to lift Gideon from the darkness. She felt something tug his body from the opposite direction. The horrifying howl continued as she jerked harder, but her strength was matched measure-for-measure by the powerful force pulling in the opposite direction. It was an evil she had never before encountered. Pure and ancient. An evil so dark she questioned her ability to fight it off. Hattie knew she was in the throes of battle for Gideon's life with the ungodly force.

"I can't hold on. It's too powerful," Gideon cried out. "Let go, Hattie, or it will pull you in with me!"

"Don't let go, Gideon. I won't let it take—"

Before Hattie could complete the sentence, her feet slid in the crumbling earth and Gideon's hand slipped from her grasp. She fell and landed on her back between the rows of bell peppers and squash, sending her cane sailing behind her. She saw Gideon descend into the darkness and scrambled back to the hole.

"Gideon!" she cried out. "Don't go. I'm here. Don't go."

But it was too late. The crater began to close as she crawled to the edge, and Gideon's eyes quickly vanished. The only thing remaining was blackness and the faint echo of the howl.

Hattie was now on her hands and knees at the spot where the hole had been. She cried while digging into the dirt, slowly accepting it was too late. Hattie sobbed into the earth, breathless with perspiration dripping from her brow.

"Not again, Lord," she said through tears. "Don't let it happen again."

Hattie's watch began to tick once again. The second hand resumed its normal course. The fog lifted and neatly hoed rows of greens, beans, and peppers surrounded her like soldiers standing guard over a wounded warrior.

The council chamber at Los Angeles City Hall was filled to capacity. Hundreds more squeezed into the balcony, and the overflow crowd in the halls pressed toward the massive double doors, each taking turns trying to convince the security guard they were important enough to enter the auditorium.

The drone of a thousand conversations drifted to the cathedral ceiling and bounced off the marble walls. A gaggle of photographers and reporters sat on the floor in front of the podium beneath the eye line of the audience. Two 300-inch monitors hung to the left and right of center stage, each beaming the live image of the empty dais.

It was almost 6:00 p.m. The room grew anxious in anticipation of the mayor's entrance. The side door opened and Mayor Camille Ernestine Hardaway entered the room just as the walls threatened to vibrate from the chatter.

The babble of a thousand words swirling in the air suddenly crashed to the floor the moment she set foot in the room. Within seconds, the only sound heard were Camille's red Prada soles walking across the 100-year-old maple wood floor toward center stage. As usual, Camille took full control simply by entering the room. Was it because she was stunning? Or was it the way her perfectly formed five-feet-nine-inch body effortlessly sliced through the air like a shard of light on a starless night. Maybe it was the chilling black Yves St. Laurent blazer and skirt, which appeared to have been sewn directly onto her body. A white ruffled collar and cuffs provided the perfect accent for the masterfully crafted suit.

Whatever the cause, Camille was in control long before she made eye contact with anyone in the room. She planted her feet confidently behind the lectern and flashed the smile that ruled the city. The audience stood reverently and applauded as cameras from the front of the room flashed furiously to capture every glint of her white smile, shimmering hair, and glistening eyes.

Camille humbly acknowledged the recognition with a nod and wave as she scanned the room with keen eyes storing every detail for future use. A mane of silky black hair framed a face far too beautiful for the rough-and-tumble world of big-city politics. Her flawless skin glowed like amber in the halo of camera flashes.

Camille allowed the ovation to run its course before she spoke. The audience took their cue and returned silently to their seats as she readied her lips to speak.

"Good evening, everyone, and thank you for joining me in my sixth State of the City address," were the first words she spoke. "I am honored to serve as the forty-third mayor of Los Angeles; a world-renowned international city that celebrates diversity and leads the way in job creation, innovation, education, health care, and the environment for our future generations."

Her sensuous tone coated the room like a layer of warm honey. Seductive undercurrents lulled even her most ardent enemies into a suspended state of unwilling submission.

Camille was born less than two miles from where she now stood. Adopted at birth by two doting parents who, from the moment they laid eyes on her, believed she was destined for greatness. No one was surprised when her IQ tested at 158 in high school. Her parents mortgaged their home to put her through college. She received an undergraduate degree in political science from UCLA in three years and a Juris Doctor from Harvard before turning twenty-four. She effortlessly passed the California Bar exam on her first attempt. There was no other place in the world she could be at this moment, other than standing center stage at city hall.

"Greetings to the president of the city council, Salvador Alvarez, and to all the members of the city council. Greetings to the many city commissioners, elected officials, department heads, and to all our honored guests here tonight."

Camille masterfully scanned the room as she spoke without notes or teleprompter. She made direct eye contact with someone in the room with every sentence. All present would have their very own two-second private audience with the mayor before the end of her State of the City address.

"At the dawn of this new year, and the third year of my second term, the state of our great city is still vital and strong. As strong financially and economically as we have ever been in our history.

"Nevertheless, we must also recognize there are still fractures in the strong foundation we have built, tears in the social fabric that, if we do not attend to with all our energies, will erode that foundation and reverse our dramatic progress."

Camille methodically increased the rate she spoke. The words soon took on the cadence of a learned Baptist preacher crossed with a seasoned politician on a winning campaign.

"Jobs and confidence are back, but our economic recovery has still left thousands of people behind.

"Our neighborhoods are revitalized and new construction is all around us, but some still look to the future, anxiously, and wonder whether there's room for them in a changing Los Angeles."

Sheridan Hardaway sat quietly in a front row, aisle seat, with fingers intertwined at his chin and legs crossed at the knee. The tip of his Gucci loafer pointed directly up at his wife and the black Armani suit wrapping his six foot four frame looked as dashing sitting as it did when he stood.

For many in the room it was difficult to decide who to look at . . . the beautiful charismatic mayor at center stage or her painfully handsome husband, with hair like luscious black whipped cream only yards away.

"Too many of our residents, people who work hard and make a decent wage, men and women squarely in the middle class, grow frustrated, as the city becomes ever more expensive and their dream of starting a family or owning a home falls further out of reach.

"This rising cost of living, the financial squeeze on our city's working- and middle-class families—these are the fundamental challenges of our time, not just for our city, but for great cities around the world."

Tony Christopoulos, the mayor's chief of staff, recited the speech word-for-word along with Camille in his head. "*And to sustain our economic recovery and this renewed confidence in our city, we must confront these challenges of affordability directly, in the Los Angeles way, big-hearted, but clearheaded."* He knew every word . . . because he wrote it.

He beamed with a silent pride in the seat next to Sheridan. His eloquent words delivered by such a ravishing and influential mouthpiece was more than the twenty-nine-year-old Harvard graduate from Dowagiac, Michigan, could have ever imagined happening in his life. Camille liked to surround herself with beautiful things, and Tony was no exception. His brilliant analytical mind alone was justification enough to trust such a young man with the important position, but his Abercrombie & Fitch body and face made it impossible for her to select any other candidate as her number one man. She trusted him with her political life.

Camille continued after another raucous ovation following her last proclamation. "One of the fundamental responsibilities of any mayor is ensuring public safety. Los Angeles remains one of the safest big cities in America. Thank you, Police Chief Nettles, Adult Probation Chief Wasserman, Juvenile Probation Chief Fullerman, and District Attorney Hansel Patterson.

"Homicides are down 30 percent from last year, among the lowest in forty years, with shootings half of what they were ten years ago. But we can do better.

"With new police and fire academies made possible by our economic recovery, we'll hire and train more first responders, from 911 dispatch operators to firefighters to police officers. Soon you'll see more officers walking a neighborhood beat, from Wilshire Boulevard to Third Street to the South Central."

Camille's glance rested an extra second on one of the reporters in the faceless clutter at the front of the room. She recognized Gideon Truman from his network news program. *What is the national media doing here?* she silently considered between promises of improved public transportation and a new baseball stadium. *That's curious.* Their eyes locked in the span of a few seconds. The two most influential people in the room exchanged an imperceptible acknowledgment of each other's powerful impact on the world.

"The new Doberman Stadium will be a multiuse indoor 175,000-seat arena," Camille continued. "It will house our beloved Los Angeles Doberman Baseball franchise, which we all lovingly refer to as 'The Dobers,' becoming the new home of the Dobers who have called Los Angeles their home since 1958. The project will be financed privately, and the land will be purchased by the city of Los Angeles. The team would be given a sixty-six-year lease for the arena."

Camille spoke for exactly one hour, six minutes, and twenty-two seconds, stopping only to allow applause following every touted accomplishment and proposed initiative. The audience collectively decided to remain on their feet at the fifty-two-minute mark. There was no reason to sit. The room and every person watching the live feed from the comfort of their home was now more in love with Camille than they were on the day they cast an avalanche of votes ranking her the U.S mayor with the highest-winning margins for two consecutive terms.

Camille stepped from behind the podium and walked to the edge of the stage headfirst into a storm of applause and cheers at the climactic conclusion. She went from one end of the stage to the other, blowing kisses to crowd and flashing the victory sign. She was a rock star and, thanks to Gideon Truman, the entire country was now watching.

The lobby at city hall quickly filled with the same faces that Camille had just shared her vision for the future of the city with. Waiters in cinched vests and ties pirouetted among the crowd balancing trays of champagne, sparkling water, and assorted hors d'oeuvres. A circle of two-story marble pillars held a mosaic concaved ceiling arched over the who's-who of the city. State and local politicians, deep-pocket Democratic donors, and corporate power brokers oozed from every crack in the Italian tiled floor. The mood was festive, and the smell of success and power was in the air. Camille delivered the speech that could easily catapult her to the governor's mansion, and everyone present knew it.

She was surrounded by a squadron of reporters, each clamoring for her attention.

"Mayor Hardaway, you've had another amazing year," one shouted over the crowd. "What do you say to the critics who said you didn't have enough political experience to run a city the size of Los Angeles?"

The question caught Camille's attention. She deemed it worthy of a response. "I'd say the facts prove they were wrong. Under my leadership Los Angeles has fully recovered from one of the worst economic downturns since the Great Depression and is now more vital and stronger financially and economically than we have ever been in our history," she replied immodestly.

"You have one year left until you're termed out," another reporter shouted from the three-deep circle around her. "What are your plans after you leave office?"

Another question warranting her attention. "I haven't thought that far ahead. I know whatever I'll do, it will be in the service of the people of this great city and state."

The reporters continued peppering Camille with questions. "Do you have plans to run for governor?" a bold member of the press asked. Another called out, "Have you considered running for senator?" She took a step toward them and the corps parted as she politely replied, "As I said, I haven't decided yet. Now if you will excuse me, ladies and gentlemen, I really must circulate. I'm neglecting my guests."

Camille moved from circle to circle in the room. She shook hands, signed autographs, and posed for selfies. It was her night, and she was in her element. She worked the room with the finesse and grace of a ballerina. A thousand eyes followed her every move. All observed and appreciated each toss of her hair and calculated flash of her smile.

Gideon Truman was no exception. He had interviewed presidents, A-list celebrities, two popes, and international dignitaries, but there was something unusual about Camille Hardaway. He didn't know exactly what. *She is undeniably beautiful,* he thought as he watched her from across the lobby. *But that isn't it.*

His keen reporter eyes followed her as she transitioned from one conversation to the next, leaving no one feeling snubbed or dismissed. Camille knew how and when to make enemies, but tonight wasn't the time. It was a time to shine and to bask in the glory of her successes.

The longer Gideon watched her, the more uneasy he grew. His stomach began to gurgle as he found himself transfixed by her every move. He couldn't take his eyes away, even when he tried. *There's something not right about that woman,* he concluded as her maneuvers brought her only three feet away. The gurgle in his gut escalated to a gentle rumble.

Camille abruptly turned on her heel and looked him directly in the eye before he could look away. "If you will excuse me," she said politely to a group of four men and one woman standing near him. "We have a celebrity with us tonight, and I wouldn't be a good mayor if I didn't pay my respects."

Camille walked to Gideon with an extended hand. "Mr. Truman," she said reaching for the hand still hanging at his side. Her rapid approach caught him unprepared. "To what do we owe the honor of having a reporter of your caliber here tonight? I hope I haven't done anything to put me under your microscope," she said with wicked smile.

Gideon regained his composure and confirmed she was even more beautiful at close range. "Not at all," he said donning his most shallow party smile. "My producer suggested I come tonight. She thought there might be a big story here."

"Big story?" she asked coyly. "Only if you think your national audience is interested in potholes and the homeless."

Gideon responded with a laugh. "No, but they might be interested in the woman who could be the first female governor of California."

"Tell your producer she shouldn't believe everything in the *Los Angeles Times*. That's a rumor they've never bothered to confirm with me."

"Well, are you running?" he boldly asked, wiping the painted smile from his face.

"I like you, Mr. Truman—"

"Please call me Gideon," he interrupted.

"I like you, Gideon, so I'll make you a promise. If I do decide to run for governor, you'll be the first to know."

"Some say it's inevitable and you've already amassed a substantial war chest."

"Maybe . . . or maybe not, but I'm certainly not prepared to confirm or deny anything tonight."

"Then what can you confirm or deny tonight?" he pressed gently.

"Handsome and persistent. I like that in a man. All right, Mr. Tru . . . Gideon. I'll give you a few hints. I have one year left in my last possible term as mayor. I'm still young. My approval ratings are off the charts, and my profile is apparently high enough to get your attention. You're the investigative reporter. Those are the clues; now let's see if you can solve the mystery."

Before Gideon could respond, Tony Christopoulos approached Camille from behind. "Excuse me, Mrs. Mayor," he said gently touching her arm, "the senator has to leave, and she asked if you would be available to take a picture with her."

"Of course," Camille said without turning around. "Gideon, this is my chief of staff, Tony Christopoulos. Tony, I'm sure you know Gideon Truman."

Gideon was able to tear his eyes from Camille for the first time since she approached him. Tony and Gideon exchanged a familiar glance. One normally reserved for chance encounters at bars on the West Side of town.

"I haven't had the pleasure of meeting Mr. Truman before," Tony said, extending his hand. "But I certainly know who you are. Loved your coverage of Mandela."

"Thank you. He was a great man," Gideon said while admiring Tony's penetrating brown eyes crowned by thick jet-black eyebrows. *Mediterranean and stunning. She does like to surround herself with beautiful men,* he thought as he recalled the image of the handsome Sheridan Hardaway on the front row.

"I was fortunate enough to have the opportunity to interview President Mandela shortly before he died," Gideon continued. "He changed the world."

Tony pried his eyes away from Gideon. "Mrs. Mayor, I'm sorry to take you away, but the senator is waiting."

"Remember what I promised," Camille said as she turned to leave. "You'll be the first to know."

Tony directed her through the crowd, gently brushing aside a gauntlet of congratulators and requests for selfies with a polite, "I'm sorry, but I promise to bring her right back."

When they reached a clearing in the crowd, Camille whispered, "He couldn't take his eyes off me the entire night."

"Who?" Tony asked cautiously.

"Gideon Truman. If I weren't a married woman . . ."

Tony laughed out loud. "You and most of the people in this room. He's gorgeous. But I suspect, Mrs. Mayor, I might be more his type than you."

"You're joking," she said with a questioning smile.

"Rumor has it he has a boy toy stashed away in his Hollywood Hills home."

"Too bad," she said dismissively. "All the handsome ones are either married, gay, or crooks. Oh well, I have Sheridan, so I shouldn't complain."

"Yes, Mrs. Mayor," Tony replied looking straight-ahead. "You do have Sheridan."

"Did you see her tonight?"

"She was spectacular. Almost too good to be true."

"I think we might have a winner."

"Have we checked out her husband yet?"

"Got the boys on it now."

A half-smoked cigarette smoldered, leaving a ghostly trail of ash where the cigarette had been. The dimly lit room had an ethereal glow from the smoke as the man behind the large oak desk spoke on the telephone.

The only light in the room came from a seventy-five-inch screen showing a live feed of Camille Hardaway charming the crowd thousands of miles away in the lobby at city hall. The unknown camera operator stealthily captured images of the mayor seen only in this smoky room, on this screen, and by this singular viewer.

"Good. We need to know everything about him. Who he's fucking. Who, if anyone, is fucking him. Finances, drugs, prostitutes, illegitimate children, lies on his résumé dating back to his first job, boxers or briefs, everything. With this one, I even want to know who his parents are fucking. Good-looking guys like him always have a shitload of secrets. Even the most seemingly insignificant indiscretion could derail the entire plan."

"Don't get ahead of the process. It isn't a plan yet. We're only at the exploratory stage."

"I understand, but I think the country is finally ready for a Camille Hardaway."

"No argument here. The real question is, is Camille Hardaway ready for the country?"

"My gut tells me she is."

"Yes, but remember, your gut has been wrong before."

"Should have listened to you on G. W., but I can't always be right."

"Wish you'd stop beating yourself up about that. We all agreed he was the man for the job."

"And he fucked us royally."

"At least our new boy is making up for it."

"Yea, but it cost him his entire first term. And he's still cleaning up the mess."

"He got us through the worst of the economic crisis."

"Barely."

"We got health-care reform. We're out of Iraq. So it hasn't been all bad."

"Speaking of which, what does he think of her?"

"He said he wants some alone time with her before she hits the national stage."

"Spoken like a true president," the caller said with a slight chuckle. "That can certainly be arranged."

"When will we get the report on her husband?"

"Should be ready in a few weeks. In the meantime, we've got two boys following him to see what a week in the life of Sheridan Hardaway looks like."

"Good."

The surging of an engine roared in the background.

"Where are you?"

"On my jet. Taking off from Long Beach Airport."

"Were you at city hall tonight?"

"I was. Had to see her in person for myself."

"Did you speak with her?"

"Too early for that. Just wanted to see if she lived up to her reputation."

"And?"

"There is no question she has what it takes to be the first black female president of the United States."

"I agree. So now it's up to us to make it happen."

Chapter 2

The black Escalade carrying Camille and Sheridan glided through the streets of Los Angeles. Wilshire Boulevard held remnants of earlier rush-hour traffic. Camille read e-mails on a pad in her lap while Sheridan checked messages on his phone. A series of electronic dings, chimes, and bings bounced off the darkly tinted windows and leather seats as e-mails, phone calls, and text messages arrived on the devices in steady intervals.

The heavily armored limousine floated like a magic carpet propelling the mayor and her husband on a cushion of air through her kingdom. It was one of the safest vehicles in the world. Ballistic proof windows, road tack dispenser, smoke screen system, and electric shocking door handles were just a few of the antikidnap devices the car boasted. After her third death threat and the first kidnap attempt, Sheridan and the head of her security insisted the city invest in the most secured vehicle on the market. Not everyone in the city was ready for a black female mayor, and the death threats proved it.

"You haven't told me what you thought of the speech," Camille said without looking away from the glowing screen.

Sheridan ignored her question and instead asked, "Was that Gideon Truman you were talking to at the reception? What did he want?"

"It was. He thinks I might make a bid for the governor's office," she casually replied.

"So . . . What did you tell him?"

"I told him not to believe everything he reads in the paper."

"Did he ask about your plans for Dober Stadium?" Sheridan impatiently goaded her to say more.

"No. Why would he ask about that?"

"Because it's the biggest project of your entire administration."

"It didn't come up," Camille replied.

"Have you decided on the location yet?" Sheridan asked casually.

"As of now, the top choice is a vacant 110 acres in Playa del Rey. It's perfect beachfront property. Stunning ocean views, close to the freeway and Pacific Coast Highway, and no immediate neighbors to oppose it."

"What about the abandoned shipyard? You seemed hopeful about that site a month ago."

"I got the preliminary assessment from the EPA last week. The shipyard is full of contaminants. Hydrocarbon spillages, solvents, pesticides, you name it. Remediation is estimated to be in the hundreds of millions and that's *before* the first brick is laid. Playa del Rey is the only real option we have at this point."

"Who owns—"

"I don't want to talk about that right now," she said interrupting him midsentence. "You haven't answered my question. What did you think of my speech?"

"Do I even need to tell you?" Sheridan replied with a smile.

"Yes."

"You were . . . OK," he said expressionless.

Camille smiled broadly and playfully slapped Sheridan's arm. "Thanks, asshole."

Sheridan feigned pain. "Ouch," he said massaging his bicep. "That hurt. You don't realize just how strong you are." The reflection in the blacked-out partition separating the driver's cab and the back of the Escalade mimicked their playful exchange.

Camille met Sheridan only seven years earlier at a fundraiser at the Getty Museum days before she was to launch her campaign for mayor. Their already substantial individual magnetism doubled by simply standing together. They were married within six months at the urging of her campaign manager. Sheridan's chiseled frame and devastatingly good looks were the perfect backdrop for Camille's campaign. His presence took the edge off her raw, sensuous power and made her a less-threatening woman for the cameras and skeptical voters.

They were the ultimate power couple—glamorous, beautiful, wealthy, and ruthlessly ambitious. No one dared cross them for fear of losing lucrative city contracts or being banished to political and social exile. No party in the city was worth attending unless they were there. No fundraiser was considered a success if the Hardaways were not present. If the Hardaways sent their regrets, every high-end event planner in the city knew they must immediately change the date to accommodate their schedules.

"Be honest now. Tell me what you really thought."

Sheridan turned off his telephone. The only light in the car came from the pad in Camille's lap and the filtered headlights from cars approaching from the opposite direction. Sheridan tossed his cell phone onto the seat and moved in closer.

"You were magnificent," he said as he moved his lips to hers. "I love you," he said, punctuating each word with a kiss—"more now than ever before."

The most powerful woman in the city could never resist Sheridan's touch. His warm breath on her neck sent a shiver down one side of her body and back up the other. Her lips quivered as he kissed circles around her open, breathless mouth.

"The driver . . ." she warned weakly.

". . . can't see a thing."

"We're almost home. Wait just a few . . ." Her words trailed into a whisper, then a sigh and faded to a sensuous moan. ". . . minutes," was her last breathless word.

Sheridan's powerful hand massaged her trembling thighs and slowly separated them. Camille made a vain attempt at resistance, but the gentle force of his hand coupled with her desire for the pleasure to come made resistance impossible.

The pampered skin of his palm caused her head to spin as it slowly moved up her leg, stopping intermittently at just the right spots to tickle and tease her tender flesh. Sheridan made it his life's mission to learn every inch of her body. He studied her like a map and in record time identified every point capable of causing her to shudder and moan in pleasure. She was helpless under his touch. Total submission was her only option.

She felt the warmth of his fingers between her legs. He now held her in the palm of his hand and could manipulate her to do and say whatever he desired. She gasped when his fingers slide beneath the moist silk of her La Perla panties.

The mayor held his hand firm to show a semblance of resistance, but when he pressed the tip of his finger inside, she shuddered and silently prayed he would continue. Sheridan knew she wanted more when he felt her hips gently gyrating on his hand. His head began the slow descent down her body, caressing and kissing her breasts, but leaving her blouse buttoned and white ruffles unruffled.

She anticipated where his lips would land through the haze slowly enveloping her. The euphoria of the State of the City address was a distant memory. Lust and passion replaced power and prestige. All she could feel was the weight of his head sliding down her body. His intoxicating musk filled her nostrils, and the sound of his lips kissing their way up her thighs was like the melodic strumming of a violin in the hands of a virtuoso.

"Baby, stop," she pleaded as he slid her panties to the floor of the limousine. "Honey, we're . . . We're almost home," she weakly protested as his lips tasted the first drop of her sweet essence.

Camille slowly slid sideways and lowered her back onto the Corinthian leather. The fabric of her Yves St. Laurent skirt formed a puddle at her waist as Sheridan's head rested between the mayor's legs. The magic carpet ride took an erotic detour as Sheridan's dancing tongue skillfully took her to secret places only he could find.

Camille could only hold on tight until the ride ended. She prayed the driver couldn't see through the blackened limousine partition as her head rolled from side to side on the seat. Sheridan was merciless as he plunged deeper and deeper. She felt the added pleasure of the coarseness of his tongue and tickle of his goatee. "Why do you do this to me, baby?" she pleaded helplessly as he maneuvered the magic carpet even higher. "Please don't, Daddy," she moaned and quaked at the exact point his tongue performed the most remarkable figure eights, pirouettes, circles, twists, and turns.

Sheridan knew the signals. The undulating hips, the twirling Pradas, the steadily increasing flow and the tightening grip on his head. In this moment she belonged to him, not the city of Los Angeles. He possessed her body and soul. There were no urgent problems only she could solve or crises demanding her immediate attention. There were no voters' hands to shake or rosy baby cheeks to kiss. There was only Sheridan and Camille Hardaway. He was the master, and she was his slave.

"You're going to make me cum, baby," she warned.

No need to tell this to Sheridan. He knew the precise moment she would be reduced to shuddering muscle spasms, tangled hair, and disheveled designer clothes.

Three . . . two . . . he counted down silently as his tongue guided the magic carpet to the highest point of the journey. *And one—*

Camille clamped down on her bottom lip to prevent a frenzied shriek of pleasure from escaping. Her hips lurched upward. Sheridan skillfully stayed in position throughout the entire series of spasms showing her no mercy. Her fingers gripped the back of his head as if she were trying to stay on a bucking bull. Her body froze at the peak of pleasure. Her hips remained suspended in the air with Sheridan planted firmly inside her. Then suddenly, her body dropped to the car seat as Sheridan gently administered the final twirls of his tongue just as a painter would the final strokes on his masterpiece.

Camille's body continued to twitch as she looked out the window and saw the landmarks indicating the mayor's mansion was only two blocks away. She quickly lifted Sheridan from between her legs, retrieved her crumpled panties from the floor, and used them to wipe away the evidence of her passion from his face.

As the car glided to a stop in the circular driveway, Sheridan dabbed the sides of his mouth with his fingers said, "Did that answer your question? You were magnificent."

Camille sat sternly at the head of the conference table in her office at city hall on Tuesday morning. The generals in her army were to her left and to her right. Chief of Staff Tony Christopoulos occupied the seat to her right. Bill Wong, the city administrator, to her left. The head of the real estate division, Scott Harrison next to him, and the new baseball stadium project manager, Ben Venabrink, faced Camille at the opposite end of the table.

The décor offered no clues that would lead anyone to conclude it belonged to the beautiful woman in the immaculate navy blue pantsuit at the head of the table. Dark mahogany panels covered the walls. She inherited the art from generations of stodgy old men who preceded her. Even the desk was a relic from the past. The only hint offered was the subtle trace of violets, blackcurrant, Bulgarian rose, and Egyptian jasmine from Camille's favorite perfume resting gently on the shoulders of everyone who entered the room.

An architectural rendering of the new ultra-modern stadium sat on an easel just over Ben's left shoulder.

"Mrs. Mayor," Ben said as he stood and walked to the easel, "the Playa del Rey site offers the perfect location for this project. There are 110 undeveloped acres overlooking the Pacific Ocean. The property has enough space for a 175,000-seat arena, which would make it the largest sports stadium in the world. The second largest being the Rungnado May Day Stadium in North Korea at 150,000 seats."

Ben removed the top rendering to reveal an aerial view showcasing the oval footprint and fully retractable roof. "Every element of this state-of-the-art, multipurpose sports and entertainment complex is of the highest quality. Per your instructions, our architects have come back with a design that, as you can see, is not only innovative by today's and even tomorrow's standards, but will stand the test of time and befits the importance of the location. Great cities have great buildings in great locations. And Los Angeles is a great city."

Camille listened but didn't react. At first glance, she looked unimpressed, but upon closer inspection one could see her fully dilated onyx pupils.

Scott Harrison took his cue in the well-choreographed presentation. He stood and continued seamlessly. "The property is owned by the Vandercliffs. An old-money family in Bel Air, the only remaining member of which is a Gloria Vandercliff. Miss Vandercliff is in her seventies and never married. She is the sole heir to a real estate fortune estimated to be well in excess of 2 billion. She isn't interested in getting rich off the city. She's an enormous Dober fan and sees this as an opportunity to give something back to the game she's enjoyed her entire life."

"For God's sake, enough about her," Camille snapped. "I don't have all day. How much does she want for the property?"

"For the entire 110 acres," Scott stammered, "Miss Vandercliff, through her attorneys, of course, is asking $120 million. The property is worth at least twice that in today's market and preliminary environmental impact studies show environmental remediation needed on the land is minimal."

Camille exchanged a knowing glance with Tony Christopoulos. They each had calculated the true value of the property before Scott gave his estimate. Tony gave Camille a slight nod of approval.

"This design incorporates feedback from regulatory agencies and citizens," Ben said referring back to the renderings. "It includes changes you requested and also recommendations from the governor."

"I don't care what that asshole thinks," Camille fumed. "He's only got one year left in office."

"This is an incredible opportunity for the region," Scott interjected. "Building a state-of-the-art, environmentally friendly event pavilion, housing with multiple public transportation options, represents smart development and an incredible economic engine. This will ensure the Dobers will remain the Los Angeles baseball team for the next fifty years.

"Going into this project, we wanted to build a world-class event center incorporating the best in design and technology," Scott said. "Now, because of the constructive feedback we've received, Dober Stadium will be a world-class waterfront park and public gathering place serving as a model of sustainable urban development.

"This design lives up to the importance of this incredible waterfront location and fuses together the vision of the Los Angeles Dobermans with the landscape of the beach and the input we've heard over the past several months from stakeholders, community leaders and—"

Camille slapped her hand on the desk. The smack reverberated off the paneled walls and caused everyone in the room to jump. "Enough of the dog-and-pony show, boys. Let's get to the bottom line. She wants $120 million for the land. How much will that cost?" she said, pointing to the rendering.

Scott yielded the floor to Ben and returned quietly to his seat.

"Approximately $1.6 billion. This latest design increases the overall footprint of the event center, includes market rate housing, expands open space, and builds an expansive new waterfront plaza for the public to—"

Camille stood abruptly from the table. "I've heard enough," she said looking at Scott. "Start negotiating with Vandercliff first thing tomorrow. Tell her Camille Hardaway wants Doberman Stadium built on her property. Offer her $80 million and if she refuses tell her we'll take it by eminent domain."

Scott looked up and said, "But, Mrs. Mayor, there are no grounds for eminent domain with this project."

Camille snapped her head in Scott's direction. "Did I ask your opinion?" she replied sharply.

The other men at the table looked relieved they were not involved in the exchange and avoided eye contact with the mayor and Scott.

"No, Mrs. Mayor," Scott replied cautiously. "You did not, but—"

"No buts," she snapped. "I want Dober Stadium located on that site. If you don't think you can make it happen, let me know now, and I'll replace you with someone who can."

"Mrs. Mayor," Tony said, unfazed by her display of force and dominance over the others in the room. "There is one other obstacle that won't be as easy to get over."

"And what is that?" she asked coldly.

"John Spalding, planning commission chair. He's made it his mission to ensure no new stadium is ever built. He has rejected all designs and locations we've floated by the commission. He feels it's a waste of tax dollars and the money should be used to build affordable housing for teachers and first responders."

"Fuck teachers," Camille said angrily. "We've already built thousands of units of subsidized housing all over the goddamn city. Isn't that enough?"

"He doesn't think it is," Tony replied calmly. "He's said privately he believes you're using this as a stepping-stone to the governor's mansion."

Camille walked to her desk and sat down. "We're done here. You leave Spalding to me," she said coldly. "Please see yourselves out."

The four men silently retrieved papers and exited the office as Camille launched into a heated exchange on the telephone with her next victim of the day.

The smell of chlorine filled the yard as Gideon Truman completed his usual 6 a.m. swim. Danny St. John sat nearby at a patio table reading the morning paper, taking leisurely sips of coffee and a eating a warm croissant.

"Your coffee is getting cold," Danny called out.

"One more lap," came Gideon's breathy reply as the water splashed over his shoulders.

Gideon's Hollywood hillside home had an unobstructed view of downtown Los Angeles. The forty-five-foot high letters of the iconic HOLLYWOOD sign looked down onto his yard from a hill in the distance. The city lay at their feet like an intricately woven carpet and the peak of the tower at city hall was just visible between the high-rises, hotels, and condominiums.

The two men lived together in the house since Danny's former lover, Pastor Hezekiah Cleaveland, was murdered by his wife Samantha. The devastating loss of Hezekiah, followed by the mysterious death of Samantha, created a bond between Gideon and Danny bound by love and tragedy.

They liked nothing more than being in each other's company. They traveled together on Gideon's assignments to exotic parts of the world. They dined at the finest restaurants, attended the A-list parties and ordered takeout from their favorite Chinese takeaway on Sunset Boulevard every Thursday night. They enjoyed the many perks of Gideon's celebrity status together, but the most enjoyable time was when they were alone in the house on the hill and safe in each other's arms. They were soul mates and no verse or brimstone-spewing televangelist could tell them otherwise.

At thirty-one, Danny was more handsome than he had been on any day prior in his life. To Gideon, he was the prototype on which God based the design for the most beautiful man since Adam. His tender brown eyes, delicately chiseled face, and chestnut skin made Gideon sigh with pleasure every time he saw him and each time was as precious as the first.

Gideon finally emerged from the pool. His skin glistened in the morning sun as remnants of the water trickled down his muscular frame onto the terra-cotta tile. He wore black Speedos on a body needing no camouflage or modesty. At forty-five, Gideon had the physique of a man half his age. The distinguished hint of grey at each temple was the only clue he wasn't twenty-five.

"Mayor Hardaway is all over the front page," Danny said laying the newspaper on the table and pouring Gideon coffee from a carafe. "How was her State of the City address last night?"

"She was amazing." Gideon said as he toweled himself dry. "I hate to say it, but for some reason she reminds me of Samantha Cleaveland."

Danny gripped the carafe tighter when Gideon said those words. He could almost hear the *whoosh* of a bullet rushing past his head—the same sound he heard on the night Samantha tried to kill him.

Danny wiped the sound from his mind and continued filling the cup. "How so?" he asked guardedly.

"As you can see, she's just as beautiful," he said pointing to her photograph on the front page of the newspaper. "She's smart. I read somewhere her IQ is in the top 2 percentile of the world, and she's powerful, but I can't shake the feeling there's something else."

"Ruthless?" Danny asked.

"I'm sure. Everyone has to sell their soul when they reach a certain level in politics. But that's not it."

"Evil?"

"Why do you say that?" Gideon asked curiously.

"I'll be honest with you. I get the same chill when I see her on television as I did when I saw Samantha. There *is* something evil about her."

Gideon sat with the towel draped over one shoulder. He paused for a moment to consider Danny's disturbing opinion. "I thought it was just me," he finally said. "I agree, there is something evil lurking behind those beautiful eyes, and I want to know what it is."

Danny looked silently into the distance. He saw Parker, his scruffy grey cat, patrolling the perimeter of the yard searching for his next furry victim.

Gideon felt Danny's concern. He reached across the table, took his hand, and said, "Don't worry. It's not the same, Danny. I don't think the mayor is a cold-blooded killer like Samantha."

"You don't know that."

"You're right, I don't, but I can't imagine anyone more evil than Samantha," Gideon said, taking his first sip of the now lukewarm coffee.

"Let someone else investigate her. Why is it your responsibility to expose her secrets?" Danny asked, almost pleading.

"I can't pass this one up. There's talk about a possible run for governor. I asked last night, but she was evasive. Promised I would be the first reporter to know if she decides to run. I want in on the ground floor of that story. The first black governor of California and the first woman. If there are skeletons, I want to be the one to find them."

Danny saw firsthand how unrelenting Gideon became when he worked on an important story. He watched Gideon doggedly pursue Samantha Cleaveland until he backed her into a corner, and it almost cost both their lives. Fortunately, someone killed Samantha before she had the opportunity to kill them.

"I know I won't be able to talk you out of this, so I'm not going to try. Just please be careful. I love you, and I don't want to lose you," Danny said softly.

"You're never going to lose me," Gideon said assuredly. "We may be paranoid about Camille, but considering all we went through with Samantha, it's understandable."

"Maybe," Danny said pausing. "But all the same, I wish you would speak to Hattie first."

"Hattie?" Gideon said. "Why Hattie?"

"Because if Camille Hardaway is up to something, Hattie will be the first to know about it," Danny said firmly. "And if she's as bad as Samantha, you're going to need Hattie on your side."

"I'm not going to run, and that is final!" Jean-Luc Fantoché shouted. *"What concern is it of yours? I love you and provide for you. Nothing more should matter. The rest you need not trouble yourself with."*

"It does trouble me," Juliette countered passionately.

"I have bought your family's freedom. Is that not enough to satisfy you?" he asked angrily.

"No, it is not enough," she snapped. "Have you forgotten, many of my friends are still slaves? An entire race of humans are owned by other human beings in this country. Their lives are not their own. Does it not trouble you?

Is your spirit not tormented in the knowledge that people are at this very moment laboring in fields of tobacco, cotton, and sugar under the cruel hand of an overseer?

"You understand the plight of the Negro," she continued pleadingly. "You are a caring and kind man. As governor, you can help to put an end to the inhumanity that has plagued this state and this country for far too long. For those reasons alone, it does indeed concern me."

Fantoché stung from the impact of her words. "Yes, it does trouble me," he said remorsefully. "But don't you understand? I cannot win. Thaddeus Barrière has declared his candidacy. He is by far more qualified and better known throughout the state than I. Public humiliation would surely follow if I dared enter my name beside such a formidable opponent."

"Thaddeus Barrière will not win," Juliette said definitively.

"That is nonsense," he replied dismissively. "You know not of what you speak, ma belle ange. He will be the next governor."

Juliette turned her back to Fantoché and walked to the fireplace with the single black candle at the center of the mantelpiece in her sights. "He will not win," she repeated resolutely. "There are powerful forces in this *country who will see him dead before allowing him to set one foot in the governor's mansion."*

"Dead?" he scoffed. "Why? Who are these forces of whom you speak?"

Juliette reached for a box of wooden matches resting on the hearth. "The forces I speak of prefer to remain in the shadows. But trust my words. They have decided Thaddeus Barrière will never be governor of Louisiana. He has made his position clear on the topic of slavery and stated he will never support the emancipation of slaves."

Fantoché studied her back intently. "These do not sound like the kind of men you should be consorting with," he said with concern. "The world of politics is no place for a woman of your delicate beauty."

Juliette ignored his words and struck the match. The sulfurous flare enveloped her in a burst of light.

"Juliette," he continued, "I implore you to distance yourself from these men."

"I cannot do that," she replied calmly. "Les roues ont été mis en mouvement. It is too late."

"Too late for what?" he asked anxiously.

Juliette extended her arm and lit the black candle. The wick crackled briefly, then settled into a slow, lingering burn. When she turned to face him, the tension in her demeanor had vanished. She looked at him with adoring eyes and said, "Do you love me as deeply as you say?"

Fantoché was relieved the intensity in her voice had dissipated and was replaced with irresistible sensuality accentuated by the glow of the candle. "I have no words to express the depth of my love for you," he said rushing to her. "I love you more than any man has ever loved a woman. You are the reason I exist."

Juliette stopped him at arm's length. "Then you will do as I say," she said calmly. "If not, I will leave this house at this very moment, taking with me only the clothes on my back and never trouble you again."

Fantoché looked at her questioningly. "You can't mean that."

His words hung between them. Juliette only responded with the cold stare of jade eyes.

A wave of panic rose from his boots and quickly filled his entire body. "Do not do this to me, Juliette. You know I cannot live without you. Why do you torture me with such cruel threats?"

Again, there was no response.

Fantoché felt his knees weaken. He feared they would collapse under the immense weight *he felt pressing down on him. His breath became short and losing consciousness became almost inevitable. His stomach threatened to spew the meal of escargot, foie gras, and sole meunière Juliette's servants had just served them. But for him, dying in a pool of vomit at the feet of Juliette Dupree would be preferable to facing the prospect of living without her.*

"I will take my life if you leave me," he said with a depth of sincerity only at the dispose of a truly desperate man.

"Then your choices are either to die or become governor. Tell me now, monsieur, which do you choose?" she asked coldly.

Juliette was so close, but he couldn't touch her. He could smell the entrancing aroma of her perfume and feel the warmth of her body, but her eyes held him helplessly at bay. The light from the candle on the mantle appeared blisteringly bright, or was it his imagination?

"You have not told me who these men are," he said, unable to conceal his weakness.

"Their identity is unimportant. Never ask me again," she commanded.

The balance of power shifted at that moment. Despite his wealth, social status, and privilege that accompanied his pink skin, Juliette had always been in control, but now he knew it as well.

"You would allow me to die?" he asked with the last ounce of his resistance.

"It is not my decision, but yours."

"Then I understand, mon chéri *Juliette,"* he said at the moment of collapse. *"For you, I will be governor."*

With her eyes alone, Juliette then gave Jean-Luc Fantoché permission to taste the sweetness of her cheek under the glow of the black candle.

It was after 3:00 in the morning. The streets of downtown Los Angeles were empty. A full moon shed unwelcomed light on homeless men huddled in doorways and fishnet stockings worn by prostitutes offering ten-dollar blowjobs to anyone who passed within twenty feet of their corners.

Camille guided the black Escalade into a working-class neighborhood in Watts. The pride of community and homeownership was evident in the well-tended lawns and the two cars in every driveway. The Watts Riots of 1965 left the area with the reputation of being crime ridden and depressed, but clearly, the residents knew otherwise.

She stopped in front of a white house on Grape Street that stood out from the others on the block. Cement lions with paws clawing at the air sat on each side of a white wrought iron gate. Gold-painted acorn finials topped each fence post, and bursts of flowers on trellises were anchored in brightly glazed pots throughout the yard. Electric pink trim outlined the windows, roof, and front door. The Creole roots of the inhabitant were apparent to all who passed the neat little house.

Camille looked to her left, then right, and checked the rearview mirror before exiting the car. It would be impossible for her to explain her presence in this part of town, in front of this peculiar house, at this hour of the night.

The moon followed her as she opened the gate and made her way hurriedly up the whitewashed walkway. The door slowly glided open before she could ring the doorbell.

No one stood in the threshold to welcome Camille. Instead, she heard a voice in the distance call out, "Come in, Camille, I'll be right out."

Camille was accustomed to such theatrics as doors opening by themselves, the occasional flickering of the lights, or the always perfectly timed "Squawk!" of the blue and gold Macaw named Louie Armstrong in the birdcage hanging in the corner of the dining room. Her favorite was the black candle that would light and extinguish itself at least once during her periodic visits.

Camille entered the house and closed the door quickly behind her. The smell of burning incense assaulted her nose as she hung her coat on the rack in the entry hall. The interior of the house was much like the exterior. Framed pictures of New Orleans's scenic points of interest, Bible verses stitched in needlepoint, and faded black-and-white photographs of long-since-dead ancestors hung on the yellowing floral wallpaper. The chairs and couch were guarded by plastic covers and finely crocheted doilies. The furniture was a mix of 1950s tables and chairs, and antiques that would fetch jaw-dropping appraisals on the *Antiques Roadshow*.

Just as Camille was preparing to sit in her usual seat, Madame Gillette Lemaitre entered the room from the kitchen.

"Honey, I had a taste for collard greens," she said wiping her hands on an apron cinched around her waist. "Sit down, sit down," she said summoning the Southern manners she learned at the knees of her mother and grandmother. "Would you like to try them? No pork at all. My doctor said I can only use smoked turkey now. Not quite the same but still does the trick."

Gillette was a sturdy woman in her sixties. She moved with the steady determination of a person half her age. Her lovely bone structure and virtually wrinkle-free skin and jade-green eyes were gifts from her Louisianan ancestors. Most assumed she was forty-five or, forty-six at the most, but her grandmother's Bible held the secret of her true age within the hallowed confines of its weathered pages.

"It's a little late for greens," Camille said as she sat on the couch.

"You know how that is. When you get a hunger for something there's no point in putting it off," Gillette said sitting in the chair directly in front of Camille. "Besides, when you live to be my age, there's no reason in denying yourself whatever gives you pleasure because soon enough, you'll be six feet under."

Camille heard a loud, "Squawk!" from the dining room as if Louie were saying *"Amen!"* to Gillette's most recent pearl of wisdom.

"What's on your mind, child?" Gillette said looking deeply into Camille's eyes. "I can see something's troubling you."

Over the years, Camille learned it was useless to hide anything from the woman who sat in front of her. She was like an open book to Gillette and deception could prove to be costly.

"You've read about the new Dober Stadium," Camille launched in.

"Yes, yes," Gillette said clapping her hands once. "It's beautiful. I hope you can get me a ticket. I would love to see it before I die. When is it going to be done?"

"That's the problem. It might not be approved by the Planning Commission," she said mournfully. "The chair, John Spalding, is opposed to it and has vowed to stop it from being built anywhere in the city."

"I saw pictures in the paper, and it's something else. Looks like a flying saucer landed right in the middle of a field. What kind of fool wouldn't want a stadium that beautiful in Los Angeles?"

"The kind of fool who would do anything to make me look bad. I'll be known as the mayor who failed if he's able to stop this project; I would never live it down."

"And if it's built?"

"If I get it built, then the sky's the limit. I can—"

Gillette raised her hand to stop Camille. "Never mind. Let's not get too far ahead of ourselves. We can only deal with one stadium at a time. Now, what is it you want from me?"

"You know what I want," Camille answered as if irritated by the question. "The same thing you did to the others. I want him stopped. I want him out of the way."

Gillette leaned back in the cushioned chair. The plastic covering burped and squeaked as she settled in. "You're sure that's the only way? Have you talked to him? Turn on the Hardaway charm," she said with a mimicking smile.

"I've tried reasoning with him, but he's irrational. He only wants to see me fail."

Gillette was silent for a few moments. Her eyes closed tight and lips pursed in deep contemplation. Camille stared at her intently and silently prayed she would come to the same conclusion.

Then she finally spoke. "This is the third time, Camille," Gillette said wearily with her eyes trained on the mayor. "You know this takes a lot out of me."

"I know it does, but I've tried everything, and this is the only option I have left. I'm desperate."

The smell of bubbling collard greens, garlic, and onions competed with the burning incense. Camille did not take her eyes off Gillette.

"What do you want done?" Gillette finally asked.

"I don't care. Just stop him," Camille said barely containing her desperation. "Heart attack, brain tumor, sex scandal. I don't care. Just stop him. And it's got to happen soon. We're starting negotiations with the property owner tomorrow."

"Don't worry, baby. I know just the thing," Gillette said reverting to her most grandmotherly tone.

"I don't want to know the details," Camille blurted. "I can't be involved."

Gillette laughed gently and said, "That's the beauty of the spirit world, baby. No one you can see is involved except the victim."

"Good."

"I'll start on it right away," the old woman said scooting forward in the chair. "Here's what I need. A picture of the Mr. Spalding. Something, anything, with his original signature on it. Do you have anything personal that ever belonged to him?"

Camille thought for a minute. "He gave me a baseball signed by Willie Mays that was part of his sports memorabilia collection."

Gillette laughed loudly. "Perfect! A symbol of the very thing he's trying to destroy."

The old woman stood. Her years were now more apparent as she struggled to her feet and walked to the mantle over the fireplace. She stood near the candle and said, "Bring everything here tomorrow."

"Yes, ma'am," Camille replied humbly. "Anything else?"

"There is one more thing," Gillette said walking toward the kitchen. "Are you sure you don't want to try my greens? Smells like they're almost done."

Chapter 3

Sheridan Hardaway drove the silver Mercedes up Sunset Boulevard past Grauman's Chinese Theatre, mammoth billboards of busty blonds, and a string of trendy restaurants. He maneuvered the car through a labyrinth of tour buses, taxicabs, and jaywalking tourists. The glitter and grit of Hollywood soon gave way to a serene palm-lined stretch of Beverly Hills.

Sheridan turned onto a nondescript side street tucked between a thicket of trees and blooming lavender jacaranda. A lush green canopy covered the narrow road. He could see the signature pink building just ahead. The Beverly Hills Hotel, despite its notoriety, still served as the discrete meeting spot for movie mogul power meetings, celebrity getaways, and clandestine assignations. It was the official no-tell motel for the rich and infamous.

Sheridan stopped the car in the arch of the circular driveway. A red-vested valet who looked like the next Hollywood heartthrob trotted to the car and opened the door. "Good afternoon, sir," he said with a dazzling capped smile. "Welcome to the Beverly Hills Hotel."

Sheridan did not reply.

"Do you have luggage to check, sir?" the well-trained man continued. "I would be happy to take them in for you."

"No bags. Just here for a meeting," Sheridan said, already feeling he had revealed too much.

"Very good, sir. I hope you have a productive meeting," the valet said, quoting directly from the Beverly Hills Hotel employee handbook.

With the last exchange, the valet leapt into Sheridan's car and carefully drove away.

"Good afternoon, Mr. Hardaway," came the second VIP greeting from a smiling woman behind the hotel desk. "Welcome back to the Beverly Hills Hotel. Your guest has already arrived. Here is your key. You are in Bungalow 8, just as you requested."

Bungalow 8 was the most desired at the hotel. It was nestled in a private grove on the grounds with a secluded path and no other bungalows nearby. It had been the favorite of Marilyn Monroe, Elizabeth Taylor, Cary Grant, and countless other celebrities who demanded complete privacy when visiting the hotel.

"Thank you," Sheridan said unimpressed. "Has the champagne been delivered?"

"Yes, Mr. Hardaway, it has. We've also taken the liberty of sending a complimentary tray of caviar, truffles, escargot, and a few other delicacies the chef thought you might enjoy."

"Please thank him for me."

"I will, Mr. Hardaway. Enjoy your stay and don't hesitate to call me if you require anything else."

Sheridan left the desk saying as few words as possible. The mauve, pink, and peach lobby was sparsely occupied with faces and voices rarely seen or heard outside of the forty-inch boxes in living rooms across the country. The official smile of Colgate Toothpaste sat near a terra-cotta fireplace waiting for its agent. The latest wannabe sipped mineral water with its publicist, and the next "It" girl walked through as though she were already carrying her Oscar in the Fendi tote slung over her shoulder.

Most who saw Sheridan walk through the lobby and exit the building knew who he was, but the unwritten rule, even decades before Las Vegas, was *"What happens in the Beverly . . . stays in Beverly."*

Sheridan walked the familiar path leading to Bungalow 8. Palm trees that saw the likes of

Denzel Washington, Kevin Costner, Whitney Houston, and every A-, B-, and some C-list celebrities since the day the hotel opened in 1912 swayed in the gentle afternoon breeze. The hotel grounds were dotted with pink bungalows. He passed a groundskeeper in green overalls who avoided eye contact and faded silently into the background as he passed on the path.

Bungalow 8 was tucked behind a seven-foot boxwood hedge. Sheridan looked over both shoulders to confirm there were no curious eyes watching as he approached the green privacy wall. The three-room cottage was elegant but simply decorated. The cream and mauve color scheme echoed the serenity of the outdoors. There was a small kitchenette to the right of the living area and a bedroom to the left. The gurgle of a fountain could be heard through French doors opened to a private deck and small backyard. A stack of newspapers and gossip magazines was neatly fanned on a glass coffee table, along with the bottle of chilled champagne, two flutes, and a domed silver tray.

"Hello," Sheridan called out in the empty room. "Where are you?"

The bedroom door opened and Tony Christopoulos emerged, wearing only a white towel around his waist. His sculpted torso glistened from remnants of water as he tousled his jet-black hair with another towel.

"I was in the shower," Tony said draping the damp towel over his shoulder. "Stopped at the gym on my way here and didn't have time to shower. Are you hungry? The caviar is delicious."

"I had lunch with Camille," Sheridan said walking to the French doors. "That's why I'm late."

"No worries. Gave me some time to relax. What kind of mood is she in?"

"Demanding as ever," Sheridan said dismissively.

"Did she mention the new developments on the stadium?"

"No, what's the latest?" Sheridan asked, turning to face the dripping man.

"She's decided on the Playa del Rey property."

"Fucking finally," Sheridan said. "It took her long enough."

"You won't have much time to act," Tony said. "She told Scott Harrison to start negotiations immediately."

"How much is she offering?" Sheridan asked as he twisted the cork on the bottle of champagne.

"Eighty million."

Sheridan froze midtwist of the cork and said, "Is she crazy? The property is worth twice that."

"But you know how she is. Instructed Scott to threaten the owner with eminent domain if she doesn't accept the offer."

"That's my Camille," Sheridan said accompanied by the loud *pop* of the cork. "Never can pass up the opportunity to fuck someone."

Sheridan poured two glasses of champagne and sat with Tony on the sofa. "Who owns it?" Sheridan asked.

"Some rich old lady named Gloria Vandercliff. She doesn't need the money. Just loves baseball and wants to help with the stadium."

"To altruistic sellers," Sheridan said raising his glass in a mock toast. "They're my favorite. Especially when I can make a few million off them."

"You mean, when *we* can make a few million." Tony interjected, forgoing the raised glass for a raised eyebrow. "Remember the deal is 70/30. I give you the insider information, and you close the deal."

Sheridan flashed a broad smile and moved closer to Tony. He placed a hand on his still moist thigh and slowly moved up his leg and under the towel.

"I remember, baby," Sheridan said seductively. "It's 70/30. A deal is a deal. You can trust me."

The white towel slowly formed a tent as Sheridan massaged Tony's thigh.

"I'm risking a lot for you, Sheridan," Tony said, trying to maintain his composure. "If Camille ever finds out about this she'll destroy me."

"I know, baby," Sheridan whispered while nuzzling Tony's neck.

"She could have me arrested."

"I know, baby," Sheridan repeated dotting Tony's neck and chest with breathy kisses.

"I could go to jail," Tony said weakly as the tent continued to rise.

"She'll never find out," Sheridan said, gently stroking Tony's solid member under the towel. "And you won't go to jail."

"What if—" Tony sputtered weakly.

"Stop talking," Sheridan said, pressing his lips to Tony's open mouth. "I want to fuck you now."

"Excuse me, Mrs. Mayor," came the disembodied voice from the intercom on Camille's desk. "Mr. Gideon Truman is here for your one o'clock."

Camille pressed the telephone speaker and said, "Give me three minutes, then send him in."

It had been a week since she met Gideon at the State of the City address. He called her two days later and requested a meeting to discuss the possibility of an on-air interview. *Is it too early to make an appearance on a national stage?* she questioned silently after hanging up from his call.

After Camille calculated the pros and cons of doing the interview, her political instincts told her it was the perfect time. *The country needs to know how I turned this city around and that Camille Ernestine Hardaway from South Central Los Angeles is building the largest sports arena in the world.*

Camille used the three minutes to check her hair and makeup in a mirror kept in the bottom drawer of the desk. A slight toss of her hair made every strand fall obediently into place. "Perfect," she said after applying generous red streaks on each lip. She fastened the top two buttons of her power blazer and fluffed the white ruffled collar. *Not too much tits,* she thought. *The girls would be wasted if it's true what they say about him.*

The double office doors swung open in exactly three minutes. Her young assistant, Megan, stood in the threshold wearing a tight pencil skirt. "Please go in," she said to Gideon and stepped aside.

"Mrs. Mayor," Gideon said, entering the room as if it were a sound stage. "So nice of you to meet me on such short notice."

"It's my pleasure," Camille responded with feet firmly planted in a power stance. *Always make them come to you,* was her rule when meeting with men. *Sets the tone for the entire exchange.* "Please have a seat. Would you like anything . . . mineral water, coffee?"

"No, I'm fine, thank you."

The next sound was the gentle *"click"* of Megan closing the office door. Their combined smiles rivaled the light pouring through the windows. They each had their A-games prepared and were ready for anything the other could possibly toss their way.

"I'll come straight to the point," Gideon said as he unbuttoned his blazer and sat on the sofa in the center of the room. "My producer and I are intrigued by you. The first female mayor of Los Angeles, one of the sharpest political minds in the country, the looks of a movie star. You are the American dream. Power, brains, and unlimited potential."

"That is very kind of you to say," Camille said forcing a modest smile.

"We want to introduce Camille Ernestine Hardaway to the country. Who she is, what motivates her, what she believes in," Gideon said as if he were pitching the perfect idea for a blockbuster movie to a studio executive. "We think the country will love you, and I want to be the man who formally introduces you to them."

"I'm still not clear why. Don't get me wrong, I love the idea of national exposure. It's good for the city, but I want to be very clear on your intentions. You have a reputation for, if you don't mind me saying," she delivered with a wicked smile, "on occasion, sensationalizing stories and exploiting high-profile scandals for ratings. I hate to disappoint you, but you won't find any skeletons in my closets. Only Channel and Dior."

Gideon laughed out loud. "You see! It's comments like that I want my viewers to hear. You have the highest approval ratings of any mayor in the country. I think people are curious about who you are and would love to see you on my show."

"Look, I don't mean to be coy. I'm sure you can understand I have to be very careful about how I'm presented."

"Of course."

"That being said," Camille continued looking him in the eye, "I will do the interview, but I want editorial control."

"The broadcast is live so that won't be possible," Gideon replied cautiously.

"Then I want to review the questions in advance."

"I'm sorry, Mrs. Mayor, but we have a strict policy against that." Gideon felt his prey slipping away. "I can, however, assure you any question I ask will be fair and direct. Nothing you won't be able to handle."

Camille was silent. Their eyes locked as each used keen intuitive powers to predict how the dance would end. Each quickly calculated they had a deal before the next word was spoken.

"All right, Mr. Truman," Camille said, breaking the stilted silence, "I'll do it."

She stood signaling the end of the meeting. "You can make the arrangements with my assistant, Megan," she said, extending her hand as he stood.

Gideon released a silent sigh. *I know you're hiding something,* he thought as he matched her firm grip with his own, *and I'm going to find out exactly what it is.*

The two exchanged parting pleasantries, leaving Camille to run the city and Gideon to begin the dangerous journey that lay ahead.

***

Hattie felt a cold shiver as she stood at her kitchen sink peeling a bowl of potatoes. She gripped the black handle paring knife tightly in one hand and a half-peeled potato in the other as the chill traveled up and down her back. She knew it was a sign, but had no clue what it was about.

"Lord," she said out loud as a steady stream of cold water from the tap splashed the brown spuds, sending droplets in every direction, "one of your children is in trouble. Whoever it is, protect them, Lord," she prayed. "Hold them in the safety of your arms. Guide their footsteps and deliver them from evil."

Hattie commenced with the peeling of the potatoes, having done all she could do with the limited information available. Ringlets of brown peel twirled under the blade and fell intact into the sink. Her hand trembled slightly, a sign she was concerned about whoever was in need of prayer.

A hymn slipped involuntarily from her lips.

"I want Jesus to walk with me.
I want Jesus to walk with me.
All along my pilgrim journey,
I want Jesus to walk with me."

The pile of potato skins grew as she continued the preparations for her signature salad. Every morsel coming from within the loving walls of Hattie's kitchen were coveted treasures: sweet potato pies, macaroni and cheese, the magical mixture of greens from her garden, smothered pork chops with gravy and biscuits kissed by an angel. They were always the most sought after dishes in the buffet lines at church events, family functions, and picnics. This particular salad would grace the table of a repast scheduled for the next day.

A pot of bubbling water stood at the ready for the naked orbs on a snow-white O'Keefe & Merritt stove. Hattie handled the potatoes as if they each had a story to tell, and she wanted to hear every word. "Love is the ingredient most folks forget," she often said. "When you love what you're cooking and who you're cooking it for, they can taste it in every bite."

She placed each potato into the boiling pot and waited with reverence until it sank to the bottom before the next spud was dropped. It took three trips from the sink to the stove before the pot was filled. Hattie wiped her moist hands on a tea towel hanging from the oven's chrome door handle and made her way back to the sink, each step accompanied by the lines of the hymn.

"In my sorrow, Lord, walk with me.
In my sorrows, Lord, walk with me.
When my heart is aching,
Lord, I want Jesus to walk with me."

A bunch of scallions fresh from the garden, newly boiled eggs with steam still rising from the shells, yellow mustard, relish, white onions, and celery waited for Hattie on a butcher block next to the sink. She skillfully sliced and diced the ingredients and formed neat piles of each on the board. The chill in her spine had not gone away but continuing the hymn was her way of saying, "I'm listening, Lord."

"In my sorrow, Lord, walk with me.
In my sorrows, Lord, walk with me.
When my heart is aching,
Lord, I want Jesus to walk with me."

Hattie knew the potatoes were done without even poking them with a knife. Steam from the boiling pot rested on the window above the sink, causing a kaleidoscope of light from the afternoon sun to bathe the room. Hands that had touched the face of God squeezed the now soft potato flesh, creating just the right balance of mashed and potato chunks. She couldn't ignore the tingling traveling from her spine down to her legs, but learned from years of experience you can't rush the Lord. *When He wants me to know, He will tell me.*

"In my troubles, Lord, walk with me," her hymn continued.

"In my troubles, Lord, walk with me.
When my life becomes a burden,
Lord, I want Jesus to—"

And then it happened. The window over the sink became cloudy. Billows poured from the edges and formed a fog through which she couldn't see.

There was no time to reach for the tea towel on the stove behind her. Hattie rested her mashed potato-covered hands on the counter and braced herself for what was to come. Slowly, she saw Gideon's face emerge through the fog. He was oblivious to the white smoke enveloping him. His bright eyes focused intently on something in the distance Hattie couldn't see. She could sense the danger waiting just beyond her view, but it was clear Gideon couldn't. He moved steadily through the haze directly toward the source of the threat.

"Don't go any closer," Hattie said softly to the window. "Danger is waiting for you over there."

Gideon couldn't hear her warning. He moved at an even faster pace than before. The fog grew darker with every step he took. Hattie felt he would soon be face-to-face with a force he couldn't possibly be prepared for.

"Turn back, boy," she admonished. "Turn back."

Her words simply bounced off the glass, unheard by the determined man in the window.

"He won't listen, Lord. Make him—"

The image of a woman appeared in front of Gideon before she could finish her plea. Hattie couldn't see her face, but immediately knew everything about her. *There's evil in her heart. She doesn't know it yet, but she's going to destroy him.* Hattie silently read the essence of the woman's soul as if it were scrolling on a ticker tape at the bottom of the window. *There are powerful forces around her and directing her every move. They will destroy anyone who gets in her way.*

The two figures were now so close their noses were almost touching. Suddenly the fog began to clear, and Hattie saw for the first time who the woman was.

"Oh, Lord, no," she gasped, lifting her potato-covered hand to her mouth. "Camille Hardaway."

Camille turned sharply toward Hattie as if she heard her name uttered from across the divide and looked Hattie directly in the eye. Camille did not speak, but Hattie heard her words clearly, "Keep out of this. This isn't your battle."

Hattie locked eyes with Camille and said firmly, "Jesus put you in my window, so that makes it my battle."

The images began to fade just as Hattie spoke the words. The two women's eyes remained locked the entire time. The billowing fog slowly subsided. Gideon and Camille were gradually replaced by the condensation from the steaming potatoes and the cooling pot of water on the stove.

The calm of her kitchen returned as quickly as it had given way to the vision in the window. Hattie looked down at the chopping block piled with onions and the bowl of soft potatoes.

"Lord, give me strength," she said. "You saved him once, and I know you will do it again."

Hattie combined the ingredients to create the perfect blend of flavors as only she, and her deceased mother, knew how. The potato salad was made all while Hattie silently prayed for the man in the window.

"Protect him, Lord," she said placing the cellophane-wrapped bowl in the refrigerator. "Protect him like only you can."

Gillette Lemaitre rolled the weathered baseball, given to her earlier by Camille, from one hand to the other on her dining-room table. A photograph of Planning Commission Chair John Spalding sat in a silver tray along with a document containing his original signature. Next to the tray was the unlit black candle.

Gillette came from a long line of practitioners. Her great-great-great-grandmother on her mother's side, Juliette Dupree, was said to have been the colored mistress of Jean-Luc Fantoché, the governor of Louisiana in 1852, and credited with getting him elected for two terms despite his blatant incompetence. Juliette Dupree made available to the governor the substantial benefits of her powers and allowed him into her bed only because he was sympathetic to the plight of Negros.

The candle flickering on the table in front of Gillette contained remnants of wax from the same candle that burned in Juliette's parlor in the French Quarter so many years ago. The black wax had been lit and protected by generations of Dupree women. Cruel plantation owners met sudden and inexplicable deaths, infertile woman gave birth, wandering husbands returned to their wives, and countless fortunes built on the backs and graves of slaves were lost overnight . . . All under the illuminating light of this black candle.

The only light in the room came from the dancing flame. Louie paced anxiously from side to side on the wooden perch in his cage. The occasional car driving past the house could be heard through the wood-shuttered windows.

Gillette closed her eyes and gently pushed the baseball across the table toward the candle. It rolled over the picture of John Spalding and the document containing his signature. When it tapped the candle, the flame suddenly flared, sending sparks and a white plume of smoke into the air. Louie released a loud "Squawk!" and doubled his pace at the sight of fiery display. "Squawk, squawk!" he continued until the fire slowly subsided and resumed its gentle dance atop the black candle.

Gillette opened her eyes and gently tapped the table three times with her open palms. The billowy fabric of her floral caftan dangled around her wrists as she continued patting in intervals of three, her eyes fixed on the flame and the fire consumed her senses. All she could see, hear, taste, smell, or feel was the yellow and blue blaze twinkling in the reflection in her eyes.

She lifted the baseball to the flame and waited patiently for the fire to consume the famous signature and yellowing leather. Soon, the black wool yarn beneath the leather began to crackle and pop in her hand. She placed the burning orb onto the silver tray and watched as it grew to a ball of fire.

She then reached for the photograph. John Spalding's ruddy cheeks and questioning eyes seemed to anticipate what was to come as she moved his face closer to the flame. Gillette lifted the bottom corner of the picture to the tip of the flame. John's face was quickly engulfed in the fire. Gillette placed it back onto the tray and removed the document containing his signature. She did the same with the paper. John's signature was soon lying on the tray burning with the picture and baseball.

The flickering flames caused Louie's shadow to dance on the wall. The black candle went dark when the baseball, paper, and photograph were fully consumed. The room was now pitch-black except for the last of the orange embers on the silver tray. The only sounds in the room were Gillette's labored breathing and Louie's claws scratching against the wood perch as he paced from side to side. Her job was done. John Spalding's fate was now sealed by the flame.

"It is, and so I let it be," were her final words.

The morning headline in the *Los Angeles Times* rushed across the city like a flood.

PLANNING COMMISSION CHAIR DIES IN FIERY AUTO CRASH

John Spalding, forty-three, died at the scene of a crash on Wilshire Boulevard near Beverly Hills, the Los Angeles Coroner's Office reported. Spalding was a school board member for more than a decade at the Los Angeles Unified School District and was then appointed to the City Planning Commission. Friends and colleagues said, "He was a pillar of this community. His whole family is so involved in Los Angeles politics, and he was a really good friend."

"We're all so shocked by this very tragic death," said Mayor Camille Hardaway. "John was an extremely friendly, hardworking, good family man," she said. "He was always cheerful, upbeat and down-to-earth. I once saw John walk clear across the street to pick up trash someone left in the road because that was the

kind of man he was. He always tried to help make Los Angeles the best city it could be." The mayor called Spalding's death a terrible tragedy for everyone in the community.

Spalding has been in the news lately because of his very public opposition to the mayor's plans for the new Dober Stadium. He was recently quoted as saying, "I am completely opposed to this waste of taxpayer money. It is nothing more than the mayor laying the foundation for her run for governor at the expense of taxpayers." Spalding went on to say, "Camille Hardaway will only build this travesty over my dead body."

Spalding is survived by his twenty-three-year-old daughter and his wife, Mayra. Spalding's roots run deep in Los Angeles. His father, Tony, was the city clerk and his aunt, Maria Ribeiro, was the city treasurer. LAPD are investigating the crash along with the California Highway Patrol. The cause of the crash has not been determined.

"Oh . . . my . . . God . . . This is perfect!" Sheridan shouted bursting into the bedroom. "Camille, look at this!"

Sheridan ran across the room with his white bathrobe trailing behind like a cape, and silk boxers barely containing his flapping member. It was just before 6:00 a.m. when the Sunday paper was delivered on their doorstep with a thud. Camille propped herself onto her elbows in bed and shook the remains of sleep from her head.

"You are not going to fucking believe this," Sheridan said, tossing the front page in her lap. "John Spalding got himself killed," he said excitedly.

Camille felt a quiver travel through her body.

"He crashed on Wilshire and went off the overpass onto the freeway. Died instantly. This is fucking amazing."

Camille reached for her reading glasses from the nightstand and read silently. As the print leapt from the front page, she could see the flickering black candle in her mind.

An autopsy is scheduled, authorities confirmed. Police said Spalding was driving west on Wilshire Boulevard when, for unknown reasons, his car spun out of control on the overpass above the 405 Freeway, crashed through the cement rail, and plummeted onto the roadway below. Fortunately, the freeway was empty at the early-morning hour and no other persons were injured in the crash.

This was the third time Camille had relied on Gillette to "handle" a vexing political problem. Her chief rival, who threatened to unseat her in her second mayoral race, dropped dead from a heart attack only days after it was announced he was gaining on her in the polls. The police officer who tried to blackmail her with information that would have surely cost her the mayor's office, and possibly land her in federal prison, was found dead of "natural causes" a week after he boldly asked for half-a-million dollars in hush money. Each "death" . . . courtesy of Gillette and her black candle.

"I guess he was right," Sheridan said standing over Camille as she read silently.

"Right about what?" she asked, never looking up from the paper.

"He said you would only be able to build the stadium over his dead body."

"Don't be crude," she snapped.

"I'm not being crude. It's the truth. He was your only real opposition. Now that he's dead, there is nothing standing between you and the stadium. It's fucking amazing," Sheridan said, laughing out loud.

Camille threw the paper to the floor, bolted out of the bed, and angrily cinched her silk robe around her waist. "This isn't funny, Sheridan. It's horrible."

"Since when do you care how you get what you want? It usually doesn't matter as long as you get your way."

Sheridan was right. There was no expense too high if Camille had a goal in her sights, and usually someone other than herself paid the price. *John Spalding's death was his own fault*, she silently reasoned. *If he hadn't been such an asshole, I wouldn't have had to involve Gillette. He left me no option.*

Dober Stadium was to be the crown jewel of her second term in office. It would be the accomplishment showcased while making the case for being the first female governor of the state. She could not—and had not—let John Spalding rob her of that dream.

"Why are you being so sensitive? The dick got what he deserved. He should have known better then to mess with Camille Hardaway."

"This isn't about me or the stadium. This is about the tragic death of a colleague."

"Colleague, my ass. He never passed up the chance to fuck you over. And you're wrong; it *is* about you. The universe knows you want the stadium, and it also knew John Spalding was the only person who could stop it. The stars always line themselves up perfectly whenever you need them to, and this is no exception.

Face it, Camille, this *is* about *you,* for *you,* and because of *you.*"

Camille looked at Sheridan coldly. "Don't ever say that again. I had nothing to do with his death."

"I'm not saying you did it," Sheridan said matching her icy stare. "I'm only saying it happened *because* of you. Let's face it. It's not the first time, is it?"

"What do you mean?" she snapped.

"Come on, Camille," Sheridan said as if he knew more than he should. "The police officer who tried to blackmail you, Robert White. He had a shot at beating you if he hadn't died, and you know it. The universe has always looked out for you, and this is no exception."

"You are being ridiculous," she replied defensively. "I don't want to talk about this anymore."

"You're acting as if you pushed his car onto the freeway. Don't worry, darling. I'll be your alibi," he said with a smile and reached for her arm. "I'll swear on a stack of Bibles I was fucking you when it happened."

Camille jerked away. "This isn't funny, Sheridan. A man is dead, and you're joking about it."

Sheridan could see he hit a nerve. He moved in closer. "Honey, I'm sorry," he said reaching for her again. He took her shoulders and pulled her to his chest. "You know I didn't mean it. I know you had nothing to do with his death. I was just kidding. It's tragic, and I shouldn't have made light of it. I'm sorry. That was very insensitive of me."

Camille recalled the first meeting with Gillette Lemaitre. Her campaign manager suggested she visit this "unusual" woman who helped a couple of his clients in the past. After a month of encouraging Camille to visit Gillette, Camille finally said yes. Not because she believed in her powers, but rather to stop him from asking.

She remembered sitting at Gillette's dining-room table and scoffing at the black candle. *It's nonsense, but I'll try anything to get an edge over Robert White,* she desperately thought at the time.

The association, however, came with a price. Camille casually chalked the first death up as a "coincidence." She dismissed the second death as an "unfortunate accident." But now, with John Spalding, she found it hard to call it anything other than murder.

This time, it felt like she had pushed the car over the edge of the road herself, even though she was miles away and asleep in her bed at the time the car burst into flames on the deserted asphalt highway, she could almost feel the heat of the blaze while clinging to Sheridan's comforting chest. She imagined the sound of John Spalding's cries of desperation when the car crashed through the railing and almost felt the agonizing pain as the flames consumed his body.

Her shoulders quivered slightly in Sheridan's arms.

"Honey, you're shaking," Sheridan said, pulling her closer. "I'm so sorry. I didn't mean to upset you."

It *was* murder, and she could no longer deny the blood of these three men was on her hands. Whether she believed in Gillette's powers was irrelevant now. Three lives had been extinguished because of Gillette Lemaitre's black candle.

The black candle, she thought, still cradled in Sheridan's arms.

"I'm fine," she said pulling away. "It's just a little upsetting."

"Of course it is, and I was being an asshole."

"No, it's me. I'm being overly sensitive," she said walking toward the bedroom door.

"Where are you going?" he asked curiously.

"I have to make a call in the study."

"Call from here."

"My notes are downstairs."

Camille left the room and moved hastily down the stairs, looking over her shoulder to ensure Sheridan had not followed as she entered her study.

The light of the candle flashed before her eyes. Her emotions seemed amplified in the confines of the quiet paneled room. The earthy smell of fear mingled with the intoxicating scent of power in her head; power over life and destiny, power to design her future any way she chose. The world seemed limitless. Anything she desired could become reality under the glow of the mysterious candle.

Chapter 4

"There's no doubt she's going to make it happen now that John Spalding is dead." Sheridan spoke on the telephone in his office on the fifteenth floor in the heart of the Financial District. The plaque on the door read "KEYCORP DEVELOPMENT."

KeyCorp Development owned five shopping malls in Los Angeles County, six 1,000-plus unit apartment complexes, 180,000 square feet of commercial space downtown, and would soon add to its portfolio, 110 acres of prime beachfront property in Playa del Rey.

Sheridan quietly set up the company during Camille's first year in office. He was the sole owner under the alias Michael Kenigrant. His 200 employees had never met the mysterious Mr. Kenigrant. The company was now worth $460 million-plus, most of which was made on deals involving city hall insider information. Camille was unaware of the corporation's existence or the vast fortune her husband had amassed during her tenure as mayor. She had no idea he used confidential information innocently passed over candlelit dinners or in the back of her limousine and occasionally just as his erect member was preparing to enter her trembling flesh.

"Tell me what you know, Brandon," Sheridan said into the telephone.

Brandon Birdsong was the only person who knew the identity of Michael Kenigrant. Brandon was Sheridan's seven-figure-a-year front man. He spoke on behalf of the reclusive "Mr. Kenigrant," oversaw the day-to-day operations of KeyCorp Development, and protected, with his life, the identity of the corporation's owner.

"Gloria Vandercliff," Brandon said in his usual succinct and efficient tone. "She's an eccentric heiress who lives in Bel Air. Never married and no children. Hasn't been off her estate in over twenty years. Inherited the Playa del Rey property, along with an estate estimated to be in the billions, from her father, a Mr. Cecil Vandercliff. The senior Vandercliff made his money in real estate and iron." Brandon took a breath and continued reciting the exhaustively researched dossier on the eccentric Miss Vandercliff. "She is a huge baseball fan and particularly of the Los Angeles Dobermans. Camille's people have already been in touch with her, and she's willing to sell the property to the city for the astoundingly low amount of 120 mill—"

"I know that already," Sheridan said, interrupting Brandon. "I need to meet her before any deals are made with the city. Set it up," he snapped.

"It won't be easy. She never leaves the house and rarely has anyone in. She's pretty batty from what I hear."

"I don't give a fuck how crazy she is. I need you to get me a meeting with her."

"Sheridan," Brandon said cautiously, "are you sure you want to touch this one? The construction of Dober Stadium is going to be watched by everyone. It's going to be one of the largest sports arenas in the world and one of the most expensive development projects the city has ever taken on. The media is going to scrutinize every aspect of this deal. If it ever comes out you owned the property and sold it to your wife, you also run the risk of it coming out you are Kenigrant and have made millions using information you've gathered from Camille. Not only could you lose everything, but you'd also probably face jail time for corruption. In addition, no one will believe your wife didn't know you owned the land. Even if she's able to talk her way out of it, her career would be left in tatters, and, of course, she could never run for governor."

"Don't you think I've already considered all that," Sheridan said angrily. "I stand to make at least 100 million on this deal, and there's no way I'm going to pass it up. She's in too deep now with the stadium plans. There's no way the city can back out now. She'll have no choice but to pay KeyCorp Development whatever price we name. Believe me, Camille's a tough girl. She can take care of herself."

"I don't doubt that," Brandon said with a hint of sarcasm. "But remember, this all hinges on whether you're able to convince Vandercliff to sell to you instead of the city."

"Don't worry," Sheridan said confidently. "I know these dizzy old money types. Stroke their egos, maybe do a little Stepin Fetchit. Let them think they're superior to you. By then, they're so drunk with power they'll do anything you want them to."

There was silence on the line. Sheridan sensed the revulsion from Brandon oozing through the receiver but quickly dismissed it as the reaction of a weak inferior whose sole job was to do his bidding and implement his commands.

"What name shall I make the appointment in?" Brandon asked, afraid of what the answer would be.

There was a brief silence before Sheridan responded. "Sheridan Hardaway," he finally answered.

Brandon released an audible gasp before he spoke. "Why take the risk now?" was his immediate reply.

"Because the payoff is worth the risk. I don't trust anyone—not even you—to handle this."

"Sheridan, you've made millions on this setup with Camille. I don't understand why you're willing to risk it all for this one deal."

"I thought you knew me better than that, Brandon." Sheridan stood from his desk and walked to the bank of windows. The city below seemed to bubble and pop at his feet. A jumble of high-rise towers dotted the horizon like buoys afloat at sea. "I'm a gambler," he continued. "The greater the risk, the greater the return, and that fucking turns me on. I've got a hard-on just thinking about it."

"Your erection aside," Brandon replied dismissively, "the expression 'moth to flame' comes to mind. But, it's your marriage, your fortune, and your funeral. Just remember the people you employ, including me. I've got a kid in college

and two more coming up behind him. I don't get
as turned on by risk as you do."

"Don't worry, Brandon," Sheridan said confidently. "I got this. Trust me."

*Amadeus moved anxiously from one side of
his perch to the other, following Juliette Dupree
as she walked past his cage to the fireplace.
The boned corset her maid had cinched tightly
around her waist while she clung to the bedpost
gave her the perfectly unnatural hourglass
form. Her blue satin dress was sprinkled with
finely embroidered flowers of yellows, pinks,
and greens on the bodice. Layers upon layers
of heavy petticoats and crinoline caused the
skirt to blossom into an enormous bell over silk
mules crafted especially for her delicate feet.*

*Amadeus remained silent for fear of disturb-
ing her concentration as she passed. Juliette
stood in front of the fireplace and looked lovingly to the black candle at the center of the
mantel. The wick sputtered and sparked at
the sight of her, but did not light.*

*"Ah," she said delightfully, "you have antici-
pated my intent."*

*Juliette gently picked up the candle, moved to
the dining-room table, and placed it directly in*

front of the chair at the head. The candle joined the other items placed there earlier.

The first was a lock of Thaddeus Barrière's hair given to her by Black Dahlia. Dahlia was the young beautiful slave charged with washing Barrière's clothes, cleaning his private sleeping chamber, and grooming his head of unruly brown hair. Dahlia had been raped and abused by Barrière from the day she set foot on his plantation. The state of Louisiana, however, did not consider it rape, as she was merely property with which he could do as he pleased. He also generously shared the sweetness of her flower with his houseguests, associates with whom he desired to gain favor, and even traveling salesmen.

Juliette would often allow Dahlia to try on the numerous gowns, gloves, and hats filling her closets and bureaus. She would spritz Dahlia with French perfume from crystal atomizers and hang glittering diamonds, rubies, and emeralds from her ears, neck, and wrists.

"Miss Juliette," Dahlia would say posing in front of the mirror, "you is the luckiest colored woman in da whole wide world. And far more prettier than any sadity white woman I eva did lay eyes on."

On the day Dahlia handed Juliette the lock of hair wrapped in a cloth napkin, she avoided eye contact and said, "I don't wan'na know what you aim on do'n wit' it, but whateva it tis, I hope it be terrible bad, ma'am. Terrible bad."

The second item on the table was a bill containing the signature of Thaddeus Barrière written in blue ink.

Juliette received the paper from Rufus Taylor. Rufus was a slave on loan from a plantation in Minton, Louisiana. His skills as a tailor were given to the owner of the local fine apparel shop in exchange for suits the plantation owner received but did not have the ready cash to pay for.

Taylor had numerous unpleasant encounters at the shop with Thaddeus Barrière. The most memorable of which happened on the day Barrière came in to complain about a button missing from a suit he'd sent to the shop for alterations.

Rufus was unfortunate enough to be alone in the shop when he arrived.

"Where is you master, nigger," Barrière stormed into the shop barking.

"He'll be back shortly, sir. May I hep you?" Rufus answered sheepishly.

"The day a nigger can help me is the day I put a bullet through my brain."

Barrière tossed the suit in question at Rufus's face causing it to wrap around his head like a shroud. "Did you work on my suit, nigger?"

"Yes, sir. Is they some sort a problem needs fixin'?"

"The problem is, you filthy animal, a button is missing. A button I especially ordered from London, and you stole it!"

"No, sir. I would nev'a steal from you, sir. On my grave, sir, never," Rufus replied.

"Don't talk back to me, boy," Barrière snapped.

The venomous words were followed by Barrière spitting in Rufus's face. "I'll see you whipped for this, boy," Barrière shouted and stormed out of the shop.

Rufus was indeed viciously whipped by the furious shopkeeper and, upon being sent back to the plantation in Minton, whipped again by his master whose outstanding debt to the tailor was not fully paid.

But before he was sent away from New Orleans, he gave Juliette the bill containing Thaddeus Barrière's signature. The same bill for the alterations to the suit with the missing button.

"I don't know what'ya plan on doin' wit' it," Rufus said quietly passing the bill to Juliette *across the counter in the shop, "but I hope it's somethin' awful bad, Ms. Juliette. Awful bad."*

The third item on the table was a miniature portrait of Thaddeus Barrière. Juliette received the little painting from the artist, Chauncey Lafayette. Chauncey was a classically trained French painter who made his living traveling from town to town with his wife Simone, painting portraits of wealthy residents. Simone was as black as the night and as beautiful as a sunset over Lake Charles.

Barrière commissioned Chauncey to paint his portrait. Simone accompanied him to the plantation as his assistant. The couple was greeted at the door by Barrière, who, upon laying eyes on Simone said, "That black bitch is not setting foot in my house."

"But, monsieur," Chauncey said through a thick French accent, "this is Simone, my assistant. You will not know she is even here."

"Get off my porch," Barrière yelled at a frightened Simone. "You come in," he snapped to Chauncey, "but send your nigger out back with the other darkies."

Lafayette spent the next four hours in the home painting a preening and disagreeable Barrière. "You ain't from round these parts, being a foreigner and all. You don't bring strange niggers into decent folk's houses in Louisiana."

When Lafayette completed the painting, he showed it to Barrière hoping to be paid quickly and leave the horrible man in his past. But upon seeing the portrait Barrière shouted, "It doesn't look like me at all. You trying to humiliate me, boy? You've made me look like a fat cow."

"But, sir," Lafayette protested, "it is unmistakably you. I took no liberties."

"Pack up your things and your nigger and get off my property," Barrière yelled. "I'll see to it you never work in New Orleans again."

The next day Chauncey and Simone arrived at Juliette's home, as scheduled by Jean-Luc Fantoché, to paint her portrait. She greeted them each with a kiss on the cheek. "Accueillir, Mr. et Mme. Lafayette," she said ushering them into her home.

The afternoon was filled with laughter. Juliette posed gracefully for the life-sized portrait while Simone and Chauncey delighted in her generous hospitality. As Chauncey put the final strokes on the painting of the beautiful woman, Juliette noticed the miniature of Thaddeus Barrière peeking from their art supply portmanteau.

"Who is that? He is not a very pleasant-looking man," Juliette asked, already knowing the answer.

"That is Thaddeus Barrière," Chauncey answered. "The unpleasantness of the painting does not nearly capture the ugliness of his soul. He is by far the vilest man I have ever met."

Chauncey recounted the humiliating experience. "And then he refused to pay me. I spit on his grave."

Barrière delivered himself to Juliette without the need for any manipulations on her part.

"He sounds horrible," she looked to the distraught Simone and said, "I am so sorry, mon précieux bijou. Do not trouble yourself needlessly. He will receive exactly what he deserves sooner than you imagine."

She then looked at Chauncey and said, "I will pay you double what you expected to receive from Monsieur Thaddeus Barrière for his portrait and will also reserve a special place in hell for his wrenched soul."

The three items now sitting on Juliette's dining-room table were accompanied by a box of wooden matches and a silver tray.

Thaddeus Barrière was a man of immense wealth and power in New Orleans and in the state. He owned hundreds of slaves and ran his cotton plantation with a cruel hand. "This great country was built on slavery," he often said. "Any man who threatens the fine and honorable institution of slavery threatens the very future of our nation."

His political path was clear. He was the former mayor of New Orleans and now served as a member of the state legislature. The governor's mansion was clearly in his sights and no one dared challenge him. That is . . . until Juliette Dupree.

She took the seat at the head of the table and studied the items painstakingly gathered. "It has been two years since I have had need of your services," she said looking at the candle. "I command you now to heed my words and, without delay, do my bidding."

Sparks sprang from the wick. "Time is of the essence. I command you to unleash your powers."

Juliette removed a match and struck it on the coarse side of the box. The flame caused flecks of golden fire to appear in her transfixed green eyes as she lit the candle. The wick burst into flames, and then settled into a gentle burn.

"Squawk! Squawk! Squawk!" came the rapturous cry from Amadeus on the perch.

The first item to be subjected to the flame was the document, which she lit from the top two corners and placed onto the silver tray. Then came the portrait of Barrière looking arrogantly up at her face glowing in the candlelight. The oil paint on the little cloth canvas made its consumption by fire a quick and dramatic deed. Finally, the lock of brown hair was placed just above the tip of the dancing flame. The hairs crackled and curled as they melted from the heat, sending a flurry of sparks into the air.

Juliette placed the burning hairs on the tray on top of the still-glowing embers of other items and said, "Thaddeus Barrière is no more. Jean-Luc Fantoché shall be the next governor of Louisiana."

The candle flame extinguished when the three items on the tray stopped burning. The room went dark except for the few orange embers on the tray. The only sound was the approving squawks from Amadeus in the cage.

"It is and so I let it be," were Juliette's final words before exiting the room.

Studio lights beamed down onto center stage of the CNN set of the *Truman Live Show* forming an effervescent pool reserved for the famous and infamous. An army of cameramen, technicians, producers, and gofers prepared for the arrival of Mayor Hardaway. Gideon sat thumbing through cue cards in a corner of the studio while a makeup artist dabbed the last bit of powder onto his glowing forehead.

"Are you almost ready, Mr. Truman?" a studio cypher asked anxiously. "We're live in five minutes."

"Is she here yet?" was his reply.

"Yes. She arrived a few minutes ago and is in makeup now. She'll be out shortly."

"Good, then, yes, I'm ready."

It had been two weeks since he last spoke with Camille in her office at city hall. Gideon had still not shaken the uneasy feeling about her. The familiar rumble in his gut returned when he heard she was in the building. *I don't know what it is, but I'll find out, even if it's live on national TV,* he thought as he stood from the chair and removed the makeup bib from his neck.

Nerves he hadn't felt for years crept from his stomach and consumed his entire body as he took his place under the hot lights. *Pull yourself together, boy,* he thought as he felt the first layer of perspiration forming on his brow. *Don't let her get in your head,* he thought, successfully willing the moisture to not form.

Suddenly he saw a woman enter the set from the dark shadows. The lights pointing directly in his eyes prevented him from seeing her clearly, but the statuesque silhouette was unmistakable. Gideon was reminded why she was one of the most popular politicians in the country as Camille moved from the darkness into the light.

Only this woman could make a basic skirt and jacket look like the manifestation of a gifted designer's ultimate masterpiece. The voluptuous curves of her hips were framed by a deep blue Punto Riso knit suit with a liquid black satin shawl collar and satin pocket flaps. The perfectly rounded mounds of her breasts peeked up from the deep "V" of a black satin shell, demonstrating to all that the power she wielded as the mayor of the great city in no way diminished the sensuous woman at her core.

Gideon stood and greeted her with an air kiss on each cheek. "Mrs. Mayor, thank you for taking the time from your schedule to do this. You look breathtaking as usual," Gideon gushed like a schoolboy.

"It's my pleasure," she responded with the confident air of a woman in control. "Is this where you want me to sit?" she asked motioning to one of the two directors' chairs on the set.

"Wherever you are most comfortable," he replied humbly.

Camille instinctively assessed the positioning of the lights and cameras and concluded the seat she pointed to would capture her best side perfectly.

The set was minimal and modern. A glossy black floor shimmered like a pool of water under their feet. Two black leather director stools, a sixty-inch monitor positioned just above Gideon's left shoulder, and a backdrop of neon-blue curtains. Gideon waited for Camille to sit before taking his seat.

Their images immediately flashed on the monitor behind Gideon. Hands of faceless crew members fumbled to attach microphones to each of their lapels. They were easily the two most stunning people in the room, and arguably, the entire city. Gideon's dark caramel skin and chiseled cheekbones were more suited for a Calvin Klein model than an investigative reporter. Camille's flawless skin, flowing black volcanic hair, and mesmeric eyes elicited the usual gasps and seconds of stunned speechlessness from all who looked in her direction.

The two exchanged preinterview banter, all while being completely aware of the effect their combined beauty had on everyone in the studio.

"I'm assuming there won't be any surprises," Camille asked rhetorically.

"Nothing you can't handle," he replied with as much sincerity as he could muster. "All the questions are straightforward with an emphasis on your plans for the new stadium."

"Almost ready, everyone," came a booming voice from an unknown place. "And we're live in 5 . . . 4 . . . 3 . . . 2 and . . ."

"Good evening, America," Gideon said to the camera. *"I'm Gideon Truman, and welcome to Truman Live."* Millions of viewers from coast to coast were now entranced by Gideon's beguiling smile. *"Tonight, my guest is Camille Ernestine Hardaway, the first woman to serve as mayor of Los Angeles, California, and, recent polls show, a politician with one of the highest approval ratings of any politician in this country since World War II. Welcome, Mayor Hardaway. Thank you for being here."*

The camera panned out to include Camille in the shot. The two sat at angles with their best sides facing the camera.

"Thank you, Gideon. It's my pleasure."

"Now, let me get this out of the way," he said with his signature boyish charm. *"At the risk of receiving thousands of e-mails and tweets accusing me of being politically incorrect or sexist, I must say you are not only one of the most popular politicians in the country, but you are also, hands-down, the most beautiful."*

"There's nothing politically incorrect about complimenting a woman," she said with a carefully portioned measure of modesty and wisdom. *"I think everyone enjoys hearing kind words. So, thank you."*

"You are most welcome. Now that I've gotten that off my chest, we can talk about things important to you and to the people of Los Angeles. As I said in your intro, you are the first female mayor of Los Angeles. How has the experience been for you?"

"I imagine it has been the same for me as it has been for every mayor preceding me. My gender has had very little impact on my ability to do the job. The people of Los Angeles have been their usual amazing selves and have supported me in most of my initiatives."

"You mean you haven't encountered opposition?"

"I'm not saying that. Opposition comes with the job. What I am saying is the opposition, support, and even indifference I've encountered, I don't believe, has had anything to do with me being a . . ."

Gideon, with lightning precision, assessed Camille as she spoke. Playing it safe and down the middle, he silently calculated. All is well in la-la land.

". . . and for that reason," Gideon tuned back in as Camille continued, "I believe Los Angeles is one of the greatest cities in the world."

"Ninety-two percent of registered voters, regardless of their party affiliation, feel you are doing a good job as mayor in your second term in office. Eighty-four percent of registered California Democrats and a staggering 68 percent of Republicans polled felt you would make a good governor. What do you attribute these amazing numbers to?"

"I think voters respond to honest and direct communication. They don't always agree with me, but they trust I'm going to be straightforward about my position, and that I will fight for what I believe in and for what I believe to be in the best interest of the city."

"And you don't think being a female has helped or hurt?" Gideon asked.

Gideon saw the subtle dilation of Camille's pupils. Her eyes tightened slightly and locked with his.

Stop wasting my time with this gender bullshit. Get to the stadium, she thought.

"I honestly don't," she replied succinctly, but with the smile that won elections.

Come on, Gideon thought. Get angry. Show the bitch hiding under that beautiful façade.

"*So now would be a good time for you to address the rumors circulating about your plans,*" he continued, unfazed by the slight change in her demeanor. "*Are you going to run for governor?*"

"*None of those rumors originated from me or anyone in my administration,*" she said, delivering the well-rehearsed reply.

Gideon smiled. "*That doesn't answer my question,*" he pressed.

"*I will be honest with you, Gideon. I am considering it. But no decisions have been made.*"

"*And what are you factoring into your decision?*"

Camille flashed a *"don't fuck with me"* look that went unnoticed by the cameras but registered 8.5 on Gideon's "shade" scale. The test of a good interviewer is to know just how close you can push a victim to the edge, and then gently guide them away from the cliff. Gideon knew he'd reached the limit with the line of questioning and decided to accept whatever answer she provided, regardless of how vague.

"*Most importantly, I need to know for myself that I was leaving Los Angeles in a better place than when I took office six years ago.*"

"*And do you feel that is the case?*"

"Honestly, I do," she responded with a dose of humility. "The crime rate has dropped to single digits. The economy is back to prebanking meltdown days. The housing market has not fully recovered, but all economic indicators tell us we are moving in the right direction and at the right pace."

"The most recent polls show a majority of voters agree with you," Gideon responded slightly loosening his grip.

"Now everyone knows you were married just before you took office," he said as if poking a bear with a stick. "Some have said it was a political move on your part to soften your public image and make you appear less threatening to women voters. How do you respond to that?"

An image of Camille in a stunning gold, form-fitting Versace gown, arm in arm with Sheridan in a sleek black Armani tuxedo flashed on the monitor behind Gideon.

You son of a bitch, was her thought. *Much too clever for such obvious bait, Camille responded with, "Nothing could be further from the truth. The idea of marriage hadn't entered my mind during my first campaign. I was focused on the issues and winning the race. I considered a relationship to be a distraction. But when I met my husband, I'm sorry for the cliché, but it was love at first sight. We married shortly after we met, and he has been my biggest supporter ever since."*

"How involved is he in your work? For example, do you consult with him on any of the bigger issues you face?"

"Unfortunately, for me, my husband, Sheridan, couldn't be any less interested in politics than he is," Camille said. "I'm afraid he leaves the running of the city to me."

"What does he do for a living?"

"He's in real estate, dealing primarily in high-end residential properties."

"I imagine he has to walk a fine line doing business in the city," Gideon poked a little harder. "Every deal he is involved in has the potential to pose a conflict of interest for you."

Camille appeared genuinely off-put by the statement. "I can assure you and the people of Los Angeles, my husband's work never intersects or interferes with the work I do as mayor."

Looks like I hit a nerve, he silently surmised. Gideon was satisfied, for the moment, by her obvious discomfort and set the stick aside. *"So tell us about your plans for the new baseball stadium," Gideon said, fully conscious of the short time remaining. "Have you identified a location yet?"*

Finally, she thought. *"I'm glad you asked. As some of your viewers may know, Angelinos love baseball. Our team, the Los Angeles Dobermans, are currently housed in an arena built in 1927 and is in desperate need of major repairs, retrofitting and renovation. In the last midterm election, the voters authorized me to move forward with building a new home for our team. Well, I'm very pleased to announce, as of this week, we have identified a location perfect for the needs of the new Dober Stadium, and the fans."*

"Congratulations," Gideon beamed. *"Where will it be?"*

"Due to the generosity of a loyal Doberman fan, who shall remain nameless for now, we will build the new stadium in Playa del Rey on 110 oceanfront acres. The site is perfect for a number of reasons, including, minimal impact on neighbors because it is an unoccupied portion of the beach, with excellent access to public transportation and plenty of space for not only the stadium and parking, but mixed development projects like housing and commercial space."

"Has the city already purchased the property?" Gideon asked cautiously reaching for the stick again.

"We are in negotiations with the owner as we speak and hope to have the deal sealed by the end of the week."

"Aren't you a bit nervous about going public with the location before you've taken pen to paper?"

"Not at all," Camille replied confidently. *"The benefactor is a long-time Dober fan and sees this as an opportunity to give something back to the team and to the city she loves."*

"Is your husband assisting with the acquisition?"

The smile that dotted the interview instantly vanished. Camille couldn't hide her displeasure, and Gideon found it difficult to contain his satisfaction from piercing her seemingly impenetrable armor. He had no idea, however, how closely his instincts brought him to the truth—and neither did she. Three silent seconds in television time seemed like hours in real time.

The two locked eyes and neither blinked. No words were exchanged, but the silence was deafening. Camille immediately recognized Gideon as a problem that may have to be dealt with if she was to become governor. *Be careful, my handsome friend, or you may become Madame Gillette Lemaitre's next victim.*

"Let me assure you and the people of Los Angeles," Camille said shifting effortlessly into campaign mode, *"my husband will in no way be affiliated with the acquisition or construction of the Dober Stadium."*

"Well, best of luck, Mayor Hardaway," Gideon said delivering one final jab of the stick. *"It has been wonderful having you on today. I do hope you will come back when you've decided whether you will run for governor."*

"I certainly will. I've already promised, you will be the first to know."

"You all heard it," Gideon said playfully looking directly at the camera. *"Thank you again to Mayor Camille Ernestine Hardaway. Stay tuned. Coming up next we'll be speaking with the lovely and talented Halle Berry about her upcoming summer blockbuster movie, Blood Alley."*

The microphones went dead, but the cameras remained on Camille and Gideon for an additional ten seconds showing a pantomimed conversation.

"Thank you, Mayor," Gideon said as a technician removed Camille's microphone. "Excellent interview."

Camille ignored the feeble attempt at a compliment and calmly said, "You're barking up the wrong tree, Mr. Truman."

"I'm sure all your husband's business dealings are aboveboard, but I hope you understand I did have to ask."

"I do understand. And you should understand, I don't appreciate being blindsided on national television. I did this interview because you assured me there would be no surprises."

"It wasn't my intent to blindside you."

"Intent or not, that is exactly what you did." Camille dropped the charming politician mask on the studio set floor with a splat. The smile that lit up the seventy-inch monitor vanished as quickly as it appeared. She looked Gideon directly in eye and said coldly, "Trust me, Mr. Truman, I am *not* the person you want to fuck with."

Chapter 5

"Sheridan Hardaway. I have a 1:00 appointment with Miss Vandercliff."

The man at the gatehouse looked like a six-foot-six brick wall tightly wrapped in a grey security guard uniform. The shirt barely contained his bulging biceps, and buttons struggled to cover his enormous chest.

The guard looked at Sheridan suspiciously. It was as if no one had ever come to the gate before. "May I see your identification please, sir?"

"License?" Sheridan exclaimed. "I didn't realize I would need it," he said retrieving his wallet from his breast pocket. Sheridan waited patiently as the half man-half wall compared the image on the license to his face. The guard walked back to the little booth and dialed a landline.

"Good afternoon, ma'am," the guard said into the tethered receiver. "Mr. Sheridan Hardaway is here to see you."

Sheridan saw the outline of the home in the distance through the eight-foot wrought iron gate. His real estate calculator kicked in automatically. *Forty to fifty million easily,* he thought as the guard returned to the car.

"Thank you, Mr. Hardaway," he said. "Is this your first visit to the Vandercliff Estate?"

Sheridan noted the man's hands looked like baseball gloves. "Yes, it is," he replied.

"Then welcome. There are a few things Miss Vandercliff would like you to know before you enter the property. You will be greeted by another member of the security staff when you reach the home. The Vandercliffs have been the target of numerous kidnapping and assassination attempts over the years so you will be searched with a handheld metal detector."

Sheridan looked surprised as the guard continued.

"If you are wearing any type of cologne, Miss Vandercliff asks you remain at least five feet away from her as she is allergic to certain chemicals found in most mass market fragrances. She does not wish to be touched in any way, so please do not attempt to shake hands. Miss Vandercliff is unusually susceptible to germs and, as a precaution, asks that all guests to the estate take advantage of the powder room you will see to the left of the foyer when you enter the residence. She asks that you wash your hands using the special antiseptic soap provided."

"Is she a germaphobe?" Sheridan asked tactlessly.

The well-trained guard ignored the question and continued his recital. "After you enter the gate, stay on this path. It will take you directly to the main entrance of the home."

The giant turned abruptly to the guardhouse on the last word. The electric gate slid open, and Sheridan drove up the path as he had been so efficiently instructed. The lush grounds of the estate were immaculate. The flagstone path sliced through the center of ten sprawling acres of the most expensive soil in California.

Towering white bark eucalyptus trees stood like sphinxes along the entire length of the winding driveway. Sheridan saw a sparkling swimming pool glimmering like a sapphire lying on a bed of green through the trees. To the left was a gazebo surrounded by a well-appointed redwood deck, tennis courts, and other houses he assumed were once used to entertain the family's rich and famous guests.

After the last sharp turn on the path, the house appeared. *Make that seventy million,* Sheridan thought when he saw the French-inspired chateau, aptly named Le Belvédère. Even from the road, the stunning 280-degree city views could be seen. Sheridan had thoroughly researched the reclusive Miss Vandercliff, including the particulars of her magnificent estate: *48,000 square feet, 5,000-bottle wine cellar, three master suites, seven additional bedrooms, nineteen fireplaces, elevator* . . . he recalled as the car slowed to a stop in front of the main entrance.

"Good afternoon, Mr. Hardaway. Welcome to Le Belvédère," a clone of the enormous gatehouse guard said as Sheridan exited the car. "If you would please follow me, Miss Vandercliff will be with you shortly."

"They grow them big in Bel Air," Sheridan joked as he followed the guard to the main entrance of the house.

"Yes, sir, if you insist," was the humorless reply.

Upon entering the house, the giant removed a handheld metal detector from his jacket and said, "Would you please place any metal objects you have in your pockets on the table. This will only take a moment."

The foyer was three stories high. A grand oak circular stairway wrapped around an eight-foot Tiffany chandelier that cried a thousand crystal tears. The *Blue Nude* by Henri Matisse hung casually on the wall directly opposite the front entrance.

"Is that . . ." Sheridan asked pointing to the masterpiece in awe.

"Yes, sir, it is. A gift to the family from Matisse himself."

The guard traced Sheridan's body with the wand that beeped at his belt buckle.

"I hope you don't expect me to take off my belt."

"No, sir, that won't be necessary. After you have utilized the facilities," the guard said, pointing to the infamous powder room, "Miss Vandercliff will join you in the living room."

Sheridan replaced the contents of his pockets and obediently entered the powder room. He ran the water in a gold basin, but a drop never touched his hands. *Fuck the crazy bitch,* he thought. *I'm more likely to catch something from her than she is from me. Just hope crazy ain't contagious.*

His senses were immediately overwhelmed by the ocean of oak accents in the living room. Gaudy French provincial décor and old-world masterpieces lined the walls like hand-sewn panels on an antique quilt. He walked to the floor-to-ceiling windows at the rear wall and gazed out over Los Angeles, the kingdom that belonged to his wife.

"Mr. Hardaway," came a soft voice from across the room, "I'm Gloria Vandercliff. Welcome to my home."

The lady of the house mirrored the grand home. The rarified heights of Bel Air had been kind to her. At seventy-one years of age, she carried her petite frame across the room like a woman of much-younger years. She was casually dressed in a flowing kaleidoscope blue, white, and yellow Emilio Pucci caftan and black Christian Louboutin cage sandals. The fashion world had clearly not left her behind. A shock of perfectly tousled blond hair took ten years off her face.

"May I offer you a drink?" she asked, pointing to a fully stocked wet bar near the window where Sheridan stood.

Miss Vandercliff stopped exactly five feet away from Sheridan to inspect the air around him. After finding no hint of cologne, she closed the distance between them.

"Thank you. Gin and tonic," he replied with his usual sense of entitlement.

"A good-looking and decisive man with good taste," she said walking past Sheridan to the bar. "I can see we're going to get along just fine. I'm sure you've been told I don't invite many people into my home."

"Yes, so I've heard."

"But when we spoke on the phone yesterday your offer intrigued me."

Miss Vandercliff returned to Sheridan with their drinks in hand. "Cheers, Mr. Hardaway," she said lifting the glass to her lips. "So tell me more about your offer," she said directing him to a nine-foot sofa in front of the fireplace.

Sheridan noted she left only three feet between them when she sat down. *I guess I passed the sniff test,* he thought.

"As I said to you on the telephone, my company, KeyCorp Development, would like to purchase your land in Playa del Rey. We are prepared to offer you a substantial amount more than what you're asking."

"You do realize I've already promised the land to . . ." she paused dramatically before continuing, "your wife?"

"Yes, I am aware of the city's interest."

"Does she know you're making this offer?"

"No."

"Then why are you doing this?" she asked already knowing the answer.

"Because I love my wife, and I want to stop her from making a mistake that could cost her the governor's race."

"So she *is* running for governor," she replied as if just being slipped a juicy bit of city hall gossip. "How could building Dober Stadium on my land prevent her from becoming governor?"

"If she isn't able to raise the additional funds for the development, or if she, for some other reason, isn't able to complete the stadium, she'll look like a fool. Her poll numbers are so strong now she doesn't need this project to become governor. She could win on name recognition and her record alone. I've tried to tell her this, but her advisors are telling her otherwise."

Miss Vandercliff listened intently before speaking. "So you're willing to invest millions to prevent your wife from making a mistake?" she asked skeptically.

"I told you, I love my wife and would do anything to protect her," Sheridan responded with such sincerity it even convinced him.

"She doesn't need much protection from what I can tell. She seems quite capable to me."

"Don't get me wrong. She is one of the strongest and smartest people I know, but I think she's in over her head when it comes to this stadium."

"And what do you intend to do with the land?"

"Maybe build low-income housing or a school for underprivileged kids. At this stage I'm not sure, but I know I have to move quickly before she makes a terrible mistake."

"What's to stop her from buying another property and building the stadium there?"

"She won't. Her real estate division has looked at every possible option in the city and this is the only location that could work."

Sheridan allowed Miss Vandercliff's brain to marinate in his last impassioned words. *Old bleeding heart probably loved the school for underprivileged kids line,* he thought, studying her face.

She stood from the sofa with drink in hand and walked to the window. "Do you know how much I'm worth, Mr. Hardaway?" she asked looking out the window.

"I imagine a great deal," he responded cautiously.

"A great deal indeed. At last count, it was just under 3 billion. So I'm surprised you think I am a fool," she added casually.

Sheridan froze when he heard the words. "Not at all. You're obviously a very intelligent woman."

"Then why else would you come into my home and lie to me?"

"Lie? I don't know what you mean. I want to buy the property to protect—"

"If you want this conversation to continue, Mr. Hardaway," she said turning abruptly to face him, "I suggest you tell me the real reason you've come here behind your wife's back."

Sheridan stood and quickly recalibrated his approach. "All right, Miss Vandercliff," he said, knowing there was nothing left to lose. "I'll tell you. My wife doesn't know I own KeyCorp Development. My intent is to purchase the property from you, and then sell it to the city for a small profit."

"Good boy," she said with a wicked smile. "Now was that so difficult? My dear late father taught me a very important lesson a long time ago that you might benefit from."

"And what was that?" Sheridan asked, sensing he was back in the game.

"Never underestimate your prey. They're usually smarter and stronger than you think."

"I must admit, I may have underestimated you," said Sheridan. "But I think I understand you now."

"To better understandings," she said raising her glass in a mock toast. "Can I freshen your drink, Mr. Hardaway?"

"That would be very nice, Miss Vandercliff. Thank you."

"Still so formal," she said with a hint of seduction. "Even after I've learned your little secret. Call me Gloria."

"Gloria," he said with a nod, acknowledging the unspoken code among thieves.

"The only reason I agreed to meet with you is because some little shit from your wife's office called and told me if I don't sell it to the city for $80 million they would take it by eminent domain. I don't like bullies, and I like being threatened even less," she practically snarled.

Gloria returned to the couch and continued. "Now, give me one good reason why I should sell my property to you and not your wife, besides that lovely smile of yours."

Sheridan calculated the change in the playing field and was more than prepared to take one for the team. He sat close to her on the couch and said slyly, "I can give you ten reasons."

"Mr. Hardaway," she smiled, "if you're saying what I think you're saying, I just might be interested."

"It's Sheridan," he said, placing his hand gently on her thigh, "and I am saying *exactly* what you think I'm saying."

Sheridan moved his hand steadily up her thigh causing the caftan to rise and expose her wrinkled knee.

"Ten reasons you say?" she asked skeptically.

"There's actually eleven," he whispered. "I was being modest."

Sheridan cupped the back of her head and pulled her to his lips. He could taste the remnants of an imported cigarette and what he guessed must be Polident. The thought of the profit he would make on the deal caused him to drive his tongue deep into her open, waiting mouth. Denture cream and stale cigarettes never tasted so sweet.

"Convince me, Sheridan," she panted. "Give me your eleven reasons."

Miss Vandercliff nimbly unzipped his fly with her bony fingers and released eleven solid reasons. Sheridan had no difficulty becoming fully aroused. The millions now within his grasp made him stand at full attention when she lowered her bleached head to his lap. Her jaws unhinged like an anaconda allowing the tip of his member to be massaged by her tonsils.

"Are those enough reasons?" Sheridan whispered while her head bobbed up and down the full length of his shaft.

Miss Vandercliff looked up with a satisfied grin and said, "Three more reasons than I expected."

Sheridan lifted her head and returned his tongue to her still-open mouth. He then pushed her back and lifted her legs, causing the caftan to form ripples of silk around her waist. He wasn't surprised to see she wasn't wearing panties. Sheridan took a deep breath and quickly lowered his head between her legs, causing her to gasp.

"Convince me, Sheridan," she moaned as the twists and turns of his skilled tongue caused her to squirm and buck under the weight of his head.

Sheridan slowed the whirl of his tongue. *Don't want to give her a heart attack before she signs the papers,* he thought.

He then lowered his pants to his ankles while Miss Vandercliff gently trembled from after-quakes of ecstasy. He guided his member into her flesh, one inch at a time.

"One reason," he said narrating. "Two reasons," as he slowly entered inch by inch. "Three reasons . . ."

With each inch her moans grew more intense. "Nine reasons. Are you convinced yet?"

"Give me two more reasons," she moaned. "I want it all."

Sheridan delivered the last two reasons with such force the gold bangles wrapping her wrists rattled like wind chimes blowing in the breeze on a back porch. Sheridan moved cautiously for fear of shattering old brittle bones, but Miss Vandercliff demanded more.

"Fuck me, Sheridan Hardaway," she barked. "Fuck me harder."

He dutifully followed her instructions and began to pound mercilessly into her dry flesh. "Is that enough to convince you?" he asked accenting every word with a plunge of his hips.

"Yes, my beautiful Mandingo," she shrieked. "I'm almost there. Keep convincing me."

"Are you going to sell it to me?" he asked in time with his thrusts. "Is this reason enough for you, Miss Gloria Vandercliff?"

The motion of Sheridan's hips quickly guided Miss Vandercliff to the height of ecstasy.

"Yes! Yes!" she finally screamed, thrashing her head from side to side. "Yes, I'll sell it to you! I'll sell it to you!"

The intercom in Camille's office buzzed at exactly 3:00.

"Excuse me, Mayor Hardaway," came the voice on the intercom. "I have a Mr. Kelsey Hunt on line one. He said it's very important he speak with you."

"What is it about?" Camille asked. "I'm busy."

"I'm sorry, ma'am, he wouldn't say, but he called on your private line and was very insistent. He said it is of national importance, and you will understand when you speak."

Camille wearily dropped her pen onto a stack of papers requiring her signature. "Put him through," she grunted.

"Yes, Mayor," came the relieved reply.

"This is Mayor Hardaway," she said politely into the phone. "How may I help you?"

"Good afternoon, Mayor Hardaway," the husky voice said. "Thank you for taking my call."

"My pleasure. What is it you wanted to discuss with me," she replied restraining her impatience.

"My name is Lazarus Hearst. Have you ever heard of me?"

"Hearst? My assistant said your name was Hunt."

"I must apologize for the slight deception, but it is best for all concerned no one is aware of our conversation."

"What is this about?" Camille grew impatient. "You've actually caught me at a very busy time."

"I understand," Hearst said calmly. "I'll get to the point of my call. I am the sole owner of Media Wise Industries, the largest media conglomerate on the planet. I control 60 percent of the media in the United States and 30 percent globally. Are you familiar with us?"

She recognized the name Hearst, one of the most influential families in the world when he said Media Wise Industries.

Hearst, a reclusive Philadelphia philanthropist, gave hundreds of millions to museums, public art collections, education, medicine, and political causes at both ends of the ideological spectrum. The only criteria was, it served to further his agenda.

Camille leaned back in her chair and simply replied, "Yes. I know the company."

"Good. Now I have another question for you. Please indulge me," he said politely. "Have you ever heard of The Committee?"

"I know of hundreds of committees. The entire city of Los Angeles is run by committees."

Hearst laughed, "Of course. I should have been clearer. I am referring to 'The Committee' comprised of the most powerful people in the country, who, among other things, have decided who the presidents of our great country have been since the early 1700s. We each bring our own unique talents and spheres of influence to the table and pool them to, in essence, run the country."

Camille's heart stopped. She placed a hand over the receiver and gasped. After catching her breath, she responded. "The Committee is a myth. I've heard of it, but everyone knows it doesn't exist," she said more in an attempt to convince herself. "There is no such group. The voters select the presidents."

Hearst laughed again, and then replied, "That is the true myth. The voters choose who we tell them to choose. And, in the rare event the people go against our wishes, we veto it by any means necessary, as were the cases with Garfield, McKinley, Kennedy, and Gore. I assure you, Mayor Hardaway, The Committee does indeed exist, and I am a member."

Camille's emotions raced between disbelief, fear, and irritation. Either this was a silly hoax, or she was actually speaking with a member of one of the most secret societies in the history of the country.

"Are you still there, Mrs. Hardaway? You can speak freely. The call was made using a point-to-point encryption key. I assure you anything we discuss will only be heard by you and me."

"Yes, I'm here."

"Good. I know you must think this is a prank, but I assure you it is not."

"And how do I know that?" she asked skeptically.

"Maybe if I told you a few things about yourself that you thought no one knew . . . Would that help?"

Camille stood from the desk and walked to the window with the cordless phone attached securely to her ear. "Like what?" she asked guardedly.

"Well, let's see . . . for example, we are aware you were molested by a deacon in your family's church when you were eight years old. No need to confirm or deny this because I know it is true, Camille. May I call you Camille?"

She did not respond. Her knees trembled slightly as Hearst continued.

"We also know you had a four-month affair with a professor while you were in law school. You became pregnant, but miscarried in your third month. Your parents never knew about it. Please accept my condolences, by the way. I know it must have been very difficult for you."

Camille stumbled back to her desk and sat down slowly. Fear was now the dominant emotion.

"I'm going to share this next one with you, but please be aware it isn't to frighten or threaten you, but simply to remove any doubts you might still have at this point."

Camille resisted the urge to hang up the phone; instead, she braced herself for the next revelation.

"We know about the role you played in the planning commissioner's untimely death," Hearst said slowly.

Gillette! Camille thought angrily. "I had nothing to do with his death," she blurted. "It was an automobile accident. If you're trying to blackmail me—"

"No, no," he interrupted. "This has nothing to do with blackmail, Camille," Hearst said measuredly. "You and I both know it is true. Do you still have the baseball signed by Willie Mays the commissioner gave you?"

Camille sat silently with her hand cupped over her mouth. A tear threatened to escape her transfixed eyes, but she willed it to not fall. "I don't know what you're talking about," she finally said weakly.

"Of course you do," Hearst said with a slight chuckle. "But I would have been very disappointed if you'd said anything other than exactly that. I assure you, your secret is safe with The Committee. We understand you had no other choice and did what you did in the best interest of Los Angeles. You should be commended."

"I did nothing," she said, evoking the most basic tenet of a good defense: *Deny everything*.

"Understood," Hearst said sarcastically. "Now let's get past that. Do you believe me, or should we end this call now? If you decide to hang up, please know you will never hear from me again, and your secrets will go to the grave with myself and each of my colleagues on The Committee. Your file will be destroyed."

"File?" she asked nervously.

"Yes, Camille. File. We know more about you than you know about yourself."

Camille sat silently. A whirl of thoughts rushed through her mind. *This is the end of my career. My poor unborn baby. I'll never be governor. I wonder, do they know about . . . I could go to jail,* she thought while Hearst gave her time to process the information.

"Camille," he finally said, "I'm assuming since you haven't hung up you would like for me to continue. Is that correct?"

"Yes," she said reluctantly. "What is this all about?"

"I'm very pleased you asked. The Committee has been watching your career very closely for the last six years, and I must tell you, we are all very impressed."

Hearst waited for a polite "thank you," but none came. "I'll come directly to the point," he continued. "We think you are presidential material, Camille. Of course, we would have to get you elected governor first. A simple formality."

The words, delivered so casually, hung in front of Camille like a noose. Breath rushed from her body as if someone had sucker punched her in the gut. Her heart pounded, and the room began to spin like a wheel around an axle. *This can't be happening,* she thought. *I'm dreaming.* She willed herself to wake up . . . but it wasn't a dream.

After a few moments, Hearst said, "May I ask what you're thinking?"

There was silence, so he continued. "I understand this may all seem a bit sudden to you, but as I said earlier, we have been watching you for a while, and we like what we see."

Again, there was silence. "Is this something you would like to explore further with us?" he asked.

Camille did not speak.

"We would love the opportunity to speak with you in person, Camille. I've taken the liberty of arranging for my jet to fly you to our Headquarters." Hearst repeated the word, "Headquarters," and laughed. "I know this must sound like a James Bond movie, but it's true; we actually do have a headquarters. Anyway, as I was saying, the jet will be waiting for you, whether or not you decide to meet with us, this Sunday night at the Long Beach Airport in my private hanger #217 at 8:00 p.m."

"Where is 'Headquarters'?" she finally asked.

"I'd rather not say at this point. But I can assure you, we will have you back in LA safe and sound on Monday morning so you can continue

the fine work you're doing for the people of Los
Angeles."

"Who are the other members?" she asked.

"Again, I cannot say."

She gave no response.

"Only two members will be there. But if all
goes well, you will meet most of the others in due
time."

"Most?"

"Yes, I'm afraid some of our members prefer
to remain anonymous. Nonetheless, we'll have a
nice chat and answer all the questions I'm sure
you must have." Hearst paused briefly, then
concluded, "I do hope you will decide to join us,
Camille. Our country needs you."

With his last words, he disconnected the line,
leaving Camille alone and dazed in her office
high atop city hall.

The teakettle on Hattie's stove began to whis-
tle at the same moment the doorbell rang. "Just
a minute," she called out to Gideon Truman who
stood at the front door. Hattie moved to the door
as quickly as her legs could carry her.

"Come in, baby," she said warmly. "Sit down,
sit down. I'm making a pot of tea."

"Is everything all right?" Gideon called out to her retreating back. "You said it was urgent on the phone."

"No, Gideon," she replied, competing with the shrieking kettle, "everything is *not* all right, and I need you to tell me all about it."

Hattie returned shortly, carrying two steaming cups, each with the white Lipton Tea label dangling from strings down the sides. Gideon was still standing in the center of the room pondering the riddle of her last comment.

She set the cups on waiting coasters on the coffee table. "Are you going to stand there gawking at me," she asked slowly lowering into a wingback chair, "or are you going to sit down?"

Gideon sat on the sofa directly across from her. A tray of lemon wedges, white sugar cubes, honey and cream was already waiting on the table.

"I didn't know how you take your tea so . . ." she said pointing to the tray, "I brought a little bit of everything."

Gideon dropped two cubes in the cup. "Hattie, why are you being so mysterious? Is something wrong with your health?"

"My health is fine. It's you I'm worried about."

"Me?" he asked in surprise. "I'm fine."

"My spirit tells me otherwise."

"What are you talking about?"

"I'm talking about Camille Hardaway," she said looking him directly in the eye.

"Oh, you saw the interview."

"Yes, I did, and I saw other things too."

Gideon felt exposed whenever he was in Hattie's presence. He knew there was no way to hide anything from her prying third eye, the eye that saw things in and around people they would prefer remained secret.

He leaned back on the sofa and asked cautiously, "What did you see?"

"How is Danny?" she asked ignoring his question. "Are you taking good care of him? He loves you, and that's what you need most in your life right now. Not more fame. You've got plenty already."

"He's doing fine. We take care of each other. I love him more now than I ever have. He means the world to me."

"That's a blessing, son. Exactly what God wants for you."

"It's interesting," Gideon said pensively. "Danny said I should speak with you about Camille Hardaway too. Have you two been talking?"

"Yes, but not about this."

"What have you seen?" he asked, leaning forward.

"What's more important is what I know your spirit has been trying to tell you about her. Have you been listening to your heart? The heart will keep you out of harm's way. All you have to do is listen. What has it told you?"

Gideon considered not telling Hattie about the grumblings in his stomach whenever Camille came near him. He quickly concluded deception was pointless, however, under the gaze of her caring eyes.

"It tells me something is evil about her. That she is a dangerous woman, and I should be careful around her."

"And are you listening to what the Lord is trying to tell you?" she asked already knowing the answer.

"Hattie, you know I love you and listen to everything you tell me, but you don't understand," he replied defensively. "This is my job. I wouldn't be where I am today if I backed away from every story that made me uncomfortable. When my instincts tell me there is a story, I have to follow it. It's what I do."

"Even if it puts your life in danger?"

"What do you mean, danger?" he asked boldly.

Hattie sighed deeply and said, "There are forces around Mayor Camille Ernestine Hardaway . . ." She paused considering her words carefully. "The only word I can use to describe it is evil, and it will consume everything in its path—including you, son," she said, deliberately omitting the more graphic details of her startling visions.

A chill rushed up his spine when he heard the words. The concern in her eyes caused him to look down to the now tepid cup of tea.

Hattie allowed him a few moments to sort his thoughts, and then continued. "You've gotten too close already, son. It's time to let her go her way, and for you to go yours."

"If you are trying to scare me, it's working," he said abandoning his usual fearless bravado. "But do you realize this woman will most likely become the first black female governor in the history of the United States. And who knows, after that . . . She could conceivably become president. If she is surrounded by such dark forces, don't you think I have a responsibility to do something about it?"

"It's not your job, son. Have you already forgotten how both you and Danny were almost killed by Samantha Cleaveland? Do you want to put Danny in danger again?"

"I would never put him in harm's way."

"I know, baby, but if you continue down this path, that's exactly what you'll be doing."

"You're talking in riddles," Gideon said with a hint of frustration. "How am I jeopardizing Danny's safety? He's not involved in my work."

"Are you being intentionally naïve?" Hattie asked. "If someone wants to hurt you but can't, the next best thing is to hurt someone you love."

"I understand. But you still haven't told me why Camille would want to hurt me. I don't have any incriminating information on her. I made her look good in my interview. I elevated her onto a national stage by having her on my program. Why would she want to hurt me?"

Hattie considered just how much information Gideon could handle before responding. "Son," she said with the full weight of her maternal instinct, "it's not only Camille. My spirit tells me there are people and spirits around her doesn't even know about. Very powerful forces in this world and in the spirit world that have plans for her future. Do you understand?"

"Yes, ma'am," he said listening intently.

"I don't know who they are yet, but mark my word, it's not for good," she continued. "They need her for something. I can feel it. But I don't know what. They want to use her power to do their bidding here on earth. It's not good, son. Not good at all."

Hattie cupped her hand to her mouth. Gideon could see she was deeply troubled. "Are you all right?" he asked leaning in closer. "Can I get you anything?"

"No, baby, I'll be fine," Hattie paused before continuing. She reached for a napkin on the coffee table and dabbed her moist upper lip. "These are evil times we live in, son. Evil times, and I know Camille Hardaway has something to do with it all."

Chapter 6

It was a perfect California evening. Five hundred of the city's richest, famous, and most powerful residents gladly paid $250,000 per head for a ticket to be in the same room with Camille and Sheridan Hardaway. The room overflowed with Givenchy, Gucci, and Valentino gowns on the arms of black tuxedos. The first private fundraiser for the new Doberman Stadium was held at the Holmby Hills estate of one of the wealthiest men in the world.

The host, tech giant Isadore Montgomery's net worth was easily greater than the combined wealth of everyone in the room. At thirty-four years of age, he was the third-richest man in the world, all because he invented a cellular telephone half the world owned and the other half wanted. Now, the planet revolved on the axis of his technological edicts. If Isadore Montgomery said the next must-have electronic gadget was tennis shoes with a DVD mounted on the toes so you can watch movies while jogging, the world would camp out for weeks at the neighborhood big box store to be the first to own a pair of "Isadore Montgomery's Movie Shoes."

Isadore designed and built the ultramodern glass mansion. The home was fitted with technology the government would not know existed for at least another ten years. The electrifying sunset seen through every glass wall on the first floor seemed to have been orchestrated just for his party.

He was the ultimate tech guru and his word was golden. Single, dull, five-foot-six, moderately unattractive, completely heterosexual, and excruciatingly shy, according to *People* magazine, Isadore Montgomery was the most eligible bachelor on the planet.

"May I have your attention please," Isadore said softly from the grand glass staircase making it appear he was riding a crystal waterfall. Music from a live band in a remote corner of the room stopped abruptly, and the crowd fell silent. "As you all know, the reason for this evening is to raise money for the new Doberman Stadium. I'm happy to announce ticket sales tonight, combined with the pledges many of you have made, we have already raised $50 million and counting," he said excitedly.

Gasps and sustained applause erupted throughout the room.

"So if tonight is any indication," Isadore continued, "I predict this city is going to have a new stadium very, very soon." The room burst into laughter and applause again.

"None of this would be possible without one very special person," he said, pausing to look in Camille's direction. "Mayor Hardaway, would you please join me up here? Now remember," he chuckled with a semismile. "I'm a little shorter than you so you'll have to stand a few steps down."

The crowd laughed on cue as Camille made her way to the stairs. Her black sleeveless Oscar de la Renta gown with a sheer overlay was streaked with trails of black embroidered shooting stars. A single strand of dazzling diamonds dangled from each ear, and more strands made a double loop around her wrist. She took her place on the glass waterfall one step below Isadore, making them the same height.

"For those of you who don't know it, the idea to build Dober Stadium came from this stunning woman standing with me," Isadore said. "Ladies and Gentlemen, I present to you the illustrious mayor of our great city, Camille Ernestine Hardaway."

As the audience greeted her with applause, Isadore kissed Camille's cheek and whispered prophetically, "The stage is yours, Mrs. President."

Camille's radiant smile gave no hint her heart had momentarily stopped beating. Isadore's words left her stunned. She watched his back as he descended the stairs, leaving her standing alone with the clapping sea of money, silicone, and couture at her feet.

When Isadore reached the floor, he turned, looked up at Camille, and winked with a wicked little smile. The applause slowly subsided, but Camille hadn't yet regained her composure. The room fell silent as she stared blankly at Isadore, who instructed her to proceed with a slight nod of his head only she could see.

"Thank you, Isadore," she heard fall involuntarily from her lips. The words snapped her out of the confusion-induced trance. She lit up and became the magnificent Mayor Camille Hardaway once again.

She opened with, "One point six billion dollars," and paused to look boldly into the crowd. "You heard me correctly. Doberman Stadium will cost the city of Los Angeles $1.6 billion. I'm not worried about raising that kind of money because, for this crowd, that's vacation mad money."

The room exploded in laughter. Charm poured from the beautiful woman and consumed the room like a flood. Camille shared the gargantuan details of the project as if they were already complete. "Fans of the Dobers will be treated to views of magnificent California sunsets over the ocean during game nights. Commercial spaces will line the perimeter of the complex offering high-end goods and fine dining experiences. The residential portion will include the finest architectural living spaces with world-class views."

By the end of her speech, the stadium complex was fully occupied and generating millions in tax revenue. The 50 million pledged before she spoke steadily climbed to 1, 2, 3, and 400 million as her smooth and confident words loosened wallets, trust funds, and investment portfolios.

Camille was greeted at the foot of the stairs by a kiss from Sheridan. Cameras flashed, enveloping the couple in a shroud of light. Samantha clung to Sheridan's arm, even when he tried to pull away, as they made their way through the adoring crowd.

"What's wrong?" he whispered in her ear under the guise of an affectionate peck on the cheek. "You're hurting my arm."

"Where did he go?"

"Who?"

"Isadore Montgomery," she snapped through a clinched smile.

"I don't see him. He left halfway through your speech. I haven't seen him since. He could be anywhere in this big-ass house.

"What happened? Did he say something to you?" Sheridan asked protectively.

"Yes," Camille said. "No . . . no. I don't know. Maybe I misheard him but . . ." she stopped midsentence and loosened her grip on his arm. "Never mind. It was nothing. Let's just shake the rest of these hands and get out of here. I want to go home."

Closed circuit cameras tucked into hidden crevices of the room, behind mirrors, in chandeliers, and transparent ones imbedded in the many windows, followed Camille as she worked the crowd. Her image was captured from every possible angle and fed to a bank of monitors in the control room buried deep within the bowels of the glass mansion.

Isadore Montgomery sat alone in the sound-proof room and watched his newest acquisition with great pleasure. "She is perfect," he said.

"Yes, I knew you would agree once you met her in person," came the disembodied voice of Lazarus Hearst. "The country will love her too."

"I'm not so sure about him though," Isadore said while studying the screen as Camille charmed another investor.

"Your instincts are right again," Lazarus said. "Preliminary reports on Sheridan Hardaway are not good. He's apparently been making millions on real estate investments using information received from Camille and her chief of staff, Tony Christopoulos, who, by the way, he also happens to be fucking."

"Oh shit," Isadore blurted. "Then she's out."

"Not necessarily. Accidents *do* happen," Lazarus said casually.

"And Americans love a widow."

"So true. Jacqueline could have been president if she'd been able to pull herself together after the assassination. We offered, but she turned us down."

"Different times," Isadore said, "America wasn't ready for a woman in the 1960s."

"America is ready for whatever The Committee tells them they're ready for," Lazarus said dismissively.

Isadore laughed. "When are you expecting the final report on him?"

"Tomorrow."

"Is she coming to Headquarters on Sunday?"

"We won't know until Sunday at 8:00 p.m. My instincts tell me she'll be there. The Committee will have to make a decision about how to deal with Sheridan before then. She has to be made aware of our plans."

"Why?"

"So rich and yet so naïve," Lazarus said. "She has to be a part of the decision if we decide to eliminate him. Her hands have to get dirty. The dirtier they are, the more control we'll have over her."

"She'll never agree to it."

"You underestimate her hunger for power. If Camille is made of the stuff I think she is, she will come to the same conclusion. Sheridan Hardaway must die."

"And what about Tony Christopoulos?"

"He can be of use to us right where he is. I'll have a little talk with him."

Gideon typed Sheridan Hardaway into the Google search engine in his office. The screen quickly blinked, and the results appeared. The page indicated there were approximately 4,380,000 results.

Gideon clicked on the results one by one, undaunted by the volume of Web sites containing the name Sheridan and/or Hardaway.

Dozens included images of the handsome man with and without Camille. Numerous articles contained his name, but most were incidental mentions in stories about his wife.

Gideon scribbled notes on a yellow pad. *"Graduated with a bachelor of art degree from Cal State Los Angeles. Born in Hawthorn, California. Real estate broker, no children."* All information Gideon already knew about him.

He scanned dozens of Web sites. The information began to repeat itself. Graduated with a bachelor of art degree from Cal State Los Angeles. Born in Hawthorn, California. Real estate broker, no children.

Maybe there really is nothing, Gideon thought as he tapped the mouse to close the fiftieth site. *Not even an outstanding parking ticket.*

Just as Gideon was about to give up, the name KeyCorp Development appeared as the next option. He found it odd Sheridan's name didn't appear in the brief synopsis on the search page.

He opened the site. It was the usual well-designed corporate Web site with smiling models who had no idea the company had used their images.

KeyCorp Development is a trusted leader in alternative investment opportunities, helping to emphasize the necessity of nontraditional assets for portfolio growth and diversification.

KeyCorp Development provides innovative alternative investment opportunities by leveraging investment program development, management, performance, and distribution experience.

Programs sponsored and managed by the KeyCorp Development group of companies have attracted equity of more than $457 million.

KeyCorp Development has sponsored fifteen fully cycled real estate investment programs.

Founded by Michael Kenigrant, KeyCorp Development is an in-house, FINRA-registered broker-dealer and member of SIPC.

Gideon read page after page of the Web site, but Sheridan's name was nowhere to be found. *Why did it come up in a search for Sheridan Hardaway?* he thought, looking curiously at screen.

"That's interesting," he said aloud. "KeyCorp Development was incorporated six years ago. The same year they were married."

His reporter instincts kicked in. Gideon went to the state of California's Web site. "Now let's see," he said speaking to himself, "who filed the original papers with the state to form the corporation."

When he entered the company name, the familiar hourglass icon appeared and began to spin as it sorted through billions of binary codes. The page finally blinked onto the screen and slowly opened inch by inch.

"OK," he said leaning toward the screen, "let's see what we've got here."

KeyCorp Development
Type: Privately Held Corporation
Formed in: Los Angeles County
Total Assets: $457,000,000
Articles of Incorporation filed by: Sheridan Hardaway

Gideon stared at the screen and read the words repeatedly to ensure his brain wasn't playing a trick.

Articles of Incorporation filed by: Sheridan Hardaway

"Son of a bitch," he said slowly. "Does Camille know about this?"

Jean-Luc Fantoché's carriage barreled down Rue des Bourbon forcing pedestrians to scurry out of its path. The coachman suddenly pulled hard on the reins and shouted, "Whoa there.

Easy now, boys," forcing the two stallions to rear up onto their powerful hind legs to stop the racing hansom cab.

Fantoché wasted no time exiting the coach. His black cape flared behind him as he ran to Juliette's front door.

"Juliette!" he called out as he leaped the porch stairs in one exuberant bound. "Let me in, Juliette. I have wonderful news!"

The front door swung open and her face caused him to stop and gaze at her beauty.

"What is it?" she asked. "Are you drunk?"

"Yes, mon chéri. Drunk on life, intoxicated by your beauty. Inebriated by my good fortune!" he exclaimed.

Fantoché rushed to her, lifted her in his arms, and twirled a full circle.

"Put me down," she said laughing. "Come in and tell me your good news."

When the door closed behind them, Fantoché shouted, "He's dead! Thaddeus Barrière is dead!"

Juliette looked at him earnestly. "Dead? When?"

"Only this morning," he said, unable to contain his joy. "He was found lying in a pool of his own bile in his bed chamber. He choked to death in his sleep."

How ironic, she thought. He lived spewing bile, and now he has died choking on the very same.

"Do you know what this means?"

"It means you are a horrible man for taking pleasure in another man's misfortune," she said with just the right balance of disapproval and admonishment. *"You should be ashamed of yourself."*

"No, my darling," he said elatedly. *"It means I will surely be the governor of our great state. I am now unchallenged on the ballot. I will win, even if I am the only man in the entire state of Louisiana who is foolish enough to cast his vote in my favor!"*

Juliette turned her back and walked to the parlor with Fantoché following close behind.

"What is the matter, my darling? I thought you would be as pleased as I. It was you who persuaded me to enter the race. I did it for you, and now your prayer has been answered. It is fate, do you not see? God has sealed my destiny. I shall be governor. Maybe even president."

Juliette remained with her back to him. "I am pleased," she said. *"It is only I cannot remove from my mind the horrible manner by which your fate has been sealed. He must have suffered terribly. Do they know what caused his death?"*

"No, only that there was no foul play involved," he said tempering his delight. *"He was alone in his bed chamber with the door locked from inside."*

Juliette looked toward the fireplace to conceal her smile. No suffering was too great for a man such as he, she thought. I only wish I could have been there to serve as a witness to his torment.

"That is good," she said turning to face him from behind a veil of pity. *"At least no innocent person will be implicated in his death."*

The remainder of Camille's week was consumed with the mundane tasks few associated with the job of mayor, such as filling potholes, ribbon cutting, and doling out proclamations. This was accompanied by an endless stream of citizens who thought she had been elected to silence their neighbor's barking dog, remove the homeless person sleeping on their corner, or install the desperately needed stop sign in their neighborhood.

Even with oversized scissors aimed at yellow ribbons and in meetings with visiting dignitaries, the conversation with Lazarus Hearst never left her mind. Was he serious? How could she know if it was actually him. Did Gillette tell him about

John Spalding? Should she go to the airport on Sunday night?

The questions seemed unending and most went unanswered. It was now Sunday evening, and she still had not decided.

"Honey," Sheridan called out from the bathroom in the master suite of the mayor's mansion, "you'd better hurry. We're going to be late for the opera. It starts at 7:00."

Sheridan emerged in a black tuxedo and saw Camille staring blankly out the window. "Camille," he shouted. "What are you doing? You're not even dressed yet. You love Tosca."

She did not respond.

"Camille," he called out again and walked to her side. "Honey," he said reaching for her arm, "are you feeling all right?"

Camille jumped at his touch. "What? I'm sorry," she blurted. "I wasn't listening. What did you say?"

"I said are you feeling all right?" he repeated with concern.

"I'm fine. Why do you ask?"

"Because I have been talking and you haven't heard a word I've said. You've been this way all week. Maybe we shouldn't go. You've been pushing yourself too hard lately."

"I'm fine, darling," she said regaining her composure and gently touching his cheek. "I just have a lot on my mind with the stadium. Give me a few minutes and I'll meet you downstairs."

"Are you sure?"

"Yes. Now go. I won't be long."

Sheridan left Camille standing in the window. *That's final. I'm not going to the airport. The entire notion is ridiculous. Headquarters, secret societies,* she scoffed. *A committee who selects the president. It's all nonsense, and I was a fool for considering it.*

Camille was silent in the back of the limousine the entire ride. Sheridan made futile attempts at getting her attention, but all fell on deaf ears.

"Do you think the Hendersons will be there tonight?" he tested.

There was no response.

"I hope we're not late. If we are, let's skip it and go to Fat Burgers."

Still no response from Camille as she looked out the tinted windows.

The limousine rolled to a stop at the foot of the main stairs leading to the Dorothy Chandler Pavilion. The driver hurried to Camille's door. She emerged, wearing a dazzling aqua-blue Oscar de la Renta gown made especially for her, with Sheridan following close behind.

"We'll be three hours," Sheridan said to the driver. "Make sure you're back here when we come out."

"Yes sir," the faceless driver said.

By 7:30, Camille and Sheridan sat comfortably in mezzanine seats overlooking the grand auditorium. The opera house was full to capacity, and everyone in the room at some point looked up to see the celebrity mayor and her handsome husband.

She faded in and out of the drama unfolding on the lavishly designed set below. Divas pouring their souls onto the stage, shedding a river of tears over unrequited love, and filling the hall with anguished arias went mostly unnoticed by Camille. Pounding overtures from the orchestra amounted to nothing more than a bothersome buzz in her ear.

What if it's legitimate? Camille thought.

President Camille Ernestine Hardaway. The words reverberated in her head to the tune of the tenor singing "E lucevan le stelle."

I could be passing up the chance of a lifetime.

Halfway through the first act, Camille looked at Sheridan and said abruptly, "I have to leave."

"What? It's just started," he responded.

Camille grabbed her beaded clutch, stood, and said, "Call the driver and tell him to meet me in front. Now."

When Sheridan motioned to stand, Camille put a hand firmly on his shoulder and snapped. "No. You stay. I'll send the car back for you."

With that, she disappeared through the curtain into the hall.

"Is something wrong?" asked a startled usher.

Camille ignored the question. Her Manolo Blahnik pumps made light of a flight of stairs leading to the ground floor. She moved swiftly through the lobby to the wall of glass doors and exited into the night with the fabric of her dress billowing behind. She quickly scanned the two deep rows of limousines. The SUV rounded the corner just as her heel touched the bottom step.

The driver made his way through the labyrinth of cars toward her. Camille reached for the door handle before the car came to a complete stop. "Is there a problem, Mrs. Mayor?" the concerned driver asked.

"Yes. I have a situation out of I town I have to attend to. Take me to the Long Beach Airport, Hanger 217."

"May I ask where you will be flying?" he asked sheepishly. "The head of your security detail will want to know."

"No, you may *not* ask," she snapped. The curt response came more from embarrassment at not knowing her destination than for the impertinence of the driver. "Tell him it was a personal matter, and I will see him tomorrow morning at city hall. Now please drive quickly. I have to be on that plane at 8:00."

"Yes, ma'am," the driver said as he turned abruptly onto the street into traffic.

The Harbor Freeway was filled with middle agers heading home for the night and their children heading out for the night. The car swerved in and out of traffic in a mad dash for the Long Beach Airport. It was now 7:52.

Camille saw the familiar landmarks and called to the driver, "I need you to drive faster."

"Yes, ma'am."

The accelerated pace turned to reckless as he swerved between lanes. Camille could hear the screeching of tires on the sharp corners leading to the airport.

The driver slowed as he approached a red light on the off-ramp.

"Don't stop," she shouted. "Keep going."

"Mrs. Mayor, I—"

"Don't talk. Drive!" she barked.

"Yes, ma'am."

The car lurched forward, full speed, through the intersection. Drivers from opposing directions slammed on brakes and fishtailed to avoid hitting the SUV.

Within seconds of the near miss, Camille heard sirens. She looked out the back window and saw flashing red lights.

"Do not stop," she instructed. "Keep going. We're almost there."

The driver didn't protest and stayed on course to Hanger 217.

At 7:57 the car, now followed closely by two police cruisers, entered the Long Beach Airport.

"There's Hanger 217," Camille said. "Turn left here."

The car swerved onto the tarmac leaving only two tires on the ground. The squad cars mimicked the daring maneuver and closed the distance between them.

"Drive into the hanger," she commanded.

The gaping entrance loomed just ahead. Fluorescent light spilled out into the night. The roar of the twelve-seat Learjet 60XR filled the cavernous space.

Once inside Camille saw the stairs at the plane's entrance begin to lift slowly off the ground.

"Stop!" she shouted to the driver.

The car screeched to a halt, enveloping the police cars in a cloud of smoke from the burnt rubber.

The officers bolted from their cars with guns pointed directly at the vehicle.

"Get out of the car, now!" one shouted aggressively. "Show me your hands!"

As the smoke settled, Camille swung open the door. The stairs on the plane stopped rising and slowly returned to the ground. Camille turned directly to the barrels of the guns. Flashing red from strobe lights on top of the cars streaked her face. "Stand down, Officers," she commanded. "I am Mayor Camille Hardaway, and you are interfering with a matter of national importance."

The officers were stunned at the sight of the mayor standing in front of them in the aqua gown. They immediately lowered their hands to their sides.

"Ma'am, is there a situation here? Are you in danger? Should we call for backup?"

Camille turned quickly on her heels and moved to the plane. "The only thing I need you to do," she shouted over her shoulder, "is move those cars so this plane can take off."

Camille moved quickly up the waiting stairs and vanished into the mouth of the plane. The stairs folded into place, and the door closed without assistance. The plane rolled steadily forward forcing the stunned officers to quickly return to their cars and clear the way for the rolling jet.

The engines revved louder as it exited the hanger onto the tarmac. Within seconds, the aircraft lifted off the runway and slowly disappeared into the Los Angeles night.

The opera ended with the usual torture, murder, and suicide of Tosca over lost love. Sheridan made his way through the crowded lobby avoiding eye contact with other patrons. Actors, who only minutes earlier were on stage, mingled among the crowd in full costume. Wait staff passed out crystal champagne glasses.

"Sheridan!" called a jolly man with white hair, black tux, and blond trophy at his side. "Where is our lovely mayor? I saw her earlier."

"She had to leave suddenly," he responded with feet still in motion. "City emergency."

"I hope everything is all right," the man said.

"Yes," Sheridan responded hurriedly over his shoulder. "Everything is fine. Enjoy the rest of your evening."

The driver was waiting for Sheridan at the entrance, just as Camille said.

"Where is she?" he asked the obviously shaken driver standing at the rear car door. "Where did you take her?"

"To the Long Beach Airport. She left in a private jet."

"Private jet?" Sheridan asked with deep concern. "What the fuck are you talking about? Where is it taking her?" he shouted.

"I don't know, sir."

"What do you mean you don't know?" Sheridan shouted again. "You allowed the mayor of Los Angeles to be taken from the city in a private plane, and you don't know where it's taking her? Are you out of your fucking mind? Did you at least *ask* her where she was going?"

"Yes, sir, but she refused to tell me. She only said to tell the head of security she'd be back at city hall tomorrow morning."

"Was there anyone else on the plane?"

"Not that I could see."

The nervous driver intentionally left out the high-speed chase through the streets of Long Beach and the guns pointing at Camille. "She was perfectly fine when she boarded the plane," were the last of the evening's accounts he would share with anyone.

Sheridan huffed into the rear of the limo. "Drive me home, you fucking idiot," he barked over the rear partition. "What the fucking kind of security are you? Allowing her to . . . I don't fucking believe this."

"Yes, sir," the driver stammered. "I'm very sorry—"

"Shut the fuck up," were Sheridan's final words to the shaken driver.

Sheridan repeatedly entered Camille's speed dial code the entire drive home.

"This is Camille Hardaway. Please leave a message," were the only words he heard.

"Camille, where the fuck are you? Call me."

"Camille, are you all right? Pick up the fucking phone."

Sheridan left a series of progressively desperate messages, the last of which was, "Camille, if I don't hear from you within the next hour I'm alerting the chief of police."

His phone immediately beeped, indicating a text message had arrived.

Sheridan quickly swiped the icon. "Do not call the police!" the text read. "I am fine. Will be home as soon as possible. Nothing to worry about. XOXO Camille."

"Where are you?" he quickly typed.

There was no reply.

Camille had never flown in a private jet though she traveled the world. Until now, first-class commercial flights had been the extent of her luxury transport. The gentle hum of the powerful engine amounted to nothing more than soothing white noise. Fine leather chairs, the color of foam on a steaming latte, caressed her body as she looked out the window into the darkness. She assumed no one other than the pilot was on the plane.

Soft music from sources unknown seemed to ooze from the walls and plush carpet. It was an aria from the opera she had just abruptly left.

That's odd, she thought. *I wonder, did they know I was just* . . . Camille dropped the line of thinking midsentence, too afraid to consider the answer.

Ten minutes into the flight, the cabin door opened. A woman appeared in the threshold.

"Good evening, Mayor Hardaway," she said graciously. "Welcome aboard *The Constitution*. My name is Angel, and I will be your attendant for the flight."

Angel wore a simple blue skirt and white blouse. Her ivory skin and sculpted face were so flawless she looked unnatural.

"Whose plane is this?" Camille asked coldly.

"I'm afraid I don't know the answer to that, ma'am," Angel replied politely. "Your flight will be three hours and fifty-five minutes. Our world-class French chef has prepared a five-course meal specifically suited to your palate. The meal includes several of your favorite dishes and a few he thought you might enjoy. We have a fully stocked bar at your disposal, including your favorite, Boërl & Kroff Brut Rose. May I offer you a glass?"

Camille hadn't fully adjusted to the woman's sudden presence and simply replied, "Yes, thank you."

"Very good, ma'am."

If Camille had not felt the slight breeze from the woman walking past, she would have sworn it was a ghost.

"Excuse me," Camille said to her just before the cabin door closed. "Where is the fight going?"

"To Louisiana, ma'am." Just saying the words tinted Angel's intonation with the slightest Southern accent. "The great city of New Orleans."

The flight, meal, and service were flawless. Angel periodically appeared and disappeared like the subtle brightening and dimming of a lightbulb. Much of the time, Camille didn't know whether or not she was in the cabin, even when she looked directly at her.

At exactly three hours and fifty minutes into the flight, Angel entered and said, "Excuse me, Mayor Hardaway. The captain has informed me we will be landing shortly. If you wouldn't mind, please fasten your seat belt."

The jet came to rest in a hanger identical to the one it departed from in Long Beach. Camille waited for Angel to appear one last time, but the interior cabin door remained closed. Suddenly, the exterior door opened and the steps lowered to the hanger floor. Camille retrieved her clutch and cautiously walked to the door. She peeked out, not knowing who or what would be waiting for her. Bright fluorescent lights and deafening silence greeted her at the opening.

Suddenly she heard a car engine start. She looked to her left and saw a black Escalade idling near the rear of the jet with a man, dressed in all black, standing at the rear open door looking up at her.

She approached the man and said, "I'm Camille Hardaway. Is this car for me?"

The driver looked at her coldly and simply replied, "Yes, ma'am, it is."

It was 2:00 a.m. in New Orleans. The streets were empty except for remnants of stubborn revelers and debris left behind from earlier that evening. The car rolled through the city at a deliberate pace. Stately homes in the Garden District reminded her of cemetery monuments lined in a row.

Camille saw the peaks of St. Louis Cathedral in the windshield ahead and asked, "Where are you taking me?"

"We're almost there, ma'am."

"You didn't answer my question," she said sarcastically.

The expressionless driver offered no reply.

The car turned onto Bourbon Street and drove slowly past the bars and restaurants still lively with patrons. Jazz chords poured from open doors and mixed in the night air with accordions playing the Zydeco two-step and trumpets belting the blues.

Flames from gas lanterns mounted at the entrances of the centuries-old structures harkened to a time long ago. The lamps offered minimal illumination but maximum Southern atmosphere for the tourist who spilled out into the night. The car finally stopped in front of 543 Bourbon Street. A short brick path covered by a trellis of weeping lavender wisteria led up to the white antebellum mansion.

Camille was startled when the driver appeared at her window and opened the door. He extended his arm toward the mansion, but did not speak. After taking a deep breath, Camille emerged from the vehicle and boldly walked through the trellis and up the stairs to the house.

Before she could reach the doorbell, the door swung open and Lazarus Hearst appeared in the threshold.

"Camille," he said heartily, "I am so pleased you decided to come. Welcome to Headquarters. Please, come in."

Chapter 7

Gideon paced the floor in his home office in boxers, T-shirt, and reading glasses tittering on the tip of his nose. The name *KeyCorp Development* appeared on every piece of paper spread on his desk and in the stacks of files on the floor. He studied yet another document as he walked between the desk and window.

Sheridan Hardaway's name only appeared on one single document in the piles of thousands of papers accumulated from public records, the Internet, and by the sometimes-borderline unethical tactics used by his own team of investigators.

Articles of Incorporation filed by: Sheridan Hardaway

Frustration increased with every step. He searched the last two days for at least one additional connection between Sheridan and KeyCorp Development. His bare feet walked over papers tossed to the floor as useless.

Gideon's concentration was interrupted when Danny entered the room.

"It's two o'clock in the morning," Danny said groggily. "Enough. Come to bed."

Gideon peered over his glasses and said halfheartedly, "In a minute, honey. I'm almost done."

Danny slumped onto the couch. "Have you found anything?"

"Not yet. There is something curious, though," Gideon said with a hint of hope. "The chief operating officer of KeyCorp is a man named Brandon Birdsong. Now, he and Sheridan are the same age, and they both graduated from Cal State LA in the same year with the same degree in business. How does a guy with only a BA, from the same state college Sheridan went to, become the COO of a multimillion dollar corporation?"

"That sounds promising," Danny said sitting up attentively on the sofa.

"There isn't one picture of Michael Kenigrant, who is named as the CEO, in any of the hundreds of articles written about KeyCorp, and he has never been quoted. Michael Kenigrant doesn't exist."

"So you think Sheridan Hardaway is Michael Kenigrant?"

"I don't 'think' he is, I *know* he is."

"But even if he is, he hasn't done anything illegal," Danny said.

"That's the point. All of the KeyCorp holdings are in Los Angeles."

"I'm not following you."

"In the last five years, KeyCorp sold properties to the city worth over $350 million. They owned each of the properties for less than two years." Gideon's gestures became more animated as he spoke.

He jumped up and retrieved a file from the floor near the desk and returned. "For example, KeyCorp sold the city the properties where three of the LA Metro lines now sit. KeyCorp acquired them only six months before selling them to the city for five times to eight times the amount they paid for them."

Gideon shuffled through the file. "Here's another one. KeyCorp bought twenty acres in South Central two years ago for pennies on the dollar. Eight months later, they sold it to the city for eight times the purchase price. KeyCorp made over 6 million in less than nine months."

"They always seem to be in the right place at the right time."

"Or they're privy to insider information on planned city projects. Either way, all roads lead back to Sheridan Hardaway."

"Even if Sheridan is Michael Kenigrant, it doesn't mean Camille is in on it."

"Of course not, but at this point, it sure looks like she is. If the whole operation were aboveboard, why would he need to conceal his identity? Even more importantly, why would he engage in an activity with even the slightest hint of impropriety? She could face a recall on those grounds alone."

Danny looked nervously at the papers in Gideon's hands. Even for him it was clear Sheridan Hardaway was Michael Kenigrant. And if Camille didn't know about KeyCorp, once she found out, there would be every motivation to make sure the information never became public.

The entire discussion recalled painful memories of Hezekiah and Samantha Cleaveland for Danny, causing knots to form in his stomach. The husband with a secret. The wife who stands to lose everything if the secret is ever made public; desperation driving her to murder.

"You already know how I feel about this whole thing," Danny said.

"I know, darling," Gideon replied pulling Danny close.

"But it's not the same. Camille is nothing like Samantha. There's no way she would commit murder. She's too smart to think she could get away with it."

"But Samantha was just as smart, and she *did* get away with it."

The image of the Foxglove flowers in Hattie William's garden, used to poison Samantha Cleaveland, flashed in Gideon's mind.

"But Samantha didn't get away with it," Gideon said in an attempt to comfort the man in his arms. "She's dead."

"Samantha is not dead because she killed Hezekiah. She died because someone finally was brave enough to stop her. The world is a better place without her. I hope whoever did it never gets caught."

"I hope not either, baby," Gideon said pressing Danny's head to his shoulder and kissing his forehead. He could see Hattie sitting in her favorite wingback chair reading her bible. "I hope not either."

"So what now?"

Gideon leaned back on the sofa and stared at the ceiling. "I'm not sure. I think I should just ask him directly if he is Michael Kenigrant."

"He'll deny it."

"Of course he will, but at least I'll have the opportunity to look him in the eye when he does. You can tell a lot when you look a man in the eyes."

"Really?" Danny said looking up at Gideon. "Then what are my eyes telling you right now?"

Gideon smiled and said, "They're saying 'come to bed, baby.'"

"Wow, you *are* good."

Danny stood up and pulled Gideon from the couch by the hand. "Come on, big guy. It's way past your bedtime."

The mansion looked just as it had over 160 years ago. French tables, chairs, and cabinets all stood in the exact same spots as when Juliette Dupree graced them with her presence.

"Squawk!"

Camille flinched when she heard the piercing cry from the next room.

"Don't be alarmed, my dear," Lazarus reassured her. "That's just our family pet."

Camille looked from the foyer into the adjoining parlor and saw the blue and gold Macaw pacing on its perch in a far corner of the room, then to Lazarus.

"That's Louis. Louis Armstrong," she said suspiciously.

"I'm sorry?"

"The bird. His name is Louis Armstrong. He belongs to . . ." she stopped midsentence. "To a constituent in Los Angeles."

"He's a relatively common breed. His name is Count Basie. His family has lived here for generations. I assure you, he has never left this room in his entire life. He was actually born in that very cage."

Camille guessed Lazarus Hearst was a man of sixty-eight or sixty-nine. Six feet tall with a slight slump. He walked steadily and deliberately. She had never seen the media mogul before, but knew of his reputation as a ruthless business-man with immense wealth. His full head of hair was snowy white with a single lock slopping over his forehead. He wore a simple grey suit with a white shirt and yellow and black stripped tie.

Camille began to grow weary of the drama she now found herself in. "I'm here, Mr. Hearst. Can you please tell me what this is all about?"

"In due time, my dear. In due time," he replied with a smile. "And please call me Lazarus. First, let me apologize for interrupting Tosca for you. I know it's your favorite. I hope the music on the plane helped make up for missing the rest of opening night."

"It was lovely," she said slowly resigning her-self to his world and his whim.

"Now come with me. I want to show you something."

Lazarus entered the parlor and walked to a portrait hanging over the grand fireplace. Camille froze in the center of the room when she saw the painting.

"Come closer, my dear," Lazarus said. "Isn't she lovely? The most beautiful woman of her day. I hope you don't mind me saying, but seeing the resemblance, it is clear you are equally as lovely as she."

The figure's dazzling green eyes with flecks of gold caused Camille's blood to run cold. She did not respond.

"Her name was Mademoiselle Juliette Dupree. This was her home for a time. She was the courtesan of the then governor of Louisiana, Jean-Luc Fantoché. He loved her very deeply. Some felt he could have even become president."

"Why didn't he?" she asked.

"Well, it's complicated, but basically, Juliette decided he wasn't the right man for the job."

Camille heard footsteps enter the room and turned sharply toward the door.

"You!" she gasped. "I should have known."

"Good evening, Camille. Welcome to Headquarters. I'm so glad you came."

The little man approached and reached for her hand. He lifted it to his lips and placed a kiss on the knuckle. "You look radiant. Is that de la Renta?"

"You already know, Isadore Montgomery," Lazarus said. "I'm afraid we are the only two members who could make our little meeting tonight, but I assure you we speak on behalf of the entire Committee."

Camille relaxed a bit upon seeing Isadore. Maybe it was the Los Angeles connection. He represented a little piece of home. She had been in his home and accepted millions of his dollars. He was a familiar face in an unfamiliar place.

"So you're a part of this, as well," she said, attempting to gain some control over the situation.

"I am," he said. "I'm actually the newest member, so much of this is as new to me as it is for you."

"Member?" she asked scrounging for information.

"Yes. The Committee," Isadore said. "May I offer you something to drink? Coffee, tea, or something stronger."

"No, thank you," she said politely.

Camille placed her beaded clutch on a nearby tea table and began to walk away, turning her back on the two men. She too was a master at theater. Turning her back showed she was not afraid and in control of her own space and movements. She walked from one fine antique to the next.

"This home is lovely," she said gently running her hand along the carved wood Rococo spine of a heavily tufted silk sofa sitting in the center of the room.

"Thank you. We like it," Lazarus said. "The home has been fitted with the latest security and technological features. If North Korea were to drop a nuclear bomb on New Orleans right now, this would be the only building remaining standing. It is fully self-contained. Whoever is fortunate enough to be in here when the bomb drops could survive without ever opening the door for a year."

"When the bomb drops?" Camille asked curiously.

"Yes, my dear, *when*. It is inevitable," Lazarus said in a casual tone. "It's only a matter of time."

Camille looked away. The matter-of-fact way he spoke of Armageddon was far too much to absorb at that moment.

"I don't get here as often as I'd like," Lazarus continued. "But when I do, I always feel like I am sitting at the center of the universe."

"Indeed we are," Isadore said with a mischievous smile.

"What do you mean?" Camille asked, turning to the two men.

Isadore looked at Lazarus for permission to answer her question, which was granted with a slight nod.

"You see, Camille," Isadore said, looking her directly in the eye, "every major decision in the past one hundred and fifty years determining the course of this country was most likely made in this very room."

"Where did she go?"

"That's the point, I don't know," Sheridan snapped. "She got on a plane and left."

"We have to call the police," Tony Christopoulos said into the phone. "This is serious."

"She sent a text from the plane and specifically said do not call the police."

"But she could be in danger." Tony began to panic. "What if she's been kidnapped?"

"She wasn't kidnapped."

"How do you know?"

"Her imbecile driver said she entered the plane alone. There was no one in the hanger except for the pilot."

"Where are you now?"

"In the limo. He's driving me home."

"Come to my house," Tony said. "We have to decide what to do."

"I'll have him take me home to my car, then I'll be right there."

Sheridan arrived on Tony's doorstep within thirty minutes of the frantic call. It was a first-floor loft on the boardwalk in Venice Beach. Vaulted ceilings, hard surfaces, and terra-cotta floors created the perfect echo chamber for the constant roar of the Pacific Ocean only steps from his open sliding glass doors.

"I don't like this," Sheridan said rushing past Tony at the front door. "I don't like it at all. Do you think she knows about Vandercliff?"

"I don't think so," Tony's analytical mind quickly deduced. "I would be the first person she'd tell if there were any suspicions about you or the project."

Sheridan clung to the ounce of relief found in the reasoning.

"It could possibly have something to do with Isadore Montgomery," Tony continued. "You saw how shaken she was after he whispered in her ear at the party. And he would certainly have a private jet. Fuck, he would have a private fleet."

Sheridan quickly replayed the scene at Montgomery's home in his head. "You're right. That does sound more plausible. Whatever he said that night threw her off her game, and she refused to talk about it."

"I say, if we don't hear from her within the next hour we have to get the police involved," Tony said. "The longer she's out of communication, the more likely she's in some sort of danger."

Sheridan followed closely on the heels of Tony's logical trail and came to the same conclusion.

"Agreed," he replied. "If something happens to Camille, the entire stadium deal is over."

"Have you bought the property yet?" Tony asked.

"Not yet. Vandercliff's attorneys are drawing up the papers now. They should be ready this week."

"What's the delay?"

"They're drawing up a contract that ensures the land is only used for the stadium. Crazy old bitch is obsessed with the team. She doesn't mind fucking over Camille, but draws the line at the goddamn Dobers."

"How did you talk her into selling the land to you? I have to admit I didn't think you had a chance."

Sheridan turned away from Tony and walked to the open patio doors. The view was nothing more than a black hole with the gentle roar of the Pacific Ocean serving as the soundtrack.

"You underestimate my charm," he said peering out into the blackness.

"I've never underestimated anything about you," Tony said to his back. "But I've heard how eccentric she is."

"Anyway, it's almost a done deal now," was Sheridan's way of bringing the topic to a quick end. "All I have to do is sign the contract this week, then sit back and wait for the city to come knocking at KeyCorp's door."

Tony sensed there was more to be told. "So you didn't say how you convinced her," he gently pressed.

Sheridan turned sharply from the doors. "Would you fucking drop it," he said angrily. "What the fuck are we going to do about Camille?"

The harsh words snapped Tony back into the present. "I still say we should call the police. She is a public official, and if there's been a kidnapping the FBI will have to be involved."

"Shit!" Sheridan yelled. "That's all I need is the fucking feds digging around in my business. It'll take them all of five minutes to connect me to KeyCorp."

"You need to calm down," Tony said moving in closer. "Why would they look into your finances?"

"Of course they will! When something happens to a wife, the first person they look at is the husband, and money is always the assumed motive."

The logic was inescapable. "Then all we can do for now is wait," Tony replied. "Text her again. Tell her you're going to call the police."

"I just fucking told you! I can't call the—"

"I understand. Just send it and see how she responds. At the very least we'll know if she's still alive."

Sheridan sent the furious text. "If I don't hear from u I'm calling the police."

The two stared intently at the phone in Sheridan's hand, waiting for a response.

Bing.

"Do not call the police! I am fine," came the glowing response.

Sheridan held the phone up as they read the message together.

"How do we know it's her?" Tony asked suspiciously.

"We don't," Sheridan replied.

"Ask a question only she and you would know the answer to."

Sheridan thought for a moment, then typed, "I need to know this is you. Tell me what we did after your State of the City address."

Sheridan turned the phone away from Tony and waited for the response.

Bing, sounded again. "You ate my pussy in the back of the limo. Do not disturb me again."

Sheridan immediately turned off the phone. "It's her," he said, dropping it into his pocket.

"What did she say?" Tony asked anxiously.

"Never mind. It's her."

It was just after 3:00 a.m. in New Orleans. Camille, Lazarus, and Isadore continued their unusual conversation in the living room at Headquarters.

"We realize this must all seem fantastic to you," Lazarus said. "But, I assure you, it's all very true."

"I must admit I'm not fully convinced," Camille said in an attempt to press the men into telling her more. "I've never been one to believe in conspiracy theories."

"Perhaps if we gave you a little demonstration," Isadore said with a boyish smile and opened a carved wooden box with pearl inlay sitting on a lone pedestal next to the sofa. A telephone like none she'd ever seen before was inside. As soon as the lid opened, an antenna with a small round satellite mounted on the tip extended from the box and began to rotate. Multiple red and white lights on a panel began to blink in no particular pattern.

"Pick it up," Isadore said playfully. "I think it might be for you."

Camille looked at the two men, then slowly lifted the receiver to her ear.

"Hello," came the voice on the line.

Camille immediately recognized the soft baritone voice.

"Is this . . .?" she asked clutching her chest.

"Yes, it is," came the reply. "And you must be Camille."

The satellite continued spinning as she spoke. "Yes . . . yes, I am."

This has to be dream, she thought looking at Isadore and Lazarus who were clearly entertained by her reaction to the voice.

"I see you finally met The Committee. Don't let them intimidate you," the president said with a slight chuckle in his tone. "They're more impressed by you than you are by them."

"And you work for The Committee?" she summoned the courage to ask.

"No, no, we work together," came the amused response. "I'm a member of The Committee, and you will be too, if all goes as planned. Once elected, U.S. presidents hold a seat on The Committee for life."

"I still don't know exactly what this plan is," she said boldly. "It's all been very cloak-and-dagger up until now."

"Well, I suspect they are anxious to tell you, so I'm going to let you all get to it. It was lovely speaking with you finally. I look forward to meeting you very soon."

The line went dead. Camille looked again at Isadore and Lazarus who by now had taken seats on the couch.

"Please sit down, Camille," Lazarus said pointing to a floral print wingback chair directly in front of them.

"The Committee is comprised of the most powerful and influential people in the country, two of which are Isadore and myself."

Camille listened intently as the story unfolded.

"Our purpose is simple," Lazarus continued. "We run this country. We decide the state of the economy. We decide when a war is needed, and when it should end. The Committee sets national priorities, and, as it relates to you, we decide who will be president."

The words reverberated in Camille's head. The casual manner in which they were delivered caused her stomach to churn. All he said was completely contrary to everything she'd been taught in high school history, college, and constitutional law courses. Conversely, she found the absolute power these men wielded to be intoxicating. It was all, and even more than she ever desired.

"Which is why you are here tonight," Lazarus continued as Isadore studied her reaction. "I will be blunt. The Committee selected you as our choice to be the first black female president of the United States of America."

The words smacked her in the face like a wet bag of sand. After recovering, she asked simply, "Why me?"

"That is an unnecessarily self-deprecating question," Isadore said. "You see, Camille, within the confines of these walls there is no room for modesty. Far too much is at stake. Your statement should have been, 'Why not.' But in answer to your question, apart from your obvious beauty, intelligence, and highly evolved and innate political acumen, you understand power and aren't afraid to use it, as you demonstrated clearly when you swiftly and decisively dispatched John Spalding."

Camille immediately leaned forward in the chair to speak, but Lazarus raised his hand to silence her defense.

"No need to deny or defend your decision. The Committee is above the law. We *are* the law,"

Lazarus said firmly. "You did what was necessary, and you handled it beautifully. Los Angeles needs a new stadium, and you are not afraid of collateral damage, if that's what it takes to make it happen. When you made that decision, we knew we picked the right person."

"Exactly," Isadore said.

The men gave Camille a few moments to absorb all they had said and that which was unsaid.

"So, you know Gillette Lemaitre?" were her first words.

"Squawk!" came Count Basie's piercing contribution from the corner of the room.

"We facilitated your introduction," Lazarus said. "I'm sure you recognized the resemblance," he said pointing to the portrait over the fireplace. "Juliette Dupree is Gillette's great-great-great-grandmother."

Camille bolted from the chair. "You set me up!" she snarled. "You spy on me. You completely invade my privacy. What gives you the right?"

"I've already told you," Lazarus said calmly . . . "We are the most powerful people in this country. The usual rules do not apply to us, and as of tonight, they don't apply to you either."

"And what if I'm not interested?" she asked with a measure of disdain. "What if I tell you to go fuck yourself?"

"Then we would drive you back to the airport," Isadore contributed. "You would return to Los Angeles, and we would all pretend this meeting never took place. You would not hear from us ever again."

"Oh, it's *that* simple," she said sarcastically. "And what if I went to the media and told them all about your little club?"

The two men laughed. "You still don't get it. *We* control the media," said Lazarus. "Besides, who would believe you? Headquarters? Secret society? It's all nonsense, right?"

Camille looked at them blankly.

"Now sit down and talk to us," Lazarus said in a fatherly tone. "We all know the idea of becoming president appeals to you, so the righteous indignation is pointless. The challenge for you is getting past your middle-class sensibilities and accepting the fact they are no longer useful to you. Once you've accomplished that, everything else will come naturally."

Camille relaxed her defensive stance and slowly returned to the wingback chair. Everything he said was accurate. Especially concerning her desire to be president. She rarely admitted it to herself. It was so farfetched she could hardly afford to entertain the notion. Governor, yes, without question. But . . . president? *"The country isn't ready yet,"* had always been her disheartened conclusion. That is . . . up until now.

"Talk to us, Camille," Isadore said. "What are you thinking right now?"

In the context of the fantastic discussion, the rules Lazarus spoke of seemed to gradually dissolve. Being in the room, with Juliette Dupree looking down on her, had the effect of creating an entirely new and magnificent canvas upon which to paint her life.

"I'm not entirely sure what I'm thinking," she said almost defensively. "I'm angry you took such liberties with my life—while at the same time, I'm honored. I feel betrayed by . . ." She stopped without completing the sentence and looked up at the portrait.

After a moment's pause she continued. "You obviously know it would be a lie if I said I wasn't interested." She paused again. "What happens if I say yes?"

"Then you would go back to Los Angeles and let us do the hard work," Lazarus said in a calm and reassuring tone. "We will ensure you become governor, and then president. We

would, of course, keep you abreast of the important developments and guide you through the
entire process."

"That's it?" she said cynically. "You're asking
me to turn my entire career over to you?"

"Basically, yes," Isadore replied unapologeti-
cally.

Camille stood again and walked to the wooden
box containing the telephone. She looked at it
intently and ran the tips of her fingers over the
pearl inlay on the lid.

"How much time do I have to think about it?"
she asked without looking at the men.

"Take as much time as you need," Lazarus
said. "There's no rush."

"There is, however, one more thing," Isadore
added slyly.

"And what is that?" she asked suspiciously.

"Sheridan," he replied.

"What about him?"

"Please sit down, Camille," Lazarus said.

"Are you familiar with a company named
KeyCorp Development?" Isadore asked.

"Yes," she said cautiously. "The city has
bought several properties from them. What do
they have to do with my husband?"

Isadore looked at Lazarus for permission to
speak, which was again granted with a gentle
nod of head.

"Camille, *Sheridan* is KeyCorp Development."

Her legal mind calculated the ramifications of the statement with lightning speed. "That's ridiculous," she said. "The CEO of KeyCorp is Michael something. Michael Kenigrant."

"Have you ever met him?"

"Of course . . . I . . . no, but my staff has met with . . ." she stopped as her brain caught up with the answer.

"Camille," Isadore said with as much compassion as he could muster, "Sheridan is Michael Kenigrant, which is why no one has ever met him."

"I suppose you can prove it," she said with her last ounce of fight.

"You'll learn quickly enough we don't say anything we can't back up," Lazarus replied. "This week, Sheridan is scheduled to sign papers to finalize the purchase of the Playa del Rey property where you plan to build the stadium. His intent is to sell it to you for three to five times what he paid for it, just as he has done with many other properties in the city."

Camille feared her legs would give way under the weight of the revelation. *This can't be!* she thought steadying herself on the wooden box. *Sheridan would never do that to me.*

"We're sorry to have to tell you this," Lazarus said, "but it's better you find out now, before we precede any further with our relationship."

Lazarus stood from the couch and walked to her side. "Are you all right? I know this must be difficult. Even powerful people are hurt when they're betrayed by someone they love."

"I'm fine," she said bravely. "But you still haven't given me any proof."

Lazarus reached into the breast pocket of his suit, pulled out a photograph, and handed it to Camille. "Is this proof enough?"

Sheridan's face was buried deep between the legs of Gloria Vandercliff. His pants were around his ankles, and she was contorted in ecstasy. Camille saw the Rolex watch she bought him the previous Christmas on the hand used to prop her legs in the air.

She looked expressionless at the picture.

"The woman your husband is performing cunnilingus on is Miss Gloria Vandercliff," Lazarus said. "Apparently, he is quite well known in certain circles for this particular skill. In this instance, he provided the service as incentive for her to sell him the Playa de Rey property. He's a liability, Camille. You will never be president if he remains in your life."

"What are you saying?" she asked. "Divorce him?"

"No, no," Lazarus said with disdain. "That would be worse than a scandal over his business dealings."

"Then what are you . . ." she began.

"You can't be serious?" she asked looking from Lazarus to Isadore, then back again.

"It's the only way," Isadore responded.

"You're insane," she interrupted.

"Are we, Camille?" Lazarus said leaving her side. "I want you to think about it before you decide."

"There's nothing to think about," she said indignantly.

Lazarus looked down at his watch and exclaimed, "Oh my, Isadore, would you look at the time. I think we should be getting Camille back home now. We have taken far too much of her time already. I did promise she would be home in time for work this morning. If she leaves now, we can have her back in LA by 8:00 a.m."

"Of course, of course," Isadore said jumping from the couch and taking her hand. "Camille, think about what Lazarus said," he advised with compassion. "When you get back to LA, talk with Gillette. I'm sure the two of you will figure out the best way to handle this."

"Squawk!"

Chapter 8

It was a stormy night at sea. The water thrashed with deadly force. Violent winds whipped the waves into cyclones almost reaching the heavens, and then cascading down currents only to be spewed up again by the spiteful ocean. A million stars looked down helplessly from the black void with pity for the souls who would soon be subjected to the wrath of the angry sea.

Hattie stirred restlessly in her bed. It was just after 3:00 a.m., and sleep had not come easy. The shallow slumber offered no refuge from the dream brewing over the tempestuous sea.

"Don't go out there," she mumbled. "It's not safe."

The sea grew angrier with each word muttered from behind the thin veil of sleep.

"No one should be out there. It's too dangerous," her almost inaudible ramblings continued.

Hattie's hands jerked in the air over the bed as if warning someone to stay away. A tress of grey hair fell from beneath her nightcap as her head rolled from side to side. Again her hands jumped into the air. "Don't go any closer."

Then she saw them. Six mounted horsemen began to rise from the sea in the eye of the cyclone. She couldn't make out their faces, but saw that the riders had human forms.

"Who . . ." she gurgled and stammered. "Who are you?"

Her body tensed watching the slow rise of the six figures from the sea. The waters calmed as if in deference to their presence. Hattie's head lay still, and her arms became rigid. The figures glowed in the starlight.

Hattie craned her neck from the pillow to get a closer look. But she couldn't see their faces.

"Who are you?" she muttered again. "Show your faces." Hattie's words were clear and distinct even in the stormy sleep.

The figures ignored her command and continued their slow rise from the deep. They released a mist that danced above their heads. The sea became deadly calm. The waves subsided and the ocean surface was now a glassy platform with only ripples around the horses' restless hooves.

Hattie waited patiently for whatever was to come next. Then, out of nowhere, a seventh

figure appeared directly in front of the equestri-
ans. Hattie saw clearly that it was a woman. She
could see the features of her face and intensely
green eyes. Even though there was no wind,
her flowing hair danced in time with the vapors
around her head. Hattie knew immediately it
was Camille Hardaway. The energy emanating
from her was unmistakable, regardless of how
the form manifested.

One of the horses broke rank and stepped
forward. The rider was also a woman and clearly
the most powerful of the group. She held a
crown in one hand. Camille moved to the side
of the horse and bowed her head as her hair
continued in the windless dance.

The powerful rider paused with the crown
directly above Camille's head and said words
Hattie couldn't hear. She slowly lowered the
crown onto Camille's head. Upon contact,
the crown began to glow, and the powerful
figure returned to her place in the line of six.

The air responded with a violent gust. Waves
crashed and whirlwinds of water formed once
again. The storm returned angrier than before.

Hattie's body reacted to the crowning with a
sudden jerk of her chest into the air.

"No!" she cried out. Hattie bolted upright
in bed, breaking the binds holding her in the

dream. "No!" she screamed into the quiet Los Angeles night.

"Where the fuck have you been. Do you know how worried I was?"

Camille entered the master suite still wearing the aqua gown from the evening before. The flight home from New Orleans was awash with anger, fear, and hope. Polite offers of tea, coffee, and freshly powdered beignets from Angel were greeted with a curt, "No, thank you." She also refused offers for sleep and instead spent the four-hour flight simmering in a stew of outrage and betrayal. Even the prospect of becoming president was overshadowed by thoughts of Sheridan's deception.

Another black Escalade greeted Camille in the hanger in Long Beach and swiftly drove her home. She calmly climbed the stairs of the mansion and saw Sheridan pulling up his boxers upon entering the bedroom. She stood framed in the doorway and simply stared at him.

Sheridan rushed to her and embraced her rigid body. "I was worried out of my mind," he said nuzzling her neck. "Where were you? I didn't know if you were dead or alive."

Camille looked coldly over his shoulder and said nothing.

"Where did you go? Are you all right? What's wrong?" he asked sensing something was amiss. "Talk to me."

Camille removed herself from his embrace. She walked to the bed, tossed her clutch onto the mattress, turned to him, and said, "I am going to ask you a question. If you lie to me there will be serious consequences."

"What is this all about?" he asked innocently. "I've never lied to you."

"What is your connection to KeyCorp Development?" she asked succinctly.

Sheridan froze when he heard the question he'd hoped would never come from her lips.

"KeyCorp? What are you talking about?"

"It's a simple question," she said firmly. "What is your connection to KeyCorp Development?" His stunned expression answered her question.

Sheridan braced his body and cocked his head to one side. "It appears you already know the answer," he replied calmly. "How did you find out?"

"How could you do this to me?" she asked.

"I did it for us. Where do you think the money for all your designer gowns came from?" he asked defensively. "The cars, the jewelry, the trips around the world. Don't you see, I did it for us? For you."

"You fool. You idiot! I could go to jail. I could lose my office. You fucking, stupid idiot."

"You're overreacting. Who else knows about it? The feds?"

"No," she snapped.

There was a hint of relief on his face. "Is it someone we can pay to keep quiet?"

Camille laughed and said, "You don't have enough money to pay these people off. But you won't have to because they will never tell anyone."

"Then what's the problem?" he asked, closing the distance between them. "If you trust whoever it is, then everything will be fine."

Camille raised her hand and slapped Sheridan hard on the cheek. His head lurched sideways from the blow.

"I'm going to let you have that one because you're upset. But if you ever raise your hand to me again—"

Camille responded to his incomplete threat with another slap landing even harder than the first. Sheridan immediately lunged at her, gripping her neck with both hands. She landed on the bed with him on top of her squirming body.

She scratched and clawed at his bare back and yelled through the pressure of his grip, "I'll kill you. You fucking idiot! I'll kill you!"

Their bodies wrestled and twisted in the fabric of her dress as they toppled off the bed and hit the floor with a loud thud. Camille landed on top. Rage exploded onto her face as she pounded his head with her tightly clinched fists. Sheridan tried to protect his face, but the assault was relentless. He bucked his hips upward and sent her flying onto her back. Then he scrambled to his feet and wrapped his powerful arm around her neck from behind. Camille's diamond earrings whipped from side to side, and her hair became a jumble of silk strands as she struggled for freedom.

Sheridan was careful to not strike her face. She was much too beautiful to damage, even in the height of anger.

"Stop it, Camille!" he yelled as she violently struggled in his arms. "That's enough. Do you hear me? That's enough!"

"You betrayed me. You made a fool of me," she shouted in return. "I'll never forgive you for this."

Camille gradually gave way to fatigue as she panted, cursed, and clawed at his face over her head. "Let me go, you bastard. Take your fucking hands off me."

When her body went limp in his arms, he released her to the floor where she lay in a puddle of silk, panting and crying, "You bastard. You fucking bastard."

Sheridan rested on his knees, but stayed on the alert should she leap from the carpet and continue her attack.

"You don't know what you've done," she said with her face buried in the carpet. "You've ruined everything."

"You said the feds don't know," Sheridan panted.

"Fuck the feds. The people who know can do far more damage to you than the feds."

"Worse than the feds?" he asked through labored breaths. "Who?"

"People who . . ." she paused and looked up at him. "You really fucked up, and I'm not going to cover for you. I have too much to lose, and I won't sacrifice one ounce of my future for you. You're on your own. Now get out!"

The governor's race of 1852 was disappointingly uneventful. After the death of Thaddeus Barrière, Jean-Luc Fantoché swept into office unopposed. The dead Barrière received a fraction of a percent of votes only because his name appeared on the ballot and there were people in the state, for their own personal reasons, who would rather see a dead man as governor than a living, breathing Fantoché.

Upon her master's untimely death, Black Dahlia was purchased by Juliette Dupree who immediately declared her a free woman. Dahlia moved to the mansion on Rue des Bourbon and worked as a lady's maid-in-waiting and for the first time in her twenty-five years earned a day's pay for a day's work. In due course she came to know the secret of the black candle. Keeping a full box of matches at the ready became the most rewarding part of living with Juliette Dupree, as was seeing the punishment meted out by the candle to some of the most ungodly creatures on earth.

Dahlia saw the destruction of mighty men and the propelling of weak men to unimaginable heights of wealth and power under the glow of the flame. Knowing its power reached far beyond what the eye could see, and was greater than any white man could even dream, gave her hope for the future. She was free, but her brothers and sisters still toiled in the burning Louisiana sun and cowered under the brutal Louisiana whip. Juliette assured her the candle would change all that. And from the extraordinary happenings witnessed behind Juliette's closed doors, Dahlia believed it was true.

Governor Fantoché soon came to know there was a cost for Juliette's love. "You killed him, didn't you?" he said to Juliette one starlit evening as he watched her standing by the fireplace. "With that," he said, pointing over her shoulder to the candle. "I know you did it."

Juliette owned his body and soul and found no need for deception or modesty. "Yes," she replied. "Surely, you did not imagine you became governor on your charm and political acumen. You didn't know the capital of the state when I met you. I, and my associates, made you governor, and if you do as I say, we shall allow you to continue amongst the living. In the course of your term as governor you will abolish slavery in this state."

The words landed so hard they almost caused Fantoché to lose his footing. "I thought you loved me."

"In a time of war and suffering," she said with a scowl, "love is a luxury I can scarcely afford."

"And if I don't do as you say?" he asked with labored defiance. "What if I refuse? What if I

take this house, the clothes, and jewelry away from you and throw you into the street?"

"Then you shall meet a fate far worse than that of Thaddeus Barrière. By nightfall tomorrow, I would have twice as much as you have given me, and the man who would replace you as governor would be in my bed. Do not underestimate the depth and reach of my power, Governor. I will destroy you as quickly as I made you. The candle is the deadliest bow in my quiver, but I assure you, there are others. I can cause your fortune to vanish in a day and leave you penniless in the street, begging for bread. Or afflict you with a slow-lingering disease, leaving you pleading for death to come. Or cause your rosy-cheeked children to die like weeds, one-by-one, at your feet. There are far more powerful men than you, Governor, who do my bidding out of love, but mostly out of fear."

Juliette delivered the last blow with such brutal force it brought Governor Fantoché to his knees. His belly filled with anguish and despair and left no room for indignation at her insolence. He was the most powerful man in the state, but the beautiful Negress who towered over him was now in complete control.

Fantoché pleaded with his eyes, but she showed no mercy. His life and the life of his children, his fortune and all he held dear was now resting in her hand, waiting to be crushed. He had seen the destruction wrought by the flame and accepted the generous benefits it bestowed. He dined at the sumptuous banquet hosted by Juliette Dupree, and now, the time for payment had come.

He didn't recognize the face standing above him. Terror gripped his heart, and the thought of her not loving him overwhelmed his senses. He could taste the bitter tang of deception on his tongue. The earthy aroma of fear assaulted his nostrils, and the tips of his fingers tingled from the touch of betrayal.

Pity, mingled with repulsion, covered her face. "You mean nothing to me," she sneered. "How a man of your limited intelligence can think I could love you is laughable. Your touch repulses me. You disgust me. The world is delivered to you on a gold platter simply because of the embryonic hue of your skin, while men of much greater character toil and suffer because of the dark hue of theirs."

Fantoché began to sob uncontrollably at her feet. "You are my world. Nothing you can say or do will alter my love for you. Tell me what you wish I should do. I am your slave," he pleaded. "Hate me, torment me with cruel words, spit in my hideous face, but do not deny me the indescribable pleasure of your touch. I cannot live without you."

Fantoché removed a small derringer from his breast pocket and lifted it up to her in the palm of his hand. "Take my revolver and put a bullet in my heart if you are to deny me your touch."

The gun lay suspended in the air between them for moments until she removed it from his extended hand. Juliette placed the barrel directly between his eyes and pressed it hard against his forehead. Fantoché closed his eyes tight and prayed death would come quickly.

"I will not grant you the gift of freedom by death," she said at the height of his anguished anticipation and dropped the gun to the floor. She stroked his cheek with the back of her hand and said, "Your love for me shall be your prison. The tasks you perform at my behest shall serve as proof of your devotion."

Fantoché released a heaving sigh of relief. "Then my only goal in life," he said collapsing to the floor and resting his tearstained cheek on her satin shoe, "from this moment on shall be to prove my devotion to you. I swear on my life, my darling, the hellish institution of slavery shall come to an end in this state."

***

Danny sat at Hattie's kitchen table while she busied herself at the stove. The room was filled with the smell of freshly baked pound cake, brewed coffee, and lemon-scented Pine Sol.

Danny often visited Hattie during the day when Gideon was working. She had become like a grandmother to him in the last year. He loved the way her home smelled. The way she looked at him when he shared thoughts she considered as products of his limited life experience. "Just keep living, baby," she would say with a knowing smile.

He'd been in her kitchen so often she already knew exactly how he liked his coffee: two teaspoons of sugar and just a drop of cream. She sliced into the pound cake on the counter and removed a hefty portion for his plate.

"Do you think about him often?" Danny asked, looking toward her back at the counter.

"Who, baby?" she replied knowing the answer.

"Hezekiah. Do you miss him as much as I do?"

Hattie joined Danny at the table and placed the cake and coffee in front of him. "Baked it this morning," she said. "I had a feeling you'd come today."

"Do you miss him?" Danny pressed on.

Hattie sat at the head of the table facing the window looking over her garden. The sun caressed their faces with a warm glow.

"I do, Danny," she finally responded. "I think of him every day. He was very important to me."

Hattie looked at Danny as he ran the tip of his finger around the rim of the coffee cup. "I know you miss him too," she said. "Trust me, it gets easier as time goes by."

Danny did not respond.

"You know that he loved you?"

"Yes, I know."

"He never told me, but I felt it in his spirit," Hattie said gently. "He never loved anyone as much as he loved you."

"How do you know that?"

"I knew everything about Hezekiah," she said proudly. "His hopes, fears, dreams. He was a troubled spirit just before he died, and it was only because of his love for you he was able to transition peacefully. He asked me to watch out for you after he was gone, to pray for you the way I prayed for him."

Danny looked up from the cup of coffee. "When did he ask you that?"

"He came to me after he passed away. He refused to leave until he knew you would be taken care of."

Danny found profound sorrow and loving comfort in her words. A tear fell from his eye as he looked at Hattie. She reached across the table and covered his hand with hers.

"Do you understand what that means?"

Danny did not respond.

"It means he delayed the call of eternal happiness and freedom from the cares and troubles of this world just for you. That's love, Danny. You meant everything to him in this world, and he still loves you in the world he's in now."

"Thank . . ." he stuttered. "Thank you, Hattie. You can't imagine how badly I needed to hear that."

"I know, baby. I know."

"He once told me about you."

"What did he tell you?" she asked.

"He didn't say your name, only that God had placed a guardian angel in his life who prayed day and night on his behalf. It made him feel safe and protected, knowing you were interceding, as he put it, on his behalf. We rarely talked about spiritual matters, but when he spoke of you, he would say, 'the prayers of the righteous availeth much.'"

Hattie matched his tear with one of her own. She reached for a paper napkin in the holder at the center of the table and wiped her cheek.

"I let him down," she said softly. "He would be alive today if I'd only warned him she was . . ." Hattie caught the words before they could escape her lips.

"She?" Danny asked, urging her to complete the sentence. "She who?"

"Never mind, Danny. It's all over now, and he's with the Lord."

"You meant Samantha," he asked gently, "didn't you?"

"Drink your coffee before it gets cold." Hattie stood from table and moved to the sink. "You haven't even tried the cake," she said with her back to him.

"She did it, didn't she?" Danny asked anxiously. "Samantha killed Hezekiah?"

Hattie turned on the faucet but did not answer. The sound of running water covered her gentle sob. Danny stood and walked to her.

"Hattie, please tell me. I need to know."

Hattie turned to face him. "She was an evil woman, Danny. Yes, baby. She killed him."

Danny went back to the table and looked out the window. "I always knew it," he said.

Hattie returned to the table. "They're both gone now, and there's nothing we can do to change that. They have to answer to the Lord. One good thing that came from all this is you now have Gideon. He loves you as much as Hezekiah did, and I know you love him too. Most people don't ever know that kind of love, and God blessed you with it twice."

"I know you're right," Danny said. "But now it feels like it's happening again. I worry about Gideon."

Hattie looked at him intently. *He's wiser than his years,* she thought. "Nothing will happen to him. I promise. God has His hand on him," she said reassuringly.

Danny looked at her with pain in his eyes. "Promise me, Hattie. Promise me you won't let anything happen to him. I would rather die than see him hurt. I couldn't go through it again."

Hattie questioned her faith. Could she make that promise? Was there a way for her to alter a man's fate? She felt helpless and weak. Then suddenly, the words rang in her ears. *"The prayers of the righteous availeth much."*

"Every time I see Camille Hardaway," Danny continued, "I get the same horrible feeling I did when I saw Samantha Cleaveland. Gideon is determined to dig up something on her. I'm afraid it could cost him . . ." he couldn't say the words.

"I'm praying for him and you, Danny," she said regaining her strength. "As hard and as much as I prayed for Hezekiah."

***

It was 7:30 Monday morning, and the Venice Beach Boardwalk slowly came to life. Vendors rolled up metal shop doors to reveal mugs, fanny packs, beach towels, and stacks of T-shirts emblazoned with palm trees and smiling suns to serve as reminders for tourists they had spent their summer vacations on the beach in sunny California.

Tony Christopoulos jogged every morning five miles up and five miles back along the boardwalk and bike path running in front of his loft and parallel to the ocean. He made it a point to never say "Good morning," or make eye contact with any of the merchants, groundskeepers, or homeless people he passed at the exact same time each day. He didn't want to be slowed down by the obligations of exchanging greetings or remembering names. This time was reserved exclusively for him. The rest of his day would soon enough be burdened with the public in his role as Camille's chief of staff.

The Santa Monica Pier marked the five-mile mark where he would turn around and head home. Pandora fed him a steady stream of divas, Chaka Khan, Whitney Houston, Mariah Carey, and Beyoncé, through the earbuds attached to his phone. He heard the familiar beep in the middle of Chaka Kahn belting, "I'm every woman, it's all . . ." indicating an incoming call.

Tony stopped and began running in place. He believed if a caller knew his private number it must be an important person.

"Hello, this is Tony," he said continuing the stationary run.

"Am I speaking with Tony Christopoulos?" the male caller asked.

"Yes, you are. Who is this?" he said as his resentment for the interruption mounted. "How can I help you?"

"Tony, we haven't met. My name is Lazarus Hearst. Are you familiar with me?"

Tony stopped in place. "*The* Lazarus Hearst?"

Lazarus released a slight chuckle and said, "Yes, I suppose I am."

"Then, yes, I know who you are, sir. How may I help you?"

"Is this a good time for you to talk? I know it's early, but this is very important."

"Yes, this is a good time. I was just leaving for work," Tony lied.

"That's unusual."

"I'm sorry? I'm not sure what you mean."

"Isn't this normally the time you take your morning run?"

Tony was puzzled by the comment. "As a matter of fact, it is. How did you know that?"

"Oh," Lazarus said calmly, "I know a lot about you, Tony."

Tony was not easily thrown, but the comment caused him to pause. "What is this about?"

"I'll get to the point so you can get back to your run. You're almost to the pier so you'll be turning back soon."

It was clear he was being watched. "Is this some sort of joke?" he asked spinning a full circle in search of who was following him. "If it is, I don't find it amusing at all."

"No, Tony," Lazarus said. His tone turned cold. "This isn't a joke. I'm calling to give you a piece of very valuable advice. It has come to my attention you are involved in a very inappropriate relationship with the husband of someone I have taken a personal interest in."

"And who are you referring to?" Tony asked summoning the remains of his dwindling bravado.

"I think you know who I'm referring to, Tony. Sheridan Hardaway, of course."

"I don't know what you're talking about," he said shakily. "I'm going to hang up now."

"I'd advise you to hear me out, Tony . . . if you value your life."

"Are you threatening me?"

"As a matter of fact, I am," Lazarus said. "Now listen very closely. Your relationship with Sheridan is over as of now. And if you don't do exactly as I instruct, your life will be over as well."

Tony's knees began to wobble.

"Camille knows nothing about your relationship," Lazarus continued. "She also doesn't know you've been feeding Sheridan information that has made him, and you, a great deal of money."

Tony made his way to a nearby bench and sat down as his knees threatened to buckle. His hand began to shake as Lazarus continued.

"And she will never know if you do exactly as I say."

Tony placed his head in his free hand and began to sob. "Yes, yes, I'll resign today. I'll disappear."

"No, I don't want you to resign," Lazarus said with a hint of irritation.

"Then what? Tell me, I'll do it. Just tell me," he pleaded.

"When you return to your loft, you'll find a package on your doorstep. It contains a telephone programmed especially for you. It will only receive calls from me and only allow you to make calls to me. Do you understand?"

"Yes," he said barely containing his sobs. "Yes, I understand."

"Keep this phone on you at all times. When you shower, jog, fuck, sleep. At all times. When I call you, I expect you to stop what you're doing and answer on the first ring. I am not accustomed to being kept waiting. You work for me now. Your sole responsibility in life from this moment on is to provide me with information on the activities of Camille Hardaway. I want to know *everything*. Who she meets with. Who her enemies and allies are. Where she goes. What her new initiatives are. Everything. I want to know it all. Stop crying and tell me you understand what I'm saying. Your life depends on it."

"I understand," Tony replied desperately.

"Good. That's very good. Now pull yourself together and run home. I don't want you to be late for work."

Camille sat in front of the little white house on Grape Street for almost ten minutes before summoning the courage to open the car door. As was the custom, she looked in every direction to ensure privacy, and then hurried up the walkway holding a small leather box. The front door opened as soon as her foot touched the first step. She paused before proceeding quickly up the stairs.

Madam Gillette Lemaitre appeared in the threshold. "Hello, Camille," she said with a broad smile. "I've been expecting you. Come in, come in."

Camille looked her in the eye and asked, "Why didn't you tell me?"

"What's important now is you know."

The women entered the foyer. Camille waited for the irksome call of the bird, but the house was silent.

"I just made myself a cup of tea," Gillette said while directing Camille into the living room. "Would you like one?"

"No," came her curt reply.

"Then sit down and tell me why you've come."

"I assumed you already knew why I'm here," Camille replied sarcastically.

"I have an idea, but I'd like for you to tell me," Gillette said calmly. "How was your trip to New Orleans?"

Gillette sat in her favorite chair with the steaming cup of tea on the side table and motioned for Camille to sit on the couch directly in front of her. Camille was still unsettled by all The

Committee knew about her life and movements.

"Sit down, girl," Gillette chided. "You're making me nervous standing over me. Relax. You know everything. You're one of us now."

"I'm *not* one of you," Camille snapped. "Whatever it is 'you' are."

Gillette laughed slightly. "I'm afraid you are, my dear. Just knowing we exist makes you one of us. No need to fight it. You've been chosen, and there's nothing you can do about it."

The edict sent a chill through Camille's entire body. Yes, she wanted to be president, but at what cost? Yes, she felt betrayed by Sheridan, but to what lengths was she willing to go for revenge?

"You still haven't told me why you're here."

"I'm here because I want answers."

"I'll do my best."

"Who are you?"

"You already know who I am."

"Don't play games with me. You know exactly what I mean," Camille replied bravely.

"All right, dear. There's no need to get upset. I am Madam Gillette Amanda Fontaine Lemaitre. I am the great-great-great-granddaughter of Juliette Adelaide Dupree, whose portrait you saw in New Orleans."

"And you work for Lazarus Hearst?"

Gillette released a hearty laugh and said, "No, no, my dear. You have that backward. Lazarus Hearst works for me."

Camille furled her brow in confusion. "*You?* That's ridiculous. Lazarus is one of the richest men in the world."

"Yes, because I made him so. Money isn't the only determining factor for power, darling. Some of the wealthiest people I know are also some of the weakest, while some of the poorest . . . well, let's just say I would never want to cross them."

"And Isadore Montgomery? I suppose he works for you as well?"

"That is correct," Gillette said.

Camille looked at her with a questioning eye and thought, *She is either delusional or completely insane.*

"Yes, darling, I know. It defies logic. Flies in the face of everything you thought you knew about the world. Two of the richest men in the world answering to a little old black woman in a two-bedroom house in Watts."

"It does seem . . . fantastic," Camille said with a patronizing tone.

"Fantastic though it may seem, I assure you it's true."

"And The Committee?"

"Ah yes, The Committee. Juliette Dupree's great grandmother formed The Committee to do her bidding. Since then, her descendants have inherited it and are charged with selecting the members and directing their actions. And I," Gillette said lifting her open palms as if presenting a gift to Camille, "am the next in line."

Camille sat in amazement. *This can't be real,* she thought.

"I can see by the look on your face you find this all hard to believe."

"You're right. I don't believe it."

"That's understandable. But before you run to call Adult Protective Services to report a batty old woman on Grape Street, I ask you to do one thing."

"What?" Camille replied hesitantly.

Gillette pointed to a circa 1970s white, slim-line telephone on a table near the kitchen door. "Pick up the phone on the table."

"Why?"

"Indulge an old lady. Pick up the phone."

Camille looked from Gillette to the telephone, then back to Gillette. The routine seemed familiar.

"Go ahead. What have you got to lose?"

Camille walked to the table and slowly removed the receiver and placed it to her ear.

"Yes, ma'am?" the baritone voice on the line said.

Camille gasped loudly and dropped the receiver to the hard wood floor. The spiral cord recoiled and caused the receiver to bounce three times with hollow thuds.

"Don't be rude, girl," Gillette said calmly from her chair. "Pick up the phone and talk to the man."

Camille stared at the receiver on the floor and could hear the muffled voice of the man saying, "Hello, hello. Gillette, are you there?"

"Go on," Gillette said pointing the receiver. "Speak with him. Maybe you'll believe him since you don't believe me."

Camille kneeled down on the floor. Her bare knees rested on the hardwood. She obediently returned the phone to her ear and said, "Hello."

"Is this Camille again?" the president said.

"Yes, it is," she replied slowly.

"This is a very good sign. I worried Lazarus and Isadore might have scared you off. All that Gillette has undoubtedly told you by now is true. She likes you, Camille. Don't fuck this up. Just do as she says and everything will be fine. I have to go now. Having lunch with my secretary of state. I'll speak with you again very soon."

The line went dead. Camille sat stunned on the floor. She looked blankly up at Gillette.

"Are you all right?" Gillette asked. "You can hang up the phone now."

Chapter 9

Sheridan frantically paced the floor in his downtown office. It was 12:30, and he hadn't spoken to Camille since the attack earlier that morning. He touched the place on his cheek where she had scratched him.

"Ouch," he snapped. "Fucking bitch."

Sheridan knew he had to move quickly. *She's probably talking to Gloria Vandercliff right now*, he thought, then said out loud, "You're not going to fuck this up for me, Camille. You owe me this for putting up with your power hungry histrionics. I got you elected. If it weren't for me, women would have never supported you. You used me," he said slamming his palm on the desk. "And now, you *owe* me."

Sheridan used his handsome face and muscular body as commodities to exchange for power, access, and money. He entered the marriage with his eyes wide open. Although they never discussed the terms, both he and Camille knew the union was not based on love.

"You silly woman," he said to her imaginary figure standing in the office. "I never loved you," he shouted. "I married you because I wanted to get as much money out of you as I could. You *knew* that! You're not innocent in all this, you bitch. I did my part, and you're going to pay me for it. Sheridan Hardaway doesn't do anything for free."

Sheridan darted to the desk, grabbed the telephone, and dialed. "Gloria," he said after composing himself. "This is Sheridan Hardaway. How are you?"

There was a brief moment of silence before she spoke. "What do you want?" Gloria Vandercliff asked curtly.

"I'm calling to find out where we are on the contract from your attorneys. I haven't heard from them and wanted to know if there was anything I can do to move our deal forward."

"We don't have a deal, Mr. Hardaway. I've changed my mind. I'm selling the land to your wife."

Sheridan struggled to maintain calm. "But we had a deal," he said. "I thought you enjoyed my eleven reasons," he tacked on with an anxious grin. "What happened? Why did you change your mind?"

Again, there was silence on the phone. "I got a call, Sheridan," she finally responded.

"A call? From who?"

"I can't say," she said nervously. "It's too dangerous for me to do business with you."

"I don't know what you're talking about," he said impatiently. "Is it the money? I'll pay you ten million more for—"

"Stop. Just stop," she shrieked. "It's *not* about the money. I don't have anything else to say on the subject. Please do not call me again."

The line went dead. "Hello. Hello. Gloria!"

Sheridan slammed down the phone. "Fucking cunt!" he shouted. "Fucking bitch!"

Sheridan immediately dialed Tony Christopoulos.

"Sheridan, I can't talk to you," Tony said before Sheridan could speak.

"Tony, what the fuck is going on? Did Camille call Gloria Vandercliff? She backed out of the deal."

"That isn't my concern," Tony said coldly.

"What do you mean, not your concern? You're in this as deep as I am."

Sheridan felt the walls of the office begin to close around him. The room seemed to grow smaller with every word spoken. Had Camille gotten to them both? Did Tony betray him? The questions darted through his mind in rapid-fire.

"Tell me what you know. Gloria said she got a call from someone. Tell me who the fuck it was!"

Tony grew stiff when he heard about "the call." The conversation earlier that day with Lazarus Hearst played in fast-forward in his mind. He felt the weight of the cell phone Lazarus delivered on his doorstep in his pocket.

"Listen to me, Sheridan," Tony said in a hushed tone. "You fucked with the wrong people this time. My advice to you is to shut down Key . . . shut down the company. Pack your bags and leave the country. You're in much deeper than you know, and there's no way out."

"What the fuck are you talking about?"

"I can't say anymore," Tony said hurriedly. "Do not call me again. Do you understand? Never."

Camille sat on the sofa while Gillette busied herself in the kitchen making another cup of tea. Her life had changed so dramatically in the last forty-eight hours, and time was needed to absorb it all. The sound of Louie's claws scratching the perch provided a soundtrack for the scene at Headquarters that played in her mind.

Doberman Stadium was steadily crumbling at her feet. Her husband made millions using information she inadvertently provided him.

And now her dream of becoming president of the United States rested in the hands of the matronly woman making her a cup of tea in the next room.

"Do you want cream or lemon?" Gillette called from the kitchen.

Camille did not respond.

"Never mind, darling. I'll bring them both."

Nothing in life had prepared her for the revelations of the last few days. There had been no course in law school covering secret societies. Sunday school curriculum didn't include tales of an old lady with a black candle who, by definition, was the most powerful person in the country, and arguably, the world. Her father never told her real power had little to do with money but everything to do with how you use and leverage the gifts you're born with.

The world she knew, studied, and mastered ceased to exist the moment she received the call from Lazarus Hearst. Her highly evolved tools of logic, reason, and deduction seemed inadequate in this strange new world. She wasn't equipped to process the information, so she resorted to the one last trick in her repertoire. Fake it until the next move is calculated.

Gillette returned to the living room with a tray of herbal tea in a chipped cup, a little ceramic cow filled with cream, and two saucers with brown sugar cubes and freshly sliced lemon wedges.

"Here you go. Drink this. It'll calm your nerves."

Camille placed the leather box next to her on the sofa. "Thank you," she said, not to be polite, but to confirm she still had the ability to speak.

"I know this is a lot to take in, but I have every confidence in you. You're doing just fine."

"Can you explain one thing to me?"

"Of course, Camille. Anything, just ask."

"Why me? Out of all the potential candidates you had to choose from, why did you choose me?"

"That's an easy one. There are no other candidates. You see, dear, you have a gift no other person on earth has. Now before you ask," Gillette said anticipating the next question, "I can't tell you what the gift is. You will have to discover it for yourself."

"How will I discover it?"

"Just by being you. The fact you are sitting here demonstrates you are on the right path. Everything you've accomplished and every step you've taken up to this moment has led you directly to me."

For the first time, Camille sensed something very comfortable about Gillette. Something familiar she couldn't quite explain.

"Who are the other Committee members?" she asked casually reaching for the cup of tea.

"Oh, honey," Gillette laughed, "committee members don't even know who all the other members are. Just know and find comfort in the fact that they will reveal themselves to you at exactly the right times in your life, at times when you will need them the most."

Camille's training in the art of investigation took over. "How did your family become the head of The Committee?" She was no longer faking it.

"My, my," Gillette said clearly amused, "straight to the heart of it. Like you, my dear, the women of my family have a particular gift. It took generations to harness the power and allow it to evolve into what it is today."

"And that gift is . . .?"

"The ability to control a man's destiny and direct his fate."

"So basically you're saying you are God?" Camille mocked.

"No, no," Gillette laughed. "Now that really would be ridiculous. We simply use the gift God gave us." Gillette slowly lifted her hand

and pointed to the black candle sitting on the dining-room table.

"The candle?" Camille whispered.

"Yes, my dear. The candle."

"Where did it come from?"

"No one really knows. The original wax has been continually blended with new wax and passed down from generation to generation. The unifying ingredient is a single drop of blood from each of the women with whom it has been entrusted. The furthest we can trace it back is to the late 1600s when our family first settled in Louisiana. Juliette, however, is credited with releasing the full extent of its power in the mid-1800s when she changed the course of the nation."

With lightning speed, Camille recalled the significant events of the nineteenth century. She looked at Gillette in disbelief and said, "You don't mean . . . ?"

Gillette smiled. "Yes, my dear. Lincoln didn't free the slaves. It was Juliette Dupree."

Camille held the warm cup of tea firmly. Her capacity to process information was depleted by this latest revelation. Despite her logic, despite her IQ of 158—placing her comfortably in the range of genius—and in spite of her position as mayor, Camille believed every word Gillette said. She'd seen, and benefited from, the power of the candle. She had spoken to the president of the United States twice. She even lit the candle. Camille searched her extensive library of reason and logic, but found no justification for not believing it was all true.

"Camille," Gillette said gently, interrupting her thoughts, "besides getting answers to your questions, why else have you come to me?"

Camille was silent.

"Are the contents of that leather box for me?"

Camille placed her hand gently on the case.

Gillette looked at her warmly and asked, "Do you think now would be a good time for us to talk about Sheridan?"

Gideon entered Tony Christopoulos's suite at city hall. The outer office was simply decorated with blue-cushioned chairs surrounding a coffee table. A large ficus tree sat in the corner, and the floors were covered with new burgundy carpet.

Gideon walked directly to the assistant sitting in front of the door leading to Tony's office.

"Good afternoon," he said to the nondescript woman behind the desk.

"Good afternoon, sir," she said with a curious smile. There was something familiar about him.

She didn't know exactly what. "How may I help you?"

"My name is Gideon Truman, I'm a reporter."

The woman looked surprised. The voice coupled with the brown skin and broad smile instantly jarred her memory.

Her back stiffened, and her smile reduced by an almost undetectable fraction. It, however, did not go unnoticed by Gideon, "Of course. Yes," she said. "I thought I recognized you."

"I don't have an appointment, but I was wondering if I might be able to speak with Mr. Christopoulos. You see, I'm working on a story about the recent boom in development in major cities around the country and wanted to get his perspective on it. I'm on a deadline, and I would really be grateful," he added with a seductive smile.

The woman nervously reached for the silent phone and quickly pulled her hand away. "I'm afraid Mr. Christopoulos is very busy today. I can have him call you later if you'd like."

"I have a few hours until my next appointment. I can wait, if that's all right with you."

The receptionist stood and said with a slight huff, "I'll see if Mr. Christopoulos is free now. Please have a seat and I'll be right back."

Before Gideon could cross his legs, Tony entered the room.

"Mr. Truman," Tony said approaching with a guarded smile and extended hand. "I'm Tony Christopoulos, Mayor Hardaway's chief of staff. We met at the State of the City address."

Gideon met Tony halfway and shook his hand. "Yes, I remember. Thank you for seeing me without an appointment, Mr. Christopoulos."

"Please call me Tony. I'm a fan of yours."

"As I told your assistant, I'm working on a story about the sudden increase in development in urban cities in the last year, and I wanted to speak with someone from this city. Several people suggested I talk to you."

"Who exactly are the people who suggested you speak with me, if you don't mind me asking?"

"To be honest, I actually don't remember. Just colleagues of yours, I suppose. But I do recall they spoke very highly of you."

The two men locked eyes. At this point, the entire exchange had little to do with the words they spoke and everything to do with what their eyes were saying.

"Really?" Tony said holding his cards close to his chest.

"Look, Mr. Christo . . . Tony, I'm kind of in a bind here. This is a small human interest story, and I'd really like to get it done quickly so I can start working on a piece about Mayor Camille Hardaway." Gideon paused briefly to allow the hint of a threat to sink in. "Would you mind if I asked you a few questions?" he asked innocently. "I promise to not take much of your time."

Tony couldn't disguise his discomfort behind the thin civil servant veneer. He diverted his eyes and looked at his Rolex two times before answering.

"I don't know," he said slowly. "I really do have a lot—"

"Just a few minutes, Tony. No more, I promise."

Tony looked over his shoulder to the assistant for help, but found her desperately trying to go unnoticed behind the desk.

"I suppose . . ." Tony finally said.

"Great! I really appreciate this."

Tony's office was more of the same—stark, beige with few furnishings. He took the seat of power behind the desk and motioned for Gideon to sit in one of the two chairs positioned in front.

"I really only have a few minutes," Tony said, minus the charm, "so let's get right to it."

"Yes, of course." Gideon decided to waste no time bringing out the big gun. "Are you familiar with Michael Kenigrant of KeyCorp Development?"

"Yes," Tony replied cautiously.

"Of course you are. The city has bought a number of properties from him. Is that correct?"

"Correct."

"Now help me understand something. I can't find any public records showing Michael Kenigrant exists. Birth certificate, driver's license, passport, school records . . . nothing. It's an unusual name, and, I tell you, Tony, I'm stumped. Can you explain that to me?"

Tony's face showed he now realized his original suspicions about Gideon were accurate. Why else would a national reporter with a reputation for investigating scandals show up unannounced on city hall's doorstep?

Tony leaned forward. "What is this *really* about, Mr. Truman?" he asked.

"By your reaction, I think you know what it's about."

"No, I'm sorry, I don't."

Gideon decided to take the risk of showing his hand early. Tony's inability to hide his emotions reduced it to a calculated risk.

"This is about Sheridan Hardaway. He's Michael Kenigrant, isn't he?"

Gideon estimated Tony blinked his eyes eight times in four seconds. *Poor guy should never play poker,* he thought.

Tony stood from the desk and said, "I don't know what you're talking about. This interview is over. Now if you will excuse me, I really am very busy."

"Does Camille know?" Gideon pressed hoping for more involuntary responses from Tony's eyes. "Either you can tell me, or she can because I am going to ask her."

"You are terribly mistaken, Mr. Truman. Now please leave."

"Is the land in Playa del Rey going to be the next deal? Is that why Mayor Hardaway wants to build the new stadium, because she and Sheridan stand to make millions?"

"If you don't leave right now, I will have my assistant call the police."

"Police?" Gideon laughed. "I think the last people you want to come in here are the police."

Tony walked aggressively around the desk and stood over Gideon.

"You really should talk to a doctor about that nervous eye twitch," Gideon said as he stood. "It could be a sign something else is going terribly wrong and," he added, "in this case, I think that may be the case."

Gideon took an aggressive step forward. "You've answered all my questions, Tony. Please tell Mayor Hardaway I'll be in touch."

***

"President! I have no desire to be president! This is madness! Utter madness!"

"Why do you question me? Have I not kept my promises to you? Against all odds, I have made you governor of this state."

"Yes, against all odds and against my will."

"Nonsense. You wanted to be governor."

"Yes, but only to please you."

Governor Fantoché paced the living room as he spoke. *"I did it to find favor with you, but now I see it was not enough. I have fought tirelessly to end slavery, yet every day you require more and more of me. Now you say president. I cannot. I do not have the strength. I will not!"*

Juliette watched him calmly from the tufted sofa as he walked nervously from one side of the living room to the other. Her jade eyes grew tighter with every word he spoke.

The governor suddenly rushed to Juliette, violently kicked the rococo coffee table from between them with his knee-high black leather boot, and knelt desperately at her feet.

"My darling, no more. Please, understand I am already well out of my depths as governor. The idea of me being president is ludicrous at best and absolutely insane at worst."

"Insane, yes, I agree," Juliette said coldly. "Your intellect is much better suited for the filthy world of a sugar baron than that of president, but you need not worry. I and my associates will guide you. We will make all the important decisions for you."

"I know what it is you want, my darling. But it is impossible. I cannot end slavery in this country as president," Fantoché pleaded. "The institution is far too deeply entrenched in our culture. It is sanctioned by the highest law in the land, the Constitution. The economy would implode. There would surely be civil war between the North and South."

Juliette stood abruptly, causing the governor to topple onto the floor. Her red silk brocaded gown with black embroidered roses slapped against his face as she made her way to the fireplace and stood in front of the black candle at the center of the mantel.

"Do you believe I fear civil war? The blood of a million white men flowing over the cotton and tobacco fields of the South would still not be enough to wash away the stain of slavery."

Fantoché looked up from the floor in astonishment. "Just because a few zealous abolitionists are willing to risk their lives and freedoms to end slavery, it is unreasonable and deeply mis-

guided to assume the average white American would do the same."

"In the South, no," she said sneering down at him. "But there are enough men of conscience in the North who would gladly fight to challenge the Constitution and end this ungodly state of oppression. By codifying slavery, the Constitution is nothing more to these honorable men than a covenant with death and an agreement with the devil."

"The South would rebel and sever the Union permanently in two."

The unlit wick of the black candle behind Juliette released a series of sparks and flashes mirroring the heated exchange between the two. Fantoché looked at the candle behind her with fear in his eyes.

"Juliette, mon chéri, do not for one moment believe I support the institution. It is an abomination before God, and I am sure our children and our children's children will pay the price for our shameless inhumanity. But what you propose is madness. How can I . . ." he paused as the candle sputtered and sparked, then burst into a robust flame.

Fantoché proceeded with his eyes darting between Juliette and the flame. "How can I alone convince the country to abruptly end an institution that is an integral part of their very existence? Our reliance on slave labor is the foundation of this economy. The cotton industry would collapse. The tobacco crops would dry in the fields. Sugarcane would cease being profitable. Can you not see it is unreasonable to make such demands of me? I am not strong enough to do as you ask."

"I advise you to choose your words to me carefully," Juliette said coldly. The burning candle caused her golden hair to glow as if illuminated from within. "Have you learned nothing from your time with me? Your only option is absolute obedience."

Fantoché slowly lowered his head, curled his hulking body into a ball on the intricately woven Persian rug, and wept. "I cannot," he cried. "I am not strong enough to do as you wish. Please, I beg you. Release me from your spell."

Camille placed the leather box in her lap and avoided eye contact with Gillette. She could almost smell Sheridan's cologne as she held the case and heard his voice softly saying, "I love you, baby." He made love to her body like no man before. He ran her bath after a day of being battered and bruised in her rough-and-tumble world. Yes, it began as a marriage of convenience; a pretty face behind the powerful woman, a prop on the stage of her life. But, somewhere along the way, she fell in love.

Somewhere between *"I do,"* and *"I don't know what I would do without you,"* her pragmatic plan morphed into passion and pleasure. But was it enough to forego access to the top office in the country? Was the ecstasy satisfying enough to sustain her in the days to come when remorse would surely haunt her? Would his tender kisses, at just the right spot on the nape of her neck, provide adequate comfort when regret came to call?

The answer to all the questions was clearly no, but Camille couldn't bring herself to cross that line. She needed him much more than even she had realized. Could she do it alone again? Who would stroke her hair on lonely nights? Who would tell her, just at the point of defeat, "Fuck'em all, baby, you can do it without them"?

But the betrayal and deceit, could she ever forgive that? The lies remained lodged in her back like poisoned daggers as she sat in front of the silent Gillette Lemaitre. How could the man who gave her so much pleasure serve an even greater portion of pain? He removed a piece of her heart with surgical precision and fed it to her daily, masked by the sweet tastes of honey and wine.

Camille guided herself systematically toward the inevitable conclusion. No, the ecstasy was not sufficient. Her neck would have to sacrifice the warmth of his kiss. She would have to remind herself to, "fuck them all," and no, forgiveness was *not* an option.

Camille lifted the case from her lap and handed it to Gillette.

"Are you sure?" Gillette asked softly.

"Yes," Camille said, tentatively considering the need to revisit the question. Her answer came quickly. "Yes, I'm sure," this time with more conviction.

"Then come with me."

Gillette placed the contents of the box on the dining-room table, along with the candle. A spray of sparks burst from the unlit wick each time she removed an item from the box. Louie looked on attentively from his perch, his head turning curiously from side to side. The room was almost completely dark as dusk arrived unannounced.

"Sit there," Gillette said, pointing to the chair at the opposite end of the table. "This time we're going to do it together."

Camille tensed at the notion. "I can't," she said softly.

"That was not a request, my dear. Sit down," Gillette said firmly.

Camille pulled the wooden chair from the table, causing the legs to screech against the hardwood floor.

The first item was a little round pillbox with a hinged top. Gillette opened it and saw a jumble of black hair clippings. "Excellent," she said. "This will do perfectly."

Camille asked Sheridan repeatedly to clean the sink whenever he shaved the beard he occasionally grew. "Honey," she called out to him on numerous mornings, "please clean the sink after you shave. There's hair everywhere."

"Let the maid do it. Give her something to complain about."

On this particular morning, Camille functioned as the maid and swept the coarse black hairs into the little pillbox and placed it into the leather case.

Gillette then removed a folded card made of roughhewn paper from the box. The edges were jagged, and the surface was a porous sandy brown with specks of lavender and rose peddles.

"My Dearest Camille," the card read. *"As a great poet once said, you are the sunshine of my life. That's why I'll always be around. You have made me the happiest man in the world by*

agreeing to be my wife. I will love and protect you until the day I die."

   XOXO,
   Sheridan

The last was a photograph Camille took of Sheridan on a trip to the Bahamas. The shirtless man stood proudly in the sand with the powder-blue water of Gold Rock Beach in the background. It was only last year the couple walked barefoot and hand-in-hand along the secluded shore, bathed in a shower of warmth and light, not another soul was in sight.

"We should move here when we retire," Sheridan said with the water lapping at their feet. "Just you and me. We'll live in a little shack right on the beach and eat lobster fresh from the ocean every day."

Was it then she fell in love with Sheridan? She would never leave the United States, and shellfish made her break out in hives. Living in a shack wasn't included in her life's master plan. But the idea he would suggest doing all those things with her, so many years in the future, served to remove yet another brick from the wall built around her heart.

Gillette passed Camille a box of wooden matches. "I want you to picture Sheridan in your mind," she instructed.

Camille closed her eyes.

"Do you see him?"

"Yes,"

"Good. Now, light the candle."

Camille opened the matchbox and removed a single spindly stick.

"Always remember, in order to get what you want, you have to give up something you love," Gillette said.

Camille struck the match on the side of the box, and the sudden flare splashed shadows of the two women and Louie onto the faded floral wallpaper. She lifted the fire to the wick which exploded into a dancing flurry of yellow, red, and blue, then simmered to a gently waving burn.

Gillette picked up the card and said, "I want you to picture Sheridan in the flame. Can you see him?"

"Yes."

Gillette moved the tip of the sentimental card to the flame, lit it afire, and placed it burning onto the silver tray. The picture came next.

"Do you still see him in the flame?"

"Yes," Camille replied simply.

"Good. Now, you take the hairs and sprinkle them over the flame."

Camille stood from the table and opened the pillbox.

"Go ahead. Don't be afraid. Pour them over the flame."

Camille saw Sheridan's face clearly in the fire. She searched her heart, but found no mercy. There was only growing contempt. She poured the hairs into her palm and placed it over the fire. Her hand slowly turned and a shower of stubble rained down over the blaze.

Sparks suddenly erupted like fireworks. Camille quickly jerked her hand away and watched the sensational, yet brief, display.

"You did well, Camille," Gillette said from her seat. "It is and so we let it be."

Tony sat alone in his office at city hall. His office was directly across the hall from Camille's and the second largest in the entire building. An efficient assistant guarded his door like a sphinx at the entrance of a king's tomb. His world was reduced to the space between these four walls ever since the call from Lazarus Hearst.

"Hold all my calls," was his morning command to the assistant. "Cancel all my meetings for the day."

The plan had been risky but elegant in its simplicity. Serve as Sheridan's eyes and ears at city hall, and in return, receive 30 percent of the profits from real estate deals between KeyCorp Development and the city. Sheridan had transferred the first million into Tony's account in the middle of the night two years earlier. It all seemed too easy and too good to be true. He went to sleep with $50,000 in credit card debt—and woke the next morning a millionaire.

Tony respected, and even admired Camille. A black woman who was one of the rare people in the world who actually was the smartest person in every room she entered. Ivy League education, beautiful, and a future even brighter than her past. He never met a person, be it a man, woman, black, or white in his hometown, Dowagiac, Michigan, or at Harvard or anywhere else, like Camille. But the thing he admired most about her was Sheridan.

On the first day he met Sheridan, their eyes communicated more than their benign words of "Very nice to meet you. Camille's told me very nice things about you." The mutual subtext to their exchange was more along the lines of, "Camille does like to surround herself with beautiful things."

The next stages of their relationship were well orchestrated by Sheridan. Political chats in the hallowed halls while waiting for Camille to wrap up a council meeting. The, "It looks like she's going to be awhile. Are you hungry? Let's grab some dinner," whispered during one of Camille's more contentious Planning Commission hearings. And finally, "Camille has decided to not go to Chicago for the convention. Would you mind if I shared your room with you? It's silly to waste taxpayer dollars on two rooms."

The night in the Chicago hotel room was the typical "straight man meets straight man" story. Camille wanted to attend the mayors convention in Chicago and asked Sheridan and Tony to accompany her. As they were preparing to leave, a mob of protesters descended on city hall outraged and fed up by the greed exhibited by Americans occupying the top tier of economic wealth.

Her advisors strongly suggested not leaving the city at such a volatile time. "It will appear you left to avoid a confrontation," they said.

"Darling," she said as Sheridan packed his bags, "they're concerned the protests could turn into riots. Would you mind going to the convention without me? I need you to represent me. Tony will be there. He'll hold your hand the entire weekend."

During that weekend, Sheridan made sure Tony held much more than his hand.

"I didn't have time to request two beds," Tony said when he and Sheridan entered their suite at Waldorf Astoria in Chicago. "I can sleep on the sofa."

"Nonsense," Sheridan snapped. "The bed is big enough for both of us. I promise I won't try anything," he said with a manly chuckle.

The evening ended early after an evening of dinner at the Tavern on the Green and drinks in the hotel bar.

"I hope you don't mind," Sheridan said as he removed his shirt preparing for bed. "I have to sleep in my boxers. Didn't pack pajamas. Thought it was going to be Camille and me. Consider yourself lucky though, I usually sleep buck naked."

Even at twenty-nine, Tony was naïve about the subtleties of latent male sexuality. He innocently replied, "Not at all. Same here."

As the night progressed, chuckles and overt exhibits of masculinity evolved into the accidental bumping of knees under the duvet, and then the gentle placing of Sheridan's hand on Tony's firm thigh. When there was no sign of resistance or repulsion from Tony, Sheridan closed the chasm of silk and cotton separating them in the bed and kissed Tony on the lips.

Neither spoke for fear of breaking the spell Chicago and Camille had cast. Male bonding quickly turned into passionate lovemaking. The noble gesture of saving taxpayers the cost of separate hotel rooms ended with Tony's orifices being stretched beyond their normal limits by Sheridan's fingers, tongue, and blood-engorged member.

Tony stared out the window of his office onto the city below. Specks of suits, cartoon lunch boxes, homeless shopping carts and hats scampered on the ground like ants. He felt trapped in the office. Trapped in the city. This wouldn't be happening if only he hadn't succumbed to Sheridan's charm and the promise of quick money.

He heard the phone in his pocket ring as he pined over the horrible turn his once-promising life had taken. Tony quickly retrieved the phone and threw it onto the desk. It stopped ringing, and he released a sigh of relief. Then it rang again causing him to jump. He picked it up and held it to his ear.

"I told you to answer on the first ring," Lazarus Hearst said tersely. "I am a very busy man, and I don't have time to wait for you to decide whether you are too afraid to speak to me. Do you understand?"

Tony slumped into the chair and said weakly, "Yes, sir."

"Good. Now what information do you have for me?"

"Nothing," Tony said honestly. "There has been nothing unusual happening. She came in this morning at 7:30 and has been in meetings ever since."

"Why aren't you in the meetings with her?"

"They were all pretty routine," he lied nervously. "Mainly disgruntled constituents. Nothing important."

"In the future, Mr. Christopoulos, you let me decide what is and is not important."

"Yes, sir."

"What else?"

"Nothing. That's it."

"Don't lie to me, Tony," the yell was accompanied by a loud pounding on wood. "I can tell by your voice there is something else you're not telling me. What is it? I don't have all day!"

"Gideon Truman knows about KeyCorp," Tony blurted. "He knows Sheridan is Michael Kenigrant."

There was silence on the phone. Then, "How do you know this?" Lazarus asked calmly.

"He came here and asked if I knew about it."

"And what did you tell him?"

"Nothing," Tony whispered nervously. "I denied I knew anything about it."

"Then what did he say?"

"He said if I didn't tell him, he would ask Camille."

"That arrogant shit works for one of my companies," Lazarus said angrily. "I never liked him but the viewers, for some unknown goddamn reason, love him."

Tony did not respond.

"Now you listen closely, Tony. Keep Gideon Truman away from Camille. Don't let her accept any requests for meetings with him."

"But I have no control over her schedule," Tony weakly protested. "There are scheduling secretaries for that."

"Well, you better get fucking control of her schedule," Lazarus said angrily. "At least for the next few days. I need some time to take care of this."

Chapter 10

The limousine stopped in front of the Beverly Wilshire Four Seasons Hotel. Black-and-white awnings dotted the front of the Italian Renaissance building. A red-vested valet immediately trotted to the car and opened the rear door. Camille stepped out and said, "Good afternoon," as if it was his vote that made her mayor.

"Good afternoon, Mayor Hardaway," the young man said. "We've been expecting you. Your party is waiting for you in the restaurant."

"Thank you," she said and walked into the hotel.

The bustling lobby was filled with clothes and faces of those who could afford the one thousand-dollar-a-night rooms. The beautiful and well-heeled walked in circles as if they had no other places to be on the sunny afternoon. All eyes were drawn to her as she walked across the lavish lobby directly to the restaurant in the far corner.

The Cut was Beverly Hill's very own five-star eatery. Camille had no desire to be there, considering all she'd been through in the last few days, but the meeting was arranged weeks earlier.

"Good afternoon, Mayor Hardaway," the woman behind the podium said. "Welcome to The Cut. Mr. Irvin is waiting for you in the private dining room. If you would follow me, please."

The two women wove through the restaurant, stopping twice for Camille to accept well wishes and "You're doing an excellent job," from other patrons.

The private dining room was dimly lit, with a single extravagantly appointed table in the center. A waiter stood at-the-ready in the corner of the room. Robert Irvin immediately stood when she entered.

When Robert Irvin, head of the Democratic National Committee, requested a meeting, the recipient did not haggle over the schedule or question why. The recipient simply said, "Yes, sir," and kissed his ring if he or she wanted a future in politics. It was his job to promote the Democratic political platform, as well as coordinate fundraising, election strategies, and select future candidates for key offices around the country.

"Camille," he said with a peck on her cheek. "So good to see you again."

"Good to see you as well, Robert. It's been almost a year."

"Yes, the last time was at the convention. People are still talking about the electrifying speech you gave."

The maître d' waited patiently for the standing exchange to run its course, and then pulled out a chair for Camille. "Your waiter today will be Jonathon," she said, pointing to the almost invisible man in the corner. "Please enjoy your meal." She said, and exited the room.

"Jonathon," Robert said kindly to the eager waiter, "would you mind leaving us alone for a moment? We'll let you know when we're ready to order."

The two sat alone in the room. Robert poured Camille a glass of white wine from a bottle sitting on the table.

"Camille, thank you for meeting with me. I know this is a busy time for you, with the stadium and all, but I'm only in town for the day and wanted to spend some time with you."

"It's always my pleasure. Although, you were a bit mysterious about what you wanted to discuss."

"First things first. Tell me about the stadium. How's that going?"

"We've had a few bumps up until now, but as of yesterday, everything is back on track. I anticipate it will be completed by the end of my term."

"That's great news," he said with a satisfied smile. "This project is a major milestone in your career."

Robert poured more wine into his glass. "So," he said coyly, "what are your plans after your term ends?"

"I haven't given it much serious thought yet."

"Camille, Camille," he said with a warm smile, "I'm not the press. This is just two old friends talking over lunch. Now, be honest. Do you plan on running for governor?"

Camille saw no point in being coy with the most powerful man in the Democratic Party. "Yes, I'm running."

"That's great news!" he said, accentuated with a clap of his hands. "Just what I hoped you'd say."

"I'm glad you're pleased."

His smile disappeared suddenly. "Oh, I am *more* than pleased. We are committed to ensuring you become governor."

"We?" she asked curiously.

"Yes, *we*. The Committee."

Camille froze when she heard the words. "You mean the DNC?"

Robert looked at her with a knowing eye and said, "No, Camille. *The Committee*."

She picked up the wineglass and leaned back in the chair. "I'm not sure I know what you're talking about."

"You've spoken to Lazarus and Isadore. Is that correct?"

Camille did not respond.

"And you've met Gillette."

She looked at him intently, but still did not speak.

"You visited Headquarters."

"You're a member of The Committee?" she asked in disbelief.

"Yes, I am," he said. "I imagine you've gathered by now The Committee is where the real power in this county is concentrated. We make the decisions, Camille, and we've decided you will be the governor of California, and, if all goes well, the president of the United States."

"What about the Republican National Committee?" she said stalling for time to absorb the grenade he dropped on the table. "I imagine they are having a similar conversation with their choice for California's governor."

Robert laughed heartily. "The head of the RNC is also a member of The Committee. Our choices are always the same. You see, Camille, at this level of politics in America, there are no Democrats or Republicans; there's only one party. And, that is, The Committee. Now," he said clapping his hands again, "let's get Jonathon back in here and order lunch. I'm starving."

"Nelson!" Karen Peters called up the mahogany staircase. "Honey, come on! You're going to be late for your game!"

"Mom!" Nelson called back, "I can't find my jersey!"

"It's in the top drawer!" she yelled.

"Winnie," Karen said to the little girl playing with a black Barbie doll in the sunroom just off the foyer, "why aren't you wearing your ballet slippers?"

"They hurt my feet," the curly haired girl replied. "They're in my bag, Mommy."

"We'll buy new ones tomorrow. Now go to the car. Your brother is almost ready."

Fairfax Station, Virginia, was home to many of Washington's power brokers. A Supreme Court justice lived to Karen's right, and the ambassador to Denmark to the left. The secluded enclave was a series of towering sugar maples, winding sidewalkless streets, brick mansions, and an endless parade of black secret service SUVs. Karen's husband of ten years, Simeon Peters, was head of Homeland Security and the love of her life. They met while he attended Princeton and she West Point and married exactly one month after graduating.

Karen was the model Washington soccer mom. Her uniform of choice was khakis, a Polo shirt, and comfortable Vans with crisp white shoelaces. By day, she shuttled eight-year-old Nelson and five-year-old Winnie between Sidwell Friends School, where they studied the three R's alongside the children of the president and other Washington spawn, and participated in soccer, ballet, and ten other extracurricular activities designed to make her children leaders, not followers. By night, Karen attended parties in Georgetown and at the White House, wearing designer gowns and discussing the most perplexing issues facing the nation while sipping American-made wines from American-blown crystal glasses.

Nelson bolted down the stairs toting a gym bag on his shoulder and a soccer ball under his arm. "I'm ready," he said skipping the last three steps. "I need ten dollars. Coach is taking us for pizza after the game."

"I'll give it to you in the car," she said hurriedly.

"Excuse me, Mrs. Peters," a middle-aged woman in a maid's uniform said, appearing in the foyer, "will you and Mr. Peters be dining in tonight?"

"No, Consuela," Karen said, reaching for her keys on a consul in the entry hall. "We're having dinner with Senator Cunningham and his wife at The Inn in Little Washington, and Nelson is going for pizza after the game. So, it's only Winnie tonight. She asked for a hamburger and fries, but please make it a turkey burger."

"Yes, ma'am."

"Remember, my mother and father are flying in tomorrow and we will be dining in," Karen said while shoveling her wallet, cell phone, and a container of mace into her purse. "My mother is allergic to wheat, so please, no wheat-based products. My father only drinks domestic wine, and he hates anything French, including bread and fries."

"Yes, ma'am."

"The party planner is coming tomorrow at 1:00 to discuss the president of Ghana's reception when he visits next month, so please tell the cook I want him to meet with us."

"Yes, ma'am."

"And one last thing before I forget," Karen said, checking her bangs in a massive gold-gilded mirror hanging in the hall, and tightening the black scrunchie around her ponytail.

"Mom," Nelson called anxiously from the front door, "we're going to be late. Let's go."

"I'm coming, honey!" Karen shouted. "I'm sorry, Consuelo, what was I saying?"

"You said there is one more thing you wanted to tell me."

"Yes, right. Winnie has a dentist appointment tomorrow, at the same time as Nelson's last game of the season. I'll need either you or Rosa to take her."

"Yes, ma'am. One of us will take her."

"Thank you, Consuela," Karen called out over her shoulder as she sprinted out door. "I don't know what I would do without you."

"Is everyone buckled in?" Karen asked, looking at Winnie in the backseat, and then to Nelson in the passenger seat of the white Suburban.

"Yes," the children replied in unison.

Just as she turned the ignition, the cell phone in her purse rang. Rule number 14 in the *Washington Wife Handbook:* Always determine the identity of a caller before deciding to ignore them. Karen pulled the phone from her purse and saw the encrypted code on the screen. A code she hadn't seen in three months.

"I'm sorry, darlings," she said unbuckling her seat belt. "I have to take this."

"Mom, no!" Nelson whined. "Coach is going to kill me if I'm late."

"I'll only be a minute. I promise."

Karen got out and walked a safe distance away from the house and car in the circular driveway. She checked over her shoulder to make sure the children hadn't exited the SUV.

"Yes," she said into the phone.

"Hello, my dear," Lazarus Hearst said. "How are you?"

"Fine, thank you."

"How's my favorite soccer player? Did he get the soccer ball I had Beckham sign for him?" Lazarus asked warmly.

"He did. Thank you."

"And your daughter? She must almost be as tall as you by now."

"Almost. She's doing well. As a matter of fact, I was just leaving to take her to ballet class."

"Then I won't keep you," Lazarus said with the understanding tone of a dad who in his life had juggled similarly demanding schedules. "I have your next assignment. Gideon Truman."

Karen Peters was one of the most gifted hired assassins in the world, and she only had one client: The Committee. In addition to marksmanship, her training at West Point included camouflage, infiltration, reconnaissance and observation, surveillance and target acquisition.

She ranked number three for the most confirmed kills in American military history at the end of her second tour of duty in the Middle East. She neutralized 243 insurgents, six high-ranking members of terrorist organizations, and three foreign officials who posed threats to United States' interests abroad. Her record for the longest distance sniper kill, when she killed two insurgents within three seconds from over one and a half miles away, had yet to be broken.

The government purged her entire military record for her protection . . . and theirs. There was no evidence of her ever having served in the armed forces. In the subsequent years, Karen honed the fine arts of death by "natural causes," accidental drownings, suicides, and her favorite, autoerotic asphyxiation. The only two people in the world who knew her distinguished credentials were Lazarus Hearst and Gillette Lemaitre, who referred to her as, "The Surgeon."

"The reporter?" Karen asked.

"Yes. I won't bore you with the details because I know you're in a hurry, but we need him neutralized."

"I don't need the particulars," Karen said, again looking over her shoulder to the wriggling kids in the Suburban. "When?"

"Tomorrow."

"Tomorrow?" Karen protested. "My son's last game of the season is tomorrow. My parents are flying in from North Carolina."

"Mom!" Nelson called out from the car.

"I'm coming, darling," Karen called back.

"I apologize for the short notice, but I'm afraid it's unavoidable," Lazarus pressed on. "The jet will be waiting for you midnight tonight and will fly you into my hanger in Long Beach. The pilot will remain at-the-ready the entire time you are on the ground and fly out of the city the moment you step back onto the plane. You'll be back home in plenty of time to catch the game and to have dinner with your parents."

"Any preference on how it's done?"

"I'll leave that up to you. No need for anything fancy. I've sent you his entire file. Bank accounts, passport, sexual proclivities, his routines . . . the works. He swims in his pool every morning at exactly 6:00 a.m. He orders Chinese food every Thursday night from Yang Chow's on Sunset, and he goes to the gym on Mondays and Wednesdays after work. Take your pick. There's plenty of opportunities for you."

The line went dead.

"I'm sorry, guys," Karen said jumping back into the SUV. "Is everyone buckled in?"

"Yes, Mother!" Nelson exclaimed impatiently. "Can we go now, *please?*"

Camille stood behind the podium on the steps of city hall. The afternoon sun covered her like gold dust sprinkled from the hand of a generous God. Cameras pointed at her from every direction, feeding the image live to televisions across the city.

On this day Camille would officially announce to the millions of her adoring constituents that she had made good on her promise. Construction of the new Doberman Stadium would begin in exactly one week. Within a year, they would be able to buy Dober Dogs and garlic fries from one of the hundreds of concession stands, purchase a luxury condominium, or watch their favorite team in comfort from one of the 175,000 cushioned seats with the beautiful California sunset over the Pacific Ocean as their backdrop.

"It has been over two years in the making," she said confidently into the cluster of microphones attached to the podium. "But this day has finally come. Exactly one week from today, the city of

Los Angeles will break ground on the new state-of-the art Doberman Stadium."

Strands of her silky black hair lifted gently in time with the breeze drifting through the city. "The stadium will be built completely without the use of tax dollars. Corporate sponsors, bonds, investors, and generous benefactors have already committed 90 percent of the $1.6 billion needed to make this dream a reality."

Gideon Truman blended in, as best he could, with the sea of reporters. He was the only person in the crowd not holding a recorder, camera, notepad, or cell phone aimed at Camille. He stood with his hands in his pockets and looked up at her disapprovingly.

Camille provided only broad-stroke descriptions of the mammoth project, intentionally omitting the pesky details so as to not confuse the masses.

"Construction will be completed in exactly one year, and we've built in an incentive for the contractor, stating that for every day they complete ahead of schedule they will receive a $10,000 bonus."

The gaggle of reporters seemed anxious for her to finish so they could pepper her with questions. She pressed on with the precisely crafted speech, punctuating each line with a dazzling smile, wave of her hand, or point of her finger. Despite their eagerness to ask questions, they each silently acknowledged she was a gifted orator and extremely pleasing on the eye.

"The people of Los Angeles made this stadium a reality. It is my honor to serve as your mayor and to be a resident of one of the greatest cities in the world."

Hands in the crowd flew into the air the instant the last word escaped her lips.

"Mayor Hardaway," one aggressive reported shouted over the rest, "some people want to name the stadium after you. What do you think of that?"

"Mayor, over here!" shouted another. "How will this success factor into your decision to run for governor?"

The barrage of questions collided in the air like fireworks. Camille carefully selected which to answer and ignored those offering no political gain. Starting with, "Doberman Stadium was the name the fans chose over fifty years ago, and it will continue to be the name fifty years from now." Then, "It will have absolutely no bearing on whether I run for governor. This isn't about me. It's about baseball and the fans who love the game."

Gideon waited patiently for the frenzy of adoration to peak, and at that precise moment shouted, "Mayor Hardaway! Gideon Truman from CNN!"

The crowd fell silent in the two seconds it took for his words to register. Local newspapers and news stations, public access channels, and free weekly throwaways were small fish in the media pond, and CNN was the whale.

Camille saw Gideon for the first time. The unpleasant memory of her last interview flashed in her mind. "Yes, Gideon?" she said forcing her smile to remain in place.

"Did your husband play a role in the purchase of the land the stadium will be built on?"

The crowd fell silent.

"Absolutely none," she answered confidently. "Next question," she said, opening the floor to the group.

But Gideon was not done.

Again the crowd fell silent, sensing more was going on between Camille and Gideon than met the eye. CNN's lens was pointed squarely at Camille Hardaway during her most significant moment of glory. Ink pens stood at the ready over notepads, and recorders were lifted high above the crowd.

"Are you absolutely sure about that?" he piped up again.

The two locked eyes as if they were standing ten paces apart and preparing to fire off a blaze of bullets until only one remained standing. It was, after all, high noon, and they were in the center of town. The crowd braced themselves in case there was suddenly a need to duck and run for cover.

"I'm sorry, Mr. Truman, but today is about Doberman Stadium," Camille said with a smile. "I would be happy to answer your questions privately some other time"; then she refocused on the group. "I'm afraid that's all the time I have for questions. Thank you all for coming and have a good day."

The press conference ended as abruptly as it began. Camille disappeared behind the main doors leaving the dazed members of the media to only guess what the cryptic exchange was really about.

She rode the elevator to her office in silence with two stunned assistants. "What was that all about?" the braver of the two asked.

Camille did not respond.

She entered her office in a huff. The cell phone rang when the oak door slammed with an echoing thud.

"Hello," she snapped.

"Don't worry about it, Camille," Lazarus said. "I've already made arrangements for Gideon Truman," and the line went dead.

The room at the Bonaventure Hotel was cold and impersonal compared to the master suite in the mayor's mansion. Sheridan checked in shortly after he and Camille found themselves rolling on the floor and pounding each other's bodies in rage.

His world had imploded, and there appeared to be no way to contain the flying debris. Playa del Rey was not going to become a part of his already-substantial portfolio. His marriage to the mayor was over, and Tony . . . was no great loss.

His dignity lay in tatters on the finely woven rug in Gloria Vandercliff's mansion, and at any minute, federal agents armed with a warrant for his arrest would surely be knocking at the door. His only option was to liquidate KeyCorp assets, leave the country, buy that shack, albeit palatial, on some remote island, and wait until the statute of limitations ran out.

Could be a hell of a lot worse, he thought, reclining on the bed and tapping the iPad icons:

Sun-drenched beaches, Rum Bahama Mamas, and lobster served by a lovely island girl, or boy, depending on his appetite at the moment.

His prospects became less and less bleak the more he thought about it. *Sure, I'll miss being in the public eye. The power. I'll probably miss that the most,* he lamented. *But at least I won't have to pretend to love her anymore.*

Or was it pretend? Sheridan looked at Camille's smiling face on the front page of the *Los Angeles Times* sitting next to him on the bed. *God, she is beautiful,* he thought. *And those lips. It was like kissing a peach. Soft, luscious, and so sweet,* he grudgingly conceded. A tent began to form in the white towel around his waist. He suddenly could smell her perfume. A warmth seemed to brush across his cheek, feeling just as it did on the many times she touched his face and said, "I love you, baby." He could almost hear her saying the words as the towel continued to rise.

He did love Camille, and tonight, sitting alone on the bed in the Bonaventure Hotel, in the middle of her city, was the first time he admitted it to himself.

"Fuck!" he said out loud. "Fucking bitch. Get out of my head."

She somehow found her way into his heart undetected. Sheridan believed he was impervious to love. "Love is for the weak and simpleminded," he often said. People who rely on love for fulfillment only do so because they are too weak and afraid to go after the things in life that really matter.

Power was Sheridan's version of love. The acquisition of it was his courtship. The use of it was his form of lovemaking, and the exploitation brought him true ecstasy and bliss. But now that the source of his wealth was depleted, he surprisingly found himself still feeling love. If his philosophy on the matters of love and romance was true, then, when there was no money to be made, there should be no emotion. The only feeling that should remain was a hunger to acquire more money.

But tonight, the only hunger he felt was for the touch of Camille's hand. The only urge was to hear her voice and to bury his lips in the deep luxurious nape of her neck. Since this was now far beyond the realm of possibility, he was left with only the void her love once filled.

The earliest flight out of Los Angeles to Florida was in the morning at 5:35. Until then, his plan was to remain in the hotel room and transfer millions from seven accounts to banks in the Bahamas, Switzerland, and the Cayman Islands. There would be enough to start over, and over, and over again.

The Bank of the Bahama's Web site appeared on the screen. Sheridan entered his username, "nadirehs," and the password, "kissmyblkass."

The page opened. "Welcome back, Michael Kenigrant," were the words at the top of the screen.

He tapped the tab, "View My Statement." As he scrolled through the five-page PDF, his spirits lifted and Camille's voice slowly faded.

$4,347,825.09 Deposited via Electronic Transfer

$1,965,662.37 Deposited via Electronic Transfer

$756,813.59 Deposited via Electronic Transfer

The list seemed endless until finally the total account balance crept up from the bottom of the screen showing $187,407,389.17 in transfers from KeyCorp accounts. *I can live with that.*

In the next fifteen minutes, Sheridan transferred an additional $127 million into the three accounts. By the time the feds connected the dollar signs, he would have vanished into thin, very rich air.

Sheridan logged off after making the final transfer. Thoughts returned quickly to Camille as soon as his head rested on the pillow: her full breasts pressing against his chest, the feel of silk when her hair brushed against his cheek, the smell of her . . . the taste of her. The towel began the familiar rise. Sheridan placed his hand under the Egyptian cotton, encircled his erect penis and slowly moved his hand up and down the full length. The insides of his eyelids served as screens upon which played the epic passion he and Camille shared.

Sheridan's breaths became shallow as he continued manipulating his now fully exposed member to the sight of Camille's legs clamped tightly around his back and his hips thrusting deep inside her. Her moans inside his head made his hand move faster and faster. "I love you, Camille," he panted out loud. "Make love to me." He could see the ecstasy on her face as he moved the camera of his mind to a bird's-eye view. Her eyes looked up as she moaned, "Fuck me, Sheridan. Fuck me harder." Her face shined as if it were glowing by the soft light of a flickering candle.

Sheridan responded to Camille's intense pleas by pounding her, and his hand, with a fury. He gaped open his mouth and thrust his head back violently onto the pillow as he crossed the threshold of no return. The milky evidence of his passion, without warning, spurted onto his heaving chest. Then suddenly his body tensed. His heart began to beat at a furious rate. His eyes bulged open as he gasped for air.

Time seemed to stand still as he stared helplessly at the ceiling. A thousand memories rushed through his mind, and all included the woman he believed he never loved. The blinding flash of cameras in the lobby of city hall on the night she announced with him at her side, "We are getting married." His hand sliding a diamond ring onto her finger and the words, "I do." Whitney Houston singing "I will always love you," as they danced their first dance as man and wife. His head buried deep between her legs in the back of the limousine.

Sheridan tried to break free from the unrelenting pull of death, but there was no escaping. His body no longer belonged to him. He lay transfixed on the bed, captive to the scenes of his love, and prayed they would never end. But the fierce pounding of his heart gradually slowed to a sporadic thump, and then sputtered to a whimpering halt. He grudgingly released his hold on life, and his body went limp on the bed. The last thing he saw was Camille's candlelit face looking at him and calling his name.

***

A collective gasp was heard over the city when the morning newspaper announced the shocking news, "SHERIDAN HARDAWAY DEAD OF APPARENT HEART ATTACK."

"Sheridan Hardaway, husband of the city of Los Angeles's glamorous mayor and rumored contender for the next gubernatorial race, died suddenly yesterday. Hardaway, forty-five, was considered Mayor Camille Hardaway's closest advisor and was a major influence in her administration. 'It appears to have been cardiac arrest,' UCLA Medical Center's Doctor Luis Calbrano told Reuters."

Tony read the paper on the deck of his condo. Early-morning joggers with ponytails bobbing behind passed as he read. A whirling Zamboni swept slowly along the bike path just below the railing. Tony stopped reading and looked out over the horizon. The corners of the newspaper shook from his trembling hands. *It wasn't a heart attack,* he thought nervously. *Lazarus Hearst had something to do with it.*

Tony could feel the weight of the telephone Lazarus gave him in the pocket of his white robe. He prayed silently it would not ring. Now, more than ever, he felt his life was in danger. He hadn't had a full night's sleep since the call from

Lazarus and was never without the phone within arm's reach. It sat on the sink when he showered. It was attached to the elastic waistband of his jogging shorts, and stared up at him from the desk in his office.

He knew it was inevitable Lazarus would one day conclude he too was a liability. *It's just a matter of time until he runs out of uses for me and decides I know too much. What if he ever thinks I'm lying to him? How can I get out of this? I want my life back. I'm a dead man walking,* were the thoughts that would race through his mind in the late hours of the night when he lay staring up at the ceiling.

"Hardaway was found dead in a suite at the Bonaventure Hotel in downtown Los Angeles by hotel staff. According to hotel records, he checked in earlier that day and did not specify a checkout date."

Danny rushed into the bathroom holding the morning paper. "Gideon!" he called over the sound of the running shower. "Gideon!" he called out again. "You are *not* going to believe this!"

Torrents of water splashed onto Gideon's glistening body. He had been up until 3:00 a.m. the previous night pouring over KeyCorp documents and trolling the Internet for more information on the company. His usual 6:00 a.m. swim, a hot shower, followed by two cups of strong coffee were the only proven ways to kick-start his days.

"I'm almost done," Gideon replied through the stream. "Give me a minute."

Danny swung open the shower door and held up the newspaper. "This can't wait. Sheridan Hardaway is dead!"

Gideon froze under the flow. "What?" he asked in disbelief, and then saw the headline.

He joined Danny in the kitchen after quickly drying off and wrapping himself in a robe. A cup of coffee waited for him on the table.

Gideon read while Danny looked on with concern.

"Sheridan and Camille married shortly before being sworn in for her first term as mayor. He was born in Hawthorn, California, and attended Cal State Los Angeles with a major in business. At times, Mayor Hardaway received criticism for her seemingly overreliance on her husband's advice on city matters. He is credited with assisting her through contentious contract negotiations with the Police Union."

"It's Hezekiah all over again," Danny said. "I told you—she's the same, if not worse than Samantha Cleaveland."

"The paper says it was a heart attack," Gideon replied. "No one else was in the room with him."

"You can't think it's a coincidence that on the day you confront her at that press conference, her husband mysteriously dies? Come on, Sheridan," Danny said. "I don't care what the paper says. Camille killed him. Just like Samantha killed Hezekiah."

Despite all the facts laid out in black and white in front of him, Gideon believed Danny was absolutely correct. Camille had something to do with it. Years of investigative reporting taught him there were no such things as coincidences.

However, for Danny's comfort he contained his emotions and censored his words. Instead, he replied reassuringly, "It happens, honey. His world was collapsing around him. The pressure must have been too much for his heart. We don't know what preexisting conditions he may have had. Believe it or not," Gideon smiled, "husbands die every day, and most do it without any help from their wives."

Hattie's morning began just as thousands had before. A half slice of grapefruit sprinkled with a teaspoon of sugar, black coffee in her favorite cup and saucer, along with her Bible and the morning paper at the kitchen table.

She took her first sip of coffee and dug the same teaspoon used to stir the coffee into the meat of a yellow grapefruit. Juice spurted with the removal of the first wedge. Her taste buds cringed in anticipation of the bitter morning tradition. The headline assaulted her eyes as she reached over the newspaper for the bible.

SHERIDAN HARDAWAY DEAD
OF APPARENT HEART ATTACK.

The bold font staring up from the table made her heart rate slow to a steady, reverent beat. Hattie read the first two lines without touching the folded paper, as if handling it would make the content true.

The words came as no surprise to her. *It was just a matter of time before she killed someone. I doubt he was the first, and he won't be the last,* she thought, and then said out loud, "God rest his soul."

Hattie picked up the paper and read.

"Mayor Hardaway has not yet made a public statement on the death of her husband. 'She must be devastated,' said Council President Sal Alvarez. 'He was good for her. She always seemed happy when they were together.' Mayor Hardaway is expected to issue a statement later today."

Hattie's thoughts turned from Sheridan to Danny and Gideon. She always included them in her potent daily prayers ever since the tragedy they shared. "Watch over them, Lord, and keep them out of harm's way." But the recent visions and dreams made her question the influence of her supplications. Gideon was Camille's—or whoever was working on her behalf—next target. Her dreams never lied, and they always came true. Someone else would die soon.

She tried to warn Gideon once, but he refused to believe it was true. *Maybe this will make him listen to an old lady,* she thought and replaced the paper with the leather-bound Bible as her choice of reading for the morning.

Four police officers were stationed outside the Mayor's mansion at 5:30 a.m. An army of the world's media camped across the street from the house the moment the story broke, only an hour earlier. Every light flicking on or off in the windows was captured by over a hundred cameras. The housekeeper peeking out of the living-room window caused a storm of flashes.

"There she is," someone shouted, and the mob's attention shifted in that direction. Then, "No, it's not her. Looked like a maid," caused the cameras to drop in disappointment. Death, grief, and sorrow were the perfect fodder for the corps when they involved a public figure, and especially one who looked like Camille and had her poll numbers.

Camille didn't leave her bedroom the entire morning. The call from the chief of police came at exactly 4:38 a.m.

"Mrs. Mayor, this is Police Chief Saunders. I'm afraid I have very bad news."

"What's happening? Has there been a terrorist attack?" she asked sitting upright in bed.

"No, ma'am. The city is fine. I'm very sorry to have to tell you this, but it's Sheridan. I'm afraid he was found dead this morning in a hotel room at the Bonaventure."

Chief Saunders tactfully left out the details of his hand gripping his penis and the dried semen on his chest. "He was alone. We checked the last call on his phone, and it was to United Airlines. He purchased a one-way ticket to Freeport, Bahamas, via Fort Lauderdale. I've taken the liberty of sending four police officers to your home. I suspect the media will be arriving there any minute now."

Camille said very little during the call. "How did he die?" was her first question.

"It appears to have been a heart attack. We won't know for sure until we get the coroner's report. It's a top priority, so we should have the results by this afternoon."

The chief waited for the tears, but they never came. Instead, his condolences were met with, "Is anyone from the media at the hotel now?"

"Yes, ma'am."

"Make sure they are kept in the lobby and not allowed up to the floor. I don't want footage of his body being taken out of the room on the news. Have them use a freight elevator and take him out through the basement."

"Yes, ma'am. Mrs. Mayor, you have my deepest sympathy. Is there anything I can do for you?"

"No, Chief. There's nothing anyone can do now. Thank you."

Camille was too stunned to cry so she did what came naturally. The first call was to Tony Christopoulos. "Tony, Sheridan is dead. I need you to go to the office now and contact every department head," she continued before he could speak. "No one is to speak to the media."

"Yes, ma'am," was his mortified reply.

"I need a statement for the press. The usual. Devastated, grief stricken, he will be deeply missed. Don't pour it on too thick. I want to sound brave, not weak."

Again, "Yes, ma'am," were the only words he could string together.

Her next move was to transfer the contents of the one account belonging to Sheridan she knew the password to. The balance was only $153,000, but she wanted to transfer it before the banks learned of his death and froze the account.

It was safer to be productive than to think about the bizarre role she played in her husband's death. *Or was it murder?* She quickly brushed the question from her mind and moved on to the next task.

"Scott, this is Camille. Have you closed the deal on the Playa Del Rey property?"

"Not yet, Mayor," Scott said groggily from bed. "I'm still waiting for the contract from her attorney." He hadn't seen the headline yet.

"I want that contract signed today. Bring it to my home before close of business. Is that clear?"

"I'll try, but—"

"No buts," she snapped. "Before the close of business today. Understand?"

"Yes, ma'am."

The more she moved, made decisions, and barked orders to confused staff members, the deeper the consequence of her actions burrowed into the hidden recesses of her soul. Memories of Sheridan grew faint. The glimmer in Gillette's green eyes from the glow of the candle dimmed, and the late-night flight to New Orleans faded into the clouds. In their absence, however, the white paint on the house at 1600 Pennsylvania Avenue seemed to grow brighter. All roads were leading her there, and tallying the cost would have to wait until after Inauguration Day.

Chapter 11

Three horse drawn carriages waited with coachmen at the ready in front of the mansion at 543 Rue des Bourbon. It was well past 2:00 a.m., and the country slept in ignorant bliss.

Juliette Dupree sat at the head of the dining-room table in the company of three members of her distinguished conclave. Etched glass kerosene lamps, mounted in each corner, and the quivering flames from a crystal chandelier above, cast ominous kinetic shadows over the room. President James Buchanan sat to Juliette's right and read the New Orleans Daily Picayune *out loud.*

Obituaries

"The Picayune *is sad to report the death of Louisiana Governor Jean-Luc Fantoché. Governor Fantoché collapsed on the steps of the State Capital only minutes after giving a speech which seemed to mark a softening in his*

administration's previously adamant stance against slavery in the South. Doctors attribute his sudden death to cardiovascular thrombosis. He is survived by his wife of thirty years, Morticia Gertrude Fantoché, and two children, Horace and Hortincia Fantoché. He is one of eleven children, including seven sisters.

"Fantoché was born on November 12, 1818, in Iberville Parish at Bayou Goula and died from unknown causes on August 31, 1857, at his home in New Orleans. Fantoché was the fifteenth governor of Louisiana. He was elected governor in 1852 and will be best remembered for his unwavering, and sometimes fanatical, efforts to assure that slavery is banned in all territories acquired from Mexico."

"But, Juliette," Buchanan questioned, tossing the newspaper to the center of the table, "why did you kill him? I don't understand. We agreed he would be my successor."

Amadeus looked curiously down from his perch and released a piercing "Squawk!" as if to chide the president for questioning the wisdom of Mademoiselle Juliette Dacian Adelaide Dupree.

"He served his purpose and was no longer of use to me," Juliette replied calmly.

"But the White House? Your plan? He was to sign the Proclamation."

"Yes, but he was far weaker than I anticipated. I made a mistake in judgment. He was
not meant to be president."

Solomon Goldman was to Juliette's left at
the dining-room table. "Then who shall replace
him?" he asked with a waxed handlebar mus-
tache tittering on his lip.

"You are the wealthiest investment banker
in the country," Juliette replied calmly. "Surely
you must know of a man capable of executing
our noble agenda."

Dahlia entered the room unnoticed by the
council. She carried a tray to the sideboard
holding an etched crystal decanter filled
with brandy and three snifters and filled the
rounded belly of each glass just as she had been
instructed by Juliette earlier that day. The only
sound from her was the gentle rustling of the
petticoat under her lavender silk brocade dress.
Juliette gave her a warm glance and nodded
"Merci." After she had placed a glass to the right
of each man, Dahlia exited the room as quietly
as she had entered.

"It took you two years, and I imagine countless torturous nights, to groom that buffoon,"
Solomon continued uninterrupted by the invisible servant, "and yet you made the unilateral
decision to snuff out his life like . . ." He paused

and looked at the black candle at the center
of the mantelpiece behind Juliette. He then
proceeded cautiously. "Well . . . like a candle.
My skin crawls at the thought of you being subjected to his brutish paws, all to no good end."

"I do not appreciate your tone, Monsieur
Goldman," Juliette said firmly. "Please do not
forget, you sit at this table at my behest. It is
I who decides the value of a man's life to our
cause—and that includes yours."

The fourth member at the table was the owner
of the largest newspaper and magazine chain
in the world, William Abernathy. Abernathy
created a media franchise that numbered
nearly forty papers in major American cities.
Any topic being debated in the country was
initiated by Abernathy. He, more than anyone,
created and controlled the American dialog and
influenced public opinion.

"I don't believe Solomon intended to question
your wisdom, Juliette," Abernathy interjected.
"This is simply a different course than we
agreed upon."

"Gentlemen," Juliette said with a hint of
threat, "please do not delude yourselves into
thinking that your opinions carry equal weight
as mine. They do not. You are here to do my
bidding. Do not allow me to regret my decision
or grow weary of your company."

"There is no need for threats," Abernathy *leaned forward and said. "We have no desire other than to please you. The threat of death is useless. You have cast your spell upon each of us, and, I am sure, countless others, under which we are gladly your slaves. We know resistance is futile and acquiescence is bliss. Our choice, of freewill and with great pleasure, is bliss. The bliss we only feel in your presence. The joy your smile brings when your wishes are manifest. The hypnotic sparkle in your jade eyes."*

"He speaks for all of us," Solomon *said humbly. "And also, I am confident, for those of The Committee who are not present tonight. I know of no greater happiness than to be in your presence. I would plead for death by your candle if you were to deny me your company."*

She was unimpressed by the current of praise and pledges of undying loyalty flowing across the table.

The influence of her beauty was undeniable. She was an exquisite free woman of color, une femme libre de la couleur. *A beauty that required no validation, coupled with the power to control a man's destiny and possess his soul, laid the world at her feet. Her true power originated generations earlier and now rested on the mantel behind her—the black candle that held life and death within the crackle of its flame.*

"Now let us put the question of loyalty behind us and never revisit it again," Juliette said to the relief of the anxious men. They were pleased to have successfully reassured her of their loyalty, and Juliette was eager to move on to the more pressing matter at hand. "Tell me who shall be the sixteenth president and abolish slavery?"

Moments of silence enveloped the room. Then Solomon spoke. "Should we consider again the congressman from Illinois? His name escapes me."

"Lincoln," Buchanan answered. "Abraham Lincoln."

"Yes, yes. Congressman Lincoln," Solomon said.

"He has no formal education and has lost numerous campaigns in the past," observed Abernathy. "Many believe he could never be president. The fear in the Republican leadership is voters would not respond to him favorably because of his off-putting and awkward manner."

"The voters will respond favorably to whomever we tell them to," was Juliette's dismissive reply. "More importantly, is he already inclined to support our agenda?"

"He owns many slaves," Buchanan said. *"But he has spoken publically on numerous occasions of his moral, legal, and economic opposition to slavery."*

"That is a very good start," Juliette said optimistically. "Très bon effet. *Bring him to me. I want to speak with the congressman face to face."*

The jet lifted off from Manassa Airfield at exactly 12:05 a.m. en route to Long Beach California. Karen Peters sat alone in the softly lit cabin. The gentle hum of the engine helped wash away thoughts of soccer games, visiting parents, and the three dozen cupcakes she promised to make the next day for her daughter's class bake sale.

The higher the plane flew the easier it became to focus on the task at hand. Her life in Fairfax Station slowly faded under the clouds. No luggage was required for this trip. She only carried a laptop and the black leather case at her feet. Nothing could link the woman on the plane to Karen Peters, wife of Simeon Peters and mother of Nelson and Winnie. At 41,000 feet, she was The Surgeon.

The internal cabin door opened and Angel appeared in the threshold. "Good evening," she said avoiding eye contact.

Her instructions were clear: "Do not engage the passenger in conversation unless she speaks to you first. Avoid eye contact. Serve Moroccan Mint Tea, a wedge of lemon, and exit the cabin immediately. Do not return unless you are called."

Karen did not respond and looked out the window into the black void as Angel placed the tea and lemon on the table next to her seat. Karen was skilled at minimizing collateral damage. Eye contact lasting one second too long could cost the alabaster flight attendant her life.

Angel suppressed the urge to ask, "Is there anything else I can get for you?" or point to the exits, "Here, here, and there," but instead, quickly locked the cabin door behind her and prayed the passenger cloaked in secrecy would not require her services the rest of the flight.

Karen studied the laptop screen.

Target: Gideon Stanley Truman
Age: 46
Marital Status: Single

Gideon Truman's life was distilled to fifty-three glowing pages on the screen. The Committee took an interest in Gideon long before Camille landed on his radar. He was the up-and-coming black reporter who worked for one of Lazarus's holdings and would undoubtedly be of use to The Committee in the future.

The screen reflected in Karen's glasses as she studied the detailed dossier.

Swims in home pool; Hollywood Hills Monday through Friday, 6:00 a.m.

Leaves for work Monday through Friday at exactly 7:30 a.m.

Works out at Equinox Fitness in West Hollywood, California, Monday and Wednesday.

Allergic to MSG and dairy products.

Sexual Orientation: Homosexual. Note: Presents as a heterosexual.

This last bit of intel was accompanied by a series of pictures of Gideon with exquisite women on his arm and one picture of him and Danny locked in a passionate poolside kiss.

Karen continued reading. "Currently living with Danny St. John, age thirty. St. John is the former lover of Pastor Hezekiah Cleaveland whose assassination was arranged by his wife, Pastor Samantha Cleaveland. Samantha Cleaveland has never been connected to the murder by authorities. Samantha Cleaveland was killed by a lethal dose of digitalis glycoside (commonly found in the foxglove plant) administered by Mrs. Hattie Williams, 12120 Bremerton Way."

A picture of Hattie Williams wearing a white Sunday hat and a wooden cane resting at her knee appeared next on the screen.

She doesn't look like a killer, Karen mused silently. *But I suppose neither do I.*

The level of detail and intrusion amazed Karen every time she read a file compiled by The Committee. Fingerprints, birth certificates, passports, arrest records, financial history, Social Security Numbers, medical records, dental records, family members . . . The list was exhaustive. If they wanted you to disappear, it could be done with the tap of one key. Your mother would have never given birth to you. College degrees earned from sweat, blood, and late-night study sessions would cease to exist. Dental records would vanish.

Or . . . Millions of dollars in Colombian drug money could appear in a bank account you never knew you had, and the Department of Homeland Security would receive an anonymous tip you were using the funds to promote global terrorism and finance bombings in Israel, Madrid, and the United States. The Committee had infinite resources and limitless options for wreaking havoc in the lives of their targets.

Karen used the next three hours to map out the quickest strategy for accessing and eliminating Gideon Truman. After all, she did have three dozen cupcakes to bake later that day.

It was 3:30 a.m. The citizens slept as the world changed around them.

"I will never understand why you choose to live here," Lazarus said looking disapprovingly around the shabby little room. "You have a villa in Tuscany, an estate in Carmel, and that lovely mansion in Virginia where I saw you last."

Lazarus sat on the sofa directly across from Gillette who was comfortable in the wingback chair with fraying fabric where her arms rested. Louis released the occasional shriek that reverberated from the floral-papered walls, bounced off the hardwood floors, and back again to its winged source.

"Because it suits my purposes for now," Gillette said. "I want to be close to Camille. She needs me. We are at a delicate phase of her grooming, and this home is the perfect setting."

"By the way, you handled Sheridan beautifully. My compliments. Heart attack by masturbation," he smiled. "So devilishly wicked."

"We have Camille to thank for that clever little twist," Gillette said reaching for a cup of chamomile tea on the table next to her. "It was she who lit the candle, and however she imagined him at that moment dictated the way he would meet his fate. She obviously wanted him to go out with a smile on his face and thinking of her. The candle doesn't do anything we don't instruct it to do. It merely reflects our desires, gives them substance, and converts them into reality."

"Nonetheless, it was worthy of Shakespeare himself."

"What did you do with the KeyCorp assets?" Gillette asked.

"All connections to Sheridan have been purged and the holdings were distributed between seven different Committee-run corporations around the world. If the government ever decides to investigate any of Gideon Truman's claims, it would take them fifty years to piece together all the parts of puzzle."

"And what about his liquid assets?" Gillette asked calmly. "The file said he had millions in five different accounts."

"The night he died, he transferred just over 300 million into three offshore banks. We retrieved it all, and now it's in your Swiss account."

"Good," Gillette said. "Well done."

"Thank you," he replied humbly. "The entire cleanup took our people less than an hour. There is now no connection between Camille and KeyCorp Development. There is, however, one loose end."

"And what is that?" she asked with a modicum of concern.

"Gideon Truman. He knows about Sheridan's little side business."

"That is very unfortunate for him," Gillette replied. "How do you plan on handling Mr. Truman? We obviously can't allow that to go unaddressed."

"It's been taken care of. The Surgeon is on her way to Los Angeles as we speak."

"Good," Gillette said with a smile. "I knew I could count on you to leave no detail unattended to."

"How was Camille when you saw her last?" Lazarus asked.

"A bit shaken, but I have complete faith in her. Camille is stronger than even she realizes. After all, she is a Dupree. Power is in her blood."

"Her lineage was never more apparent to me than when I saw her standing next to Juliette's portrait at Headquarters. The resemblance is remarkable. I've sometimes wondered why your sister never told Camille about her pedigree." Lazarus commented curiously.

"That's because no one alive knows except you and me." Gillette leaned back as if she were preparing to tell a bedtime story to a child. "You see, my mother gave birth to three girls before I was born. She was only fourteen years old at the time. One was Camille's birth mother. Another was named Florence Weaver."

"Florence Weaver?" Lazarus questioned. "Why does that name sound familiar to me?"

"Florence Weaver was Samantha Cleaveland's mother."

"So Camille and Samantha are first cousins, and you are their aunt."

"Yes," Gillette said bitterly. "That is, until Samantha was killed. I had such great plans for her," Gillette said with a hint of regret. "Such a waste."

"And the third girl?" Lazarus asked.

Gillette hesitated, then answered with a slight scowl. "The third is Hattie Williams."

"Ah . . . yes, Hattie," Lazarus said in a sympathetic tone.

"The state placed the triplets into the Children's Aid Society. Mother never saw them again, and the three never knew the others existed. Camille's mother died in child-birth, and she was adopted by the couple who raised her. Lovely people. So you see, I am the only person who knows her true lineage. Camille is the heir to the candle and The Committee, and she is destined to be the most formidable of us all."

"Does she know yet?"

"No, it's too soon."

"Then when?" Lazarus asked reaching for a cup of tea on the coffee table separating them. "Now seems as good a time as any. She already knows most of our secrets."

"Most," Gillette said. "But not all. In due time."

"And what do you plan on doing about Hattie?" Lazarus asked returning to the vexing subject. "She is the one remaining person who could disrupt the entire plan."

Gillette couldn't disguise her displeasure with the topic. "Hattie killed Samantha, but I will not let her interfere with my plans for Camille," she said firmly. "My sister and I will have to sort out our relationship in a completely different realm. One in which, unfortunately for me, we are on equal footing."

Hattie sat on the edge of her bed with perspiration on her face. She reached for a loose

Kleenex on the nightstand and dabbed her brow and upper lip. It was 4:10 in the morning and sleep had been unkind.

Gideon visited her dream, but he perished in the night before she could shake the chains of sleep. She saw a dark angel flying over the city searching for Gideon. It glided silently through the night, with eyes like red stars searching the horizon for Gideon on the earth below.

The angel's slow descent resembled a bird of prey when she spotted Gideon. *"She?"* Hattie pondered in her sleep. Gideon roamed the earth unaware that at any moment his life would be snatched away.

The dark angel's velocity increased to lightning speed as she descended, causing the rapid clapping of her wings to echo in Hattie's dream. Then, with surgical precision, Gideon was violently plucked from the earth and carried away, helplessly screaming and flailing in her mighty claws, deep into the night.

I have to call him, she thought looking at the florescent green numbers on the nightstand. *Today is the day.*

"I can't let the same thing happen to him that happened to Hezekiah. I have to warn him, Lord."

It had been almost a year since Hattie saw the last vision of her beloved pastor, Hezekiah Cleaveland, in her kitchen window, beaten and killed by the equestrian of death. Only two days later, Hezekiah lay bleeding on the pulpit from gunshots to the head and chest.

She never told him, and the guilt brought her a depth of pain and remorse she never knew existed. "I should have told him," she rebuked herself on so many nights. "He would be alive today if I'd only warned him."

Hattie rummaged through the nightstand and found the business card Gideon gave her with his private cell phone number.

"Call me anytime, day or night, if you ever need me," Gideon told her. "Danny and I love you, Hattie. You are very important to us."

She picked up the telephone and dialed his number.

After four rings, Gideon answered. "Hattie," Gideon said fully alert, "are you all right?"

"No, I'm not all right," she said slowly. "Baby, I'm sorry to call you at this hour, but it's very important."

"Do you need me to take you to the hospital? I'll be right there. Give me ten—"

"No," she interrupted. "I don't need you to come here. Gideon, your life is in danger. You have to be careful."

Danny stirred in the bed next to Gideon. "Who is it?" he asked groggily.

Gideon placed his hand over the phone and mouthed, "It's Hattie."

Danny bolted upright. "What's happening? Is she all right?"

"Hattie, you sound very upset. Are you sure you don't want us to come over?"

"I know you think I'm a crazy old lady, but, son, you have to listen to me. She's going to try to kill you today."

"She? Who?"

"I don't know for sure, but it's a woman, and I think it must be Camille Hardaway."

"Camille Hardaway?" Gideon replied in disbelief. "How?"

"From the air," Hattie said, doubting the words herself as they slipped from her lips. "I know it sounds crazy, but she's going to descend from the air. Listen to me, son. Your life may depend on it."

"I am listening to you, Hattie," he said, humoring her. "I will be very careful today. I promise. Now, I think you should go back to bed and try to rest. It's almost 4:30."

"Promise me you'll be careful."

"I promise. Now get some rest. I'll check on you in the morning."

"What did she say?" Danny asked after Gideon disconnected the line.

"She had a bad dream." Gideon saw the concern in Danny's eyes and responded accordingly. "It was nothing. Just a nightmare, and it shook her up pretty good. She'll be fine. I'll go by and check on her later today."

Danny knew it wasn't the entire story. Hattie was not a hysterical old woman who cried wolf in middle of the night. She called to warn Gideon about something. He vowed to call her himself in the morning to find out exactly what had distressed her so.

The sun rose slowly from the east, casting haunting shadows on the canyon below and signaled birds to begin their morning serenade. It was 5:57 a.m. and the hills grudgingly came to life around Gideon's home. The giant "HOLLYWOOD" sign at the peak looked down on Gideon's pool in the distance and anticipated his arrival.

Steam rose from the cold, chlorinated water evaporating in the morning sun. The water rippled at the touch of Gideon's toe as he gauged the level of shock he would feel when he plunged in for his morning swim.

Gideon loved—and hated—the ritual. Loved how invigorated he felt when it was over and hated how it felt while he was thrashing in cold water. Forty laps across the length of pool was the only proven way to assure he'd be alert and ready for the world waiting for him below.

Gideon took a deep breath and dove headfirst into the water. The shock of his 98.6 degrees slicing into the 60-degree blue liquid elicited the usual response in his head of . . . *Why the fuck do I do this?*

He swam through the water on his usual path down the center of the pool. Water splashed in his wake from his arms lifting and crashing and feet flapping behind. Black Speedos clung to his waist and provided no protection from the chill. His weightless body slowly acclimated to the cold and settled into a comfortable medium between the two extremes.

On his fourth lap Gideon looked up and saw Danny standing at the edge of the pool. Gideon stopped and dog-paddled in the water. "Get in," he said through labored breaths. "The water's great."

"I think I will," Danny replied to Gideon's surprise. "Let me get my suit. I'll be right back."

Danny joined Gideon only once before on his morning swim. The shock was too much for him before his first cup of coffee, but today was different. He wanted to be close to Gideon.

Maybe it was the call from Hattie at 4:00 in the morning.

Danny returned quickly wearing his black Speedos. Gideon looked up and saw yet another reason why he loved him. *God, I love you so much,* he thought as Danny lowered his foot into the water and recoiled quickly in reaction to the cold.

Gideon had never been in love in his entire forty-six years. He purposefully didn't allow himself to get close enough to anyone and never allowed anyone to get close to him. Until meeting Danny his entire focus was on career. The gentle wounded spirit had awakened something in Gideon he didn't know existed . . . The capacity to love, nurture, and be loved.

Theirs was a quiet, knowing passion. There was no courtship. Danny moved into Gideon's home shortly after Hezekiah Cleaveland was killed. He was shaken, damaged, and afraid. Afraid he would be Samantha Cleaveland's next victim. Gideon comforted him, protected him, and reassured him he was safe in his arms.

As the weeks went by the bond they shared transformed into a deep and comforting love. Danny needed Gideon, and now Gideon needed him. He needed to love someone, to protect them from the cruelty the world so indiscriminately

meted out to the just and unjust alike. He could
see himself in Danny's eyes. He could feel his
own warmth in Danny's embrace. For the first
time, Gideon existed beyond the one-dimen-
sional television screen and outside the reach of
the cameras. He was alive for the first time, and
it was only because Danny made it so.

"You have to jump in," Gideon said laughing
while treading water at the center of the pool.
"Get the shock over all at once."

Danny flashed a distressed smile, took a deep
breath, and plunged feet-first into the water.

Karen Peters lifted the briefcase above her
head and tossed it gently onto the curve of the
first forty-five foot "O" in the "HOLLYWOOD" sign.
Wearing all black, gloves, combat boots, jeans,
and a turtleneck, she raised her hands and with
little effort hoisted her five-feet-six-inch body
onto the curve in white metal.

Los Angeles was at her feet. She looked out
and saw signs the city was slowly coming to life.
Buses rolled along empty streets. Lights slowly
blinked off along the roads, and in the cluster
of downtown high-rises encased in a halo of fog
in the far distance. The first smattering of
morning commuters made their way along the
maze of freeways. There was an unobstructed
360-degree view of the entire metropolitan

area from the San Fernando Valley to the hills of Palos Verdes and East Los Angeles to Santa Monica and to the ocean beyond.

Karen knelt down onto the curved surface and scanned the immediate surroundings. She was completely alone, apart from a squirrel scampering on the ground nearby. The only sound heard was the gentle breeze in the grass six feet below. She reached up, tightened the black Scrunchie holding her ponytail neatly in place, and then unsnapped the locks on the briefcase.

Gideon and Danny swam in opposite directions and passed each other at the center of the pool. Synchronized splashes cascaded up as Danny matched Gideon stroke for stroke. Gideon was pleased to share this time with Danny. Anytime they were together he was a very happy and content man.

Suddenly they heard Gideon's cell phone ring in the kitchen through the open French doors. Gideon swam quickly to the edge and lifted himself from the water.

"I better answer it," he said walking to the house. "It could be Hattie."

Danny treaded water and watched Gideon disappear through the doors. Minutes passed and Gideon had not returned. *I hope she's all right,* he thought. *I'd better go by this morning and check on her*. He then resumed his trek across the length of the pool.

Karen removed the butt of an American-made Knights SR-25 rifle from the case. She nimbly attached the barrel and telescope and inserted the twenty-round magazine. Each click of metal against metal echoed off the canyon walls below. Once assembled, she set the rifle at her feet and removed binoculars from the case.

Gideon's house was in her sights within seconds. She recognized the Spanish terra-cotta tiled roof and footprint from the satellite images supplied by Lazarus. Karen saw Gideon in the pool and swiftly calculated the target was one and eight-tenths kilometers away.

"Perfect," she whispered, "I like a man with regular habits. Thank you, Mr. Truman, for making this easy for me."

"Hattie," Gideon said answering the phone standing at the kitchen table, "I was going to call you in a few minutes. How did you sleep the rest of the night?"

"I didn't sleep," she said calmly.

Gideon could hear the scratchy tones of gospel music from the old radio in Hattie's kitchen. "We were worried about you last night."

"Don't leave the house today, Gideon. If you have to get out, then you and Danny should come to my home. I'll cook for you. It isn't safe for you today."

"Hattie, I have to go to work, darling," he said basking in her love and concern. "I'm interviewing the vice president today."

Hattie was silent.

"Hattie," Gideon said responding to her obvious concern, "I assure you I'm going to be fine. How about this, right after the interview, Danny and I will come over and we can have dinner together?"

Still no response.

"Hattie, darling, are you there?"

"I'm here. After the interview come straight here. At least I know you and Danny will be safe if you're here."

"I will. I promise, now stop worrying. I'll be fine."

Karen lifted the rifle to her cheek and secured the butt snuggly against her shoulder. She positioned a black-gloved finger on the trigger and looked through the scope.

Her target swam away from her toward the house.

"One," she counted out loud.

Karen placed one knee on the white metal "O" and her elbow held the rifle steady on the other.

"Two."

The telescope keyed on the swimming figure. She moved the barrel until the back of his head appeared in the exact center of the opaque bull's-eye. Water rushed over him as he glided an inch below the surface.

"Three."

Karen squeezed the trigger. A puff of air jetted from the barrel as the bullet launched and began the three-quarter mile journey from her hand to the target. A millisecond before impact Danny suddenly dipped below the water's surface. In exactly two and a half seconds the figure bobbed to the surface. She couldn't tell where the bullet impact had been but knew she hit her mark from the ring of red forming around the still body.

Karen watched him closely for ten seconds through the lens. There was no movement, and the red slowly spread with the ripples to the edges of the pool. The kill was confirmed. She quickly disassembled the weapon and placed it piece by piece, along with the binoculars, back into their appointed places in the case. She jumped from the "O," case in hand, ran down the hill, and vanished into the wooded canyon.

"It was Hattie," Gideon said as he exited the kitchen. "She's still a bit shaken up from her dream last night. I told her we . . ."

Gideon first saw the red. It took four seconds for the scene to fully register.

"Danny!" he called out racing to the edge of the pool and diving in. "Danny!"

With the limp body in tow, he paddled to the shallow end of the pool and lifted Danny in his arms. His legs flailed as Gideon carried him quickly up the stairs and laid him on the cement. They each glimmered from water. Blood flowed onto the cement.

"Danny!" he cried, cradling the man he loved in his arms. "Oh, God, please don't let him die."

The UCLA Level I Trauma Center pulsed with the city's latest batch of victims. The mournful cries of sirens provided the soundtrack for births, deaths, and every imaginable malady in-between.

Gideon Truman bolted from a chair in the waiting room when the Emergency Room doctor approached. "Are you Mr. Truman?" the doctor asked. "Gideon Truman?"

"Yes," Gideon answered anxiously.

Earlier that morning Gideon had ridden in the ambulance as it raced up Sunset Boulevard, and watched helplessly as paramedics worked to stop the flow of blood. Hours had since passed without any word on the condition of the man he loved.

"Good morning, Mr. Truman. I'm Dr. Banks. Mr. Danny St. John has you listed on his medical directive as his next of kin. Is that correct?" he asked, referring to a medical chart.

A blood-smeared accident survivor rolled by on a gurney surrounded by a team of doctors and nurses working frantically to bring the man back from the brink of death as they spoke. "Forty-one-year-old male," a paramedic shouted to the medical crew. "Found on the side of a cliff on Pacific Coast Highway. Had to use a helicopter to airlift him back up to the highway. Broken right and left femurs, hip, and both arms. Possible spinal injury." The life-and-death exchange faded into insignificance as the crew raced by.

"Yes, that is correct," Gideon answered the doctor while bracing himself for the worst possible news.

"Are you his brother?" the doctor asked matter-of-factly.

"No," Gideon said, brushing aside all concerns about revealing the true nature of their relationship. "No, I'm his lover," he answered blindly tossing fear to the wind. "Is he alive? Please, God, tell me he's alive."

"Yes, sir, he is alive," the doctor said removing a scrub cap ringed with perspiration. "He's being moved from surgery now to the Intensive Care Unit."

Gideon dropped his head into his hands and wept. "Thank God. That bullet was meant for me. I wouldn't have been able to live with myself if he had . . . Whoever did this thought it was me in the pool. This is all my fault. I was supposed to protect him."

"If the bullet had entered half an inch higher it would have damaged the part of the brain called the medulla oblongata located in the brainstem here," the doctor said reaching over his shoulder pointing to a spot at the base of his skull. "The medulla connects the brain to the spinal cord and regulates autonomic functions like the heart rate, respiratory rhythm, swallowing, coughing, and sneezing. Half an inch lower, he would have been permanently paralyzed and . . . well, we would be having a very different conversation right now."

Gideon's brain reduced the doctor's words to an indecipherable buzz after hearing, "Yes, he is alive." The doctor's mouth moved, but Gideon struggled to process the words. "He's alive" pounded in his skull like a clapper against the walls of a brass bell.

"He lost a lot of blood, so he'll be very weak for a few weeks," the doctor continued, after noticing the streaks of red on Gideon's shirt. "Mr. St. John is AB negative which is a somewhat rare blood type, but fortunately, we were able to find a match. We removed the bullet but there will be a permanent scar just under the hairline."

"Will there be any permanent damage?" Gideon asked, wiping his moist cheek with a trembling hand. "Have his speech or motor skills been affected?"

"The bullet entered in such a way that we were able to remove it without damaging any of the surrounding tissue. Mr. St. John is a very lucky man. There doesn't appear to be any permanent damage at this point, but we'll have to wait to see the extent of his injury."

"When can I see him?"

"I'll have a nurse take you to him as soon as he's settled in ICU."

"Thank you," Gideon said with relief. "This has been a nightmare."

"I understand. Now if you'll wait here, I'll tell the nurse to come for you when he's ready."

As the doctor turned to walk away Gideon called out, "Thank you, again, Dr. Banks. Thank you for saving Danny's life."

The doctor responded with a slight smile over his shoulder and disappeared into the maze of corridors.

"Mr. Truman," came a commanding voice from behind Gideon. "I'm Detective Guthrie, Los Angeles Police Department. May I have a few words with you?"

Gideon turned quickly and was standing eye to eye with a police identification card and a pair of blue eyes peering over the leather wallet.

"I know this is a difficult time for you, Mr. Truman. I promise to only take a few minutes."

"Of course," Gideon said struggling to transition from medical to law enforcement.

"Would you like to sit down, Mr. Truman?" the detective asked pointing to two chairs in the waiting room.

"Sir, can you please tell me what happened this morning in your backyard?" the detective asked with his pen poised over a small spiral notepad.

Gideon rubbed his eyes as if he was trying to activate his memory. "It was a few minutes after 6:00. I was in the pool. I swim every morning at 6:00. I had been in for about two or three minutes before Danny came out on the deck. He never swims with me . . . well, almost never. I asked him to join me and . . ." Gideon's voice faded as the role he played in Danny's near death pressed down on his chest.

"Take your time, Mr. Truman, and try to remember everything. It's very important."

"I told him he should get in with me. He agreed and said he had to change into his swimsuit. A few minutes passed and I swam a few more lengths of the pool. Then he came back out, put his toe into the water and commented on how cold it was. I told him to jump in to get the shock over quickly."

The detective continued scribbling unintelligible notes on the pad. "And then?"

"Well, then," Gideon paused again and took a deep breath. "Then he jumped in and started swimming in the opposite direction. We passed each other a few times at the center of the pool. Then my phone rang. It was in the kitchen on the island. I had to take it because a friend of ours called earlier that morning, about 4:00 a.m., and I thought it might have been her."

"And who was that friend?" the detective asked looking up from the pad.

"Hattie. Hattie Williams. She had a vis . . . nightmare and was upset."

"Thank you, sir. Go on."

"I got out of the pool and answered the phone."

"And was it Miss Williams?"

"Yes, as a matter of fact, it was," Gideon answered cautiously. "But she doesn't have anything to do with this."

"I'm sure she doesn't, sir. Just wanted to know who was on the call. Is it normal for Ms. Williams to call you at that hour of the morning?"

"No. She had a difficult night. Anyway, I was on the phone for no more than two or three minutes, and when I came out. I saw . . ."

The image of Danny floating facedown in the pool flashed in Gideon's mind. Ripples of red surrounded his motionless body.

"Would you like some water, Mr. Truman?"

"No," Gideon said brushing the picture from his mind. "I'll be fine. I jumped in and swam to him. He was unresponsive when I lifted his head from the water. I pulled him to the shallow end, carried him up the stairs, and laid him on the deck. I could see he was still breathing. I held him for a few seconds and ran back inside to my phone and called 911. The paramedics arrived in less than five minutes."

"Did you hear or see anything unusual on or around your property before or after you got out of the pool?"

"No."

"Do you have any idea who might have wanted to harm Mr. St. John?"

"No. The only person who would have wanted to hurt Danny is dead."

"And who is that, Mr. Truman?" the officer asked suspiciously.

"It's not important. I shouldn't have brought it up. Besides, I don't believe Danny was the intended target. It was me they were trying to kill."

Detective Guthrie looked up again. "You believe they were trying to kill you? Why?"

"Do you know who I am, detective?"

"Yes, sir, I do. I'm very familiar with your work, and so is the mayor," the detective said as if divulging a secret. "She is very concerned and instructed the police chief to commit every available resource to this case."

Gideon froze when he heard the words. If Hattie's premonition from the night before was correct, it was Mayor Camille Ernestine Hardaway who was behind the assassination attempt. "I'm glad to hear that," he replied, barely concealing his suspicion.

"Is there someone in particular you think might have done this?" Detective Guthrie continued.

Gideon avoided eye contact and said, "No . . . no one in particular. It could have been any one of millions of people who watch my show every night. Every word that comes out of my mouth seems to anger someone in this country."

"I suppose that narrows it down a bit," the detective said sarcastically. "It appears to have been a professional, Mr. Truman. This was not done by an amateur. The gun used was a high-powered rifle fired anywhere from a half mile to two miles away."

Gideon looked startled. "You mean a contract hit?"

"Yes, sir."

Detective Guthrie continued speaking, but Gideon could only hear Hattie's warning from the night before. *"She's going to try to kill you today,"* Hattie had said after waking from the nightmare. *"It's a woman, and I think it might be Camille Hardaway. She's going to descend from the air. Listen to me, son. Your life may depend on it."*

"If what you said earlier about you being the actual target is correct," Detective Guthrie continued, "then when they find out they shot the wrong person, I think it's reasonable to assume they will try again."

As the detective spoke, a nurse approached. "Mr. Truman," she said ignoring the officer, "Danny is in ICU now. You can see him, but only for a few minutes. Please follow me."

Gideon was eager to see Danny, and also to end the interview with Detective Guthrie. "Do you have any more questions, detective?"

"I do, but it can wait. One last thing, though, it's clear that you are in danger. I suggest you either leave the city for a while, or if you're not able to, please consider hiring private security, at least for a while."

"Thank you. I'll consider it. You know how to reach me. Please call if you have more questions."

Gideon didn't wait for a response as he followed the nurse through the waiting room and down a long corridor.

The nurse paused in front of a set of double doors at the end of the hall. "Don't be alarmed when you see him, Mr. Truman. It looks worse than he actually is. Dr. Banks is one of the best neurosurgeons in the country. Danny was very fortunate he was available. Please limit your visit to a few minutes." The nurse pushed open one of the doors and stepped aside.

Gideon was greeted with the familiar steady beep of the electrocardiogram attached to Danny's chest. The *beep . . . beep . . . beep* sliced to his core. It meant the love of his life was tittering precariously between life and death. The neon green line formed jagged peaks and valleys with each beat of his heart. Gideon's pulse fell in sync as he approached the bed.

A nurse and doctor stood at each side of the bed checking wires and IVs running from Danny's skull, arms, mouth, and chest to an orchestra of blinking, beeping, and purring machines. White gauze with remnants of blood formed a turban around his head.

The nurse and doctor gave Gideon a comforting smile and walked past him to the door. "It's very important that he not move, Mr. Truman," the nurse said. "Please don't touch him. I'll be right outside the door if you need me."

Gideon moved closer and placed his hand on the bed only a fraction of an inch away from Danny's. His breathing was labored and eyelids fluttered as if he were in the deepest state of REM sleep.

"Hello, baby," Gideon said softly. "I'm here."

Danny slowly opened his eyes when he heard the familiar voice.

"Don't move, honey. The nurse said you have to stay still."

"What happened?" Danny asked weakly.

A tear dropped from Gideon's eye. "You were shot, baby. In our pool this morning."

Danny looked puzzled. "Shot by who?"

Gideon leaned in to Danny's ear and whispered, "I don't know for sure yet, but I promise you, baby, when I find out who did this I'm going to destroy her."

Chapter 12

The funeral service for Sheridan Hardaway was held that morning at New Testament Cathedral. The 25,000-seat crystal cathedral was filled from the top row down to the front of the sanctuary. The structure was considered a jewel on the landscape of the city. Ten stories of jutting walls constructed of 500,000 rectangular panes of glass woven together by threads of steel formed a patchwork quilt of light and blue sky.

Camille sat on the front row dressed in black from the birdcage veil and waist-length Armani tortoise-button jacket and skirt to the lambskin gloves and Jimmy Choo pumps. Tony Christopoulos sat nervously to her left staring blankly ahead at the mahogany coffin. Camille asked him to sit with her. He was the only person she trusted to be at her side at a time like this.

"Sheridan liked you, Tony," she told him on the telephone the night before. "He would want you to be on the front row with me."

The voice of a baritone soloist filled the sanctuary.

"But if the storms don't cease
And the winds they keep on blowing, blowing
in my life
My soul has been anchored in the Lord."

Camille dabbed a tear at the corner of her eye. Yes, she killed him, but she did love him. She loved standing next to him at the podium on the steps of city hall. She relished the hundreds of times they appeared together on the covers of magazines and front pages of newspapers. Nevertheless, it didn't make up for the betrayal.

Her life changed in the time it took to strike the match and light the candle. She didn't shoot Sheridan or stab him in the heart, but the method was irrelevant. What mattered was she killed her husband, and, sitting somberly with the eyes of the world focused on her head, she felt a hint of remorse.

Do you or don't you want to be president? Camille silently questioned. There was no point in waiting for a response. The answer was always yes. *Then this is the price that must be paid.*

The words Gillette said on the night she lit the candle echoed in her mind. *In order to get what you want, you have to give up something you love.* Sheridan, of all people, would understand this fundamental truth. After all, he had given up her trust and love in exchange for profit.

Camille was introduced to a world of power she, and the rest of the world, never knew existed. Lazarus Hearst controlled her destiny, and Gillette controlled her soul. She decided on the morning the call came from the police chief the right decision had been made. Her husband, her soul, and her destiny were fair exchange for the office of the president of the United States. Her initial feelings were confirmed while sitting in front of the coffin. Remorse was brushed aside, and only hope for a powerful and bright future remained.

I'm sorry, darling, she said to Sheridan. *I had no other choice. If you were alive I'm sure you would understand.*

The baritone sang only for Camille.

"You see, I realize that in this life, you're gonna to be tossed

By the winds and the currents that seem so fierce."

Tony's knee bobbed up and down nervously. Camille touched his arm reassuringly and whispered, "It's going to be all right, Tony. You and I are going to be fine. Let's just get through this."

Tony found no comfort in the words. He could feel Lazarus's eyes burning a hole in the back of his head. *I doubt he's here,* he thought, *but I know he's watching.* He could feel the weight of the ever-present cell phone in his pocket. *Please don't vibrate. Not here. Not now.*

Tony couldn't help but acknowledge the very real possibility it could be him lying in a coffin next. Lazarus would no longer require his services. Camille would find out about his relationship with her dead husband or learn of his involvement with KeyCorp Development. It didn't matter which happened first. He was a dead man in all possible scenarios.

The organ chords bounced off the glass walls amplifying the already-palpable grief in the sanctuary.

The Learjet soared over the Grand Canyon. Karen rested in the plush leather seat. The Committee made her a millionaire ten times over, but her family lived on her husband's $348,000-a-year salary from the Department of Homeland Security.

Karen typed a message on a server accessed only by Lazarus Hearst and Gillette Lemaitre. "Mission accomplished," it said. "Will wait for next assignment."

The cryptic response appeared immediately on the screen. "Accomplished?"

Karen looked puzzled. She paused for a moment, then typed, "Yes, accomplished. The target has been neutralized."

Moments passed with no hint of a reply. Then the shocking words appeared. "We are very disappointed in you."

Disappointed? Karen had never seen or heard the word used in connection to anything she touched in her life. The doting mother. The attentive wife. The elegant hostess. The perfect soldier and flawless killing machine. *Disappointed?*

Karen was mystified. "Please clarify," she tapped.

At that moment the cabin door slowly opened and Angel cautiously looked out.

"Do not disturb me!" Karen snapped before Angel could take the first step. "Turn around and close the door now if you value your life."

The cabin door quickly closed. All that could be heard was the clicking of the lock and the purr of the plane engine.

There still was no reply on the screen. "Again, please explain," she implored with a flash of fingers across the keyboard.

The notion of failure had still not entered her mind. The concept was too foreign for her to grasp.

Then the words appeared.

"GT is alive. Wrong target hit."

The green letters on the glowing screen hit her between the eyes as if they were fired from her own custom-made Glock at close range. She blinked to adjust her eyes. *It must be the lights in here,* she thought as she reread the words.

"GT is alive. Wrong target hit."

Karen's hands began to shake as she raised them over the keyboard. The only response she could form was, "Not possible. The kill was confirmed."

The reply came quickly.

"Report from LAPD source is Danny St. John was the victim, and he is still alive as well. Return to your cover immediately and await further instructions. Conversation is over." The screen went black at the moment her cell phone rang. She closed the laptop and picked up her phone from the table.

"Mommy?"

"Hello, honey," she said barely containing her trembling vocal chords. "I'll be home a few—"

"The game is in three hours. Is Consuelo taking me?" Nelson interjected with a hint of irritation.

"No, I'll be home long before then."

"Good. She doesn't understand the game very well."

"How was school today?" she asked, teetering precariously between loving mother and cold-blooded killer. "I'm sorry I wasn't there to take you this morning."

"That's okay. Consuela took us."

"Where is Winnie?"

"She's in the solarium doing her homework."

Karen loved the thrill of the hunt, the kill, the weight of the rifle on her shoulder, the smell of a recently fired weapon. But the rush was always tempered by the guilt of missing even a single moment of her children's lives. She ached at the thought of Winnie sitting alone in the solarium doing her homework and Nelson worrying Mommy wouldn't make his soccer match.

"Tell Winnie I'll be home soon and we'll bake her cupcakes for school after your game. I love you. Make sure you're ready when I get there. And remember, nana and pawpaw are coming to visit tonight, so please make sure your room is clean."

"I will," Nelson grumbled.

"I love you, honey," Karen said.

"I love you too, Mommy."

***

The song caused tears to flow from almost everyone in the auditorium during the funeral service. No one was immune to the sorrow of the grieving, beautiful widow.

Lazarus sat quietly in an office on the second floor of Headquarters. A cigarette burned in an ashtray on the desk. He watched the mahogany coffin on an eighty-inch monitor mounted across the room.

"Camille looks lovely," came the voice of Isadore Montgomery from sources unknown. "Love the birdcage veil. Nice touch."

"Always the fashion critique," Lazarus said with a smile.

"Is this the work of The Surgeon?" asked Robert Irvin, the second disembodied voice in the room.

"No. Looks like it, but it wasn't."

"Then who? Have you hired another assassin?" Isadore asked.

"No. Gillette and Camille handled this one."

"Camille?" Robert responded with surprise. "How?"

"The candle."

"Excellent," Isadore said. "She belongs to us."

"There is no doubt she'll be president," Robert interjected.

"No, boys. There is no doubt now," was Lazarus's definitive reply.

Camille gracefully dabbed another tear she managed to squeeze free.

Hattie fell to her knees on the kitchen floor, the wind sucked from her lungs. A bolt of pain shot up her leg on impact.

"No!" she cried out. "No, Lord, not again."

She saw the dark angel in the window above her sink. Its wings clapped in victory as it burst into the air from the depths of a turbulent sea. It soared high over the city and disappeared from Hattie's sight into the clouds.

"It's her," Hattie gasped. "I know it's her."

Hattie struggled to her feet and made her way to the telephone hanging on the wall. She furiously dialed Gideon's number. The phone rang three times before greeting her with, "This is Gideon Truman. Please leave a message."

Hattie pressed the button hard and dialed again.

"This is Gideon Truman. Please leave a message."

"Gideon, this is Hattie," she said still breathless. "Call me, baby. I need to hear your voice."

Hattie walked slowly to the kitchen table and collapsed into the plastic upholstered chair. She placed a hand on the Bible and opened it. The thin, translucent pages flapped open and fell randomly to Revelation 13.

She read in horror. *"And I stood upon the sand of the sea, and saw a beast rise up out of the sea, having seven heads and ten horns, and upon his horns ten crowns, and upon his heads the name of blasphemy."*

Hattie clasped her mouth with a trembling hand and prayed out loud, "Give me strength, Lord, to stop this evil."

It was a postcard-perfect Southern California day. The sun reflected off the glassy surface of the Pacific Ocean and covered Dober Stadium in a warm embrace. Snowy white seagulls pirouetted and danced in uniform as if their synchronized maneuvers were choreographed especially for the momentous occasion.

It was opening day at the new Dober Stadium, and every one of the 175,000 seats were filled with citizens who had waited anxiously for a year and a half to be the first to see the Dobers play in their new home. A tangible hum of chatter, laughter, and sporadic bursts of applause and cheers filled the air. Concessionaires shoveled hot dogs, salted pretzels, peanuts, and goo-covered nachos by the ton over counters to the ravenous hordes.

The arena was built in record time. It was exactly twelve months to the day since Camille plunged a gold shovel into the ground with her black Christian Louboutin pumps and declared to the world, "Doberman Stadium is officially under construction."

She now stood triumphantly in front of the feverish crowd. "This is a great day for the city of Los Angeles," her amplified voice echoed off the surrounding hills. "Thanks to all of you, our beloved Dobermans have a home that will be theirs for generations to come."

The fans leaped to their feet and burst into hoots, applause, whistles, and fist pumps in the air. Camille stood firmly behind home base. Her red Giuseppe Zanotti sneakers were the first ever to leave prints in the freshly smoothed clay. Locks of coiffed hair spilled from beneath the Doberman baseball cap she wore proudly. The only things separating her from the adoring mass were the 100,000 square feet of Bermuda grass, a cordless microphone, and the brim of the cap.

"They said it couldn't be done!" she shouted. "And we said . . ." Camille held the microphone up and pointed it to the audience who chanted in unison, "Yes, we can!"

"They said we'll never raise the enough money to build it, and we said . . ."

"Yes, we can!"

"They told us we wouldn't finish construction in time for the opening season game, and we said . . ."

"Yes, we can!"

The euphoric volley of words and recital of promises kept continued until Camille whipped the crowd into an almost uncontrollable frenzy of excitement. She was the mayor of the people, and they loved her more today than ever before.

"Without further delay," she said, "I am honored to be the very first mayor to say in this new Doberman Stadium: Let the game begin!"

Camille was consumed by an avalanche of applause. If the crowd's reaction to her words was a barometer of her popularity, she would definitely have a 100 percent approval rating on this day.

Gillette, Lazarus, Isadore, and Robert watched Camille start the game on a floor-to-ceiling monitor in the Headquarters basement in the French Quarter. It was one of the most secure rooms on the planet. The bunker was built to survive a multimegaton nuclear detonation within one nautical mile. A round acrylic conference table with a hollow center sat in the middle of the room with thirteen high-back leather chairs, one for each Committee member. Walls filled with row upon row of buttons and blinking lights, twenty-four-hour newsfeeds from all the major world news networks, CCTV monitors following the every move of heads of state and persons of interest around the globe, and other sundry gizmos and gadgets needed for the weighty task of running the county surrounded the table. The room's perimeter included three-ton Swiss-made doors, five-foot-thick walls, a six-foot-thick steel-reinforced concrete ceiling, and two escape tunnels. The extreme design provided ample assurance that only persons with the proper retina scans could enter or exit the room. The mansion aboveground on Rue de Bourbon served as a quaint and homey setting for generations of Committee members, but the 1,000-square-yard bunker ten stories belowground was clearly command center.

Four members present sat around the conference table at equal distances from each other. The only source of light in the dim room came from the massive screen and the blinking wall of buttons and lights. The darkness gave the illusion of the room having no floor and no ceiling.

"She is magnificent," Gillette said studying the life-size image of Camille tossing out the first ball in Dober Stadium on the screen.

"This is going to be a slam dunk," Lazarus echoed.

"Agreed. But, first things first. We have to make her governor," was Isadore's contribution to the exchange.

Lazarus smiled and said. "That's already been taken care of."

"Are the ballot machines programmed?" Gillette asked. "I don't want to have to deal with another Florida fuckup."

"Yes," came Lazarus's defensive response. "We got the top programmers at Apple working on them now. I assure you, the majority of votes will go to Camille."

"Have we lined up her Republican competition?" Gillette continued the direct line of questioning.

"Yes," Robert Irvin answered quickly. "Christi Wedgewood is going to be the Republican front-runner. She's the CEO of CompuCo. Never held public office and doesn't know her ass from a hole in the ground. We've convinced her she can win. Wasn't hard. The woman's ego is almost as big as her bank account."

"Excellent," Isadore said. "I know her. Camille will destroy her."

"She won't have to," Robert replied. "Christi has a shitload of skeletons in her closet, all just waiting for us to open the door and send them crashing down on her, including a lesbian lover in Puerto Rico, a husband who frequents trans-sexual prostitutes on Hollywood Boulevard, and three undocumented workers on her household payroll. We're going to start leaking the stories a few months before the general election. She'll start to unravel on her own like a cheap sweater. Camille won't have to lift a finger."

"By this time next year, Camille Ernestine Hardaway will be the governor of California and one step closer to the White House."

"Don't let her get to you," Danny said, cautiously. "Baby? Gideon, did you hear me?"

Gideon stared intently at the television screen as Camille beamed on opening day at Dober Stadium.

Danny's recovery from the gun shot had been slow and steady. Two weeks in the hospital was followed by months of Gideon doting, and waiting on him hand and foot in their Hollywood Hills sanctuary. The house was under 24 hour surveillance by a private security firm hired by the network. An armed, highly trained security guard accompanied them both whenever they left the house.

"Gideon," Danny said again, this time accompanied by a gentle hand on his shoulder. "Turn her off."

Gideon looked up lovingly at Danny who was now standing behind his chair. "I'm not going to let her get away with it. She almost took you away from me. She has to pay for that."

"You still don't know that she had anything to do with it. It's almost been a year and nothing else has happened. The only reminder is the little scar. It's over, baby, you have to let it go."

"It's not over. What happens when the network decides to stop paying for our security? We'll be sitting ducks. I'm not going to just wait for her to try it again," Gideon said, touching Danny's hand on his shoulder. "Next time we may not be so lucky,"

Hattie wiped her dining room table in concentric circles with the white cloth doused with furniture polish. She could see her reflection in the glasslike finish of the wood grain and smell the scent of Lemon Pledge that filled the room.

The words of a hymn accompanied each swipe of the rag.

"There is a fountain filled with blood drawn from Emmanuel's veins;

And sinners plunged beneath that flood lose all their guilty stains.

Lose all their guilty stains, lose all their guilty stains;

And sinners plunged beneath that flood lose all their guilty stains."

Hattie sang the words and interspersed a hum here and a whisper there.

"The dying thief rejoiced to see that fountain in his day;

And there have I, though vile as he, washed all my sins away.

Washed all my sins away, washed all my sins away;

And there have I, though vile as he, washed all my sins away."

As she completed the final arc of the last circle on the wood, she felt a rush of blood to her head. At first she assumed she had reached her daily quota of furniture wax vapor, but it quickly became apparent there was something more supernatural in the works.

Hattie's reflection in the table slowly faded and gave way to the face of a woman that she did not recognize. The face looked up directly into her eyes. Hattie sensed something familiar about the woman. An innocent, almost loving expression on the face seemed to say, "I mean you no harm," but Hattie was not so easily deceived.

Months of prayers and supplication after Danny's near death had prepared her for moments like this. She had prayed for strength to face any evil that might be placed in her path and today would be the first test of her faith. She did not back away from the table but instead, planted her feet firmly on the round Sears and Roebuck braided area rug.

"Who are you?" Hattie asked out loud.

There was no response.

"Tell me who you are," Hattie demanded.

Then she heard the words, "I am Madame Gillette Lemaitre."

Gillette Lemaitre continued with an unspoken dialogue. *I'm not your enemy,* her eyes gently conveyed. *I have no qualm with you.*

Hattie responded out loud with a firm, "I rebuke you in the name of Jesus."

This was met with a look of disappointment from Gillette. *You don't want me as an enemy. This is not your battle,* was the next unspoken message from the table came.

Hattie was undaunted. She looked defiantly at Gillette with a clear, yet unspoken, response to what she rightly perceived as a threat. *This is my battle, and I am prepared to fight.*

Gillette's face suddenly turned cold, hard and menacing. The gentleness vanished, and was replaced with hate and loathing. Hattie heard the audible words, "You have been warned."

The face in the table slowly vanished and was replaced with Hattie's own reflection in the high gloss.

She relaxed her warrior stance, took a deep breath and resumed forming circles with the rag on the table as if to wipe away any remnants of the mysterious Madame Lemaitre. The words of her hymn filled the room once again.

"Dear dying Lamb, Thy precious blood shall never lose its power

Till all the ransomed church of God be saved, to sin no more.

Be saved, to sin no more, be saved, to sin no more;

Till all the ransomed church of God be saved, to sin no more."

The tower clock in St. Louis Cathedral struck twelve just as the carriage rolled past and

turned onto Rue des Bourbon. Stars dotted the midnight sky like embers from a wildfire burning below. Rays from a full moon followed the coach as if they were anticipating an assignation that would change the course of the world forever.

A stone-faced coachman pulled the reigns and maneuvered the two steeds to a gentle halt in front of the mansion. The street fell silent as the clatter of hooves and scrape of wagon wheels against the cobblestone faded into the night.

When the horses settled, the driver climbed from the box and opened the door. Silent moments passed before the top of a stovepipe hat appeared from the cabin. Threadbare black pants and worn black boots soon followed, and the six-foot-four inch man unfolded onto the street. He stood erect and surveyed the unfamiliar surroundings.

A redwood pergola covered in wisteria arched over the brick path leading to front doors lit by flames from a gas lantern. The oak double doors swung open and Dahlia appeared in the threshold. Her petticoat rustled as she bowed her head and moved aside to make way for the lanky man. "Good evening, sir," Dahlia said humbly but with a confidence rarely seen in a Negress of her time. "Welcome to the home of Mademoiselle Juliette Dupree. She is expecting you. Please come in."

The man bowed his head in acknowledgment of Dahlia's gracious greeting, removed his top hat, and cautiously crossed the threshold. With each step, he absorbed every inch of his surroundings, searching for some clue as to where he was and why he had been summoned two days earlier from his home in Springfield, Illinois.

The telegram vibrated with urgency:

It is of the highest importance that you agree to meet with my associate Juliette Dupree of New Orleans [Stop] A train ticket awaits you at the Springfield Union Station [Stop] A private carriage will be in New Orleans to take you to Mademoiselle Dupree [Stop] The future of our country rests upon your prompt attention to this matter [Stop].

President James Buchanan Jr.

He never entertained the thought of not complying with the request. Now standing in the foyer, the intent of the meeting was no clearer than when he first received the telegram.

"May I take your hat, sir?" Dahlia asked, jarring him from his contemplation.

"No, my dear," he replied warmly. "I feel more comfortable keeping it close at hand."

"Very well, sir. If you would follow me into the parlor, Mademoiselle Dupree will be with you shortly."

Dahlia gently lifted her full bell-shaped skirt just above her ankles and led the way to the parlor. Shadows cast by quivering candles and kerosene lamps filled the grand room. The lavishly furnished home assaulted his senses.

The home was like none he'd ever seen. It was worlds away from the manure-packed tobacco and hemp fields of Kentucky and the acres and acres of billowing bales of Illinois wheat. Was it, in fact, a two-day train ride from Springfield to New Orleans, or had his mind played a trick and allowed him to be whisked across the Atlantic and deposited in a Parisian villa?

"Sir," Dahlia interrupted his thoughts again. "Sir?"

The man looked at her, startled. "I'm sorry, my dear. Did you say something?"

"Yes, sir, I said, would you like a brandy? Miss Dupree has the finest Kentucky brandy."

"No, thank you. I'll just wait for your mistress."

"Yes, sir," Dahlia responded with a bow and turned to exit the room.

"What is your name?" he called out as she reached the door.

Dahlia knew from experience when a white man took the time to ask a Negro woman her name it could only be for one of two reasons. He either wanted to punish her for some unknown offence or take advantage of her tenderness in the most ungodly manner.

"Sir?"

"Your name, girl. What is your Christian name?" he asked gently, sensing her uneasiness.

At the young age of nineteen Dahlia had seen the cruelest side of God's creation. The side that would whip her without mercy in the fields by day and rape her brutally in the bedroom at night. The inhumanity that would spit in her face, then require her to wash the face of their children. Her skin was dark as burnished leather and soft and luxurious to the touch as pure silk. Hours of toil in the smoldering Louisiana sun defied the norm and made her more beautiful with each passing day.

Dahlia looked him directly in the eye and summoned the courage acquired after a year of living in the mansion and responded, "Dahlia, sir. My name is Dahlia Louise Guillaume."

Lincoln studied her closely. "That is an appropriate name for such a beautiful flower. You are the property of Mademoiselle Dupree?"

"No, sir," she said defiantly.

"Then who? Who is your master?"

*"I am une femme libre de la couleur, sir," she
replied in flawless French.*

*"fem libra color?" he said mangling the words
with his Kentucky drawl. "What is that, pray
tell me?"*

*Dahlia looked him directly in eye and said,
"It means I have no master. I am a free woman
of color."*

*The man was unable to conceal his confusion.
A black woman—dressed in fine clothes—looking
him directly in the eye—declaring unapolo-
getically that she had no master . . . The pieces
did not fit the color paradigm of his home only
600 miles away. He looked around the room
to regain his bearing. Maybe I am in Paris, he
thought.*

*"Will there be anything else, sir?" Dahlia
said, interrupting his thoughts for the third
time is less than five minutes.*

*"No, no," he mumbled, focusing back on her.
"I will wait for Miss Dupree. Thank you."*

*Dahlia nodded her head in a silent acknowl-
edgment of the powerful impact of her words
and left the room.*

"Squawk!"

The loud screech caused him to turn abruptly.

"Squawk!" came again.

He looked to the source of the commotion in a far corner of the room. The blue and gold Macaw paced anxiously from side to side on its perch in a cage.

"Do not be rude, Amadeus. Mr. Lincoln is our guest."

The voice caused Abraham Lincoln to turn quickly back to the door.

Juliette Dacian Adelaide Dupree stood in the threshold. The sides of her pomegranate red silk brocade gown brushed the door frame as she entered. Embroidered gold flowers dotted the skirt and bodice while white lace cuffs spilled out of the sleeves and burst from the plunging neckline revealing her pillowy breasts and deep cleavage through the delicately woven lattice.

Lincoln froze when he saw the Creole beauty. Her honey-toned skin seemed to absorb every particle of light from the flickering candles. Her jade-green eyes bound his hands and feet and rendered him speechless. Loosely curled cascades of golden hair hinted of her African roots. He had never before seen such beauty, and the effect left him paralyzed in the center of the room.

Juliette approached with an extended hand. "Welcome to New Orleans, Mr. Lincoln. I am Juliette Dupree."

A glittering pear-shaped diamond on her fin-ger caught his eye as he successfully persuaded one foot to take a step forward. Lincoln wiped his hand self-consciously on his trousers for fear of contaminating the stunning creature with any remnant of Illinois dirt under his fingernails.

He removed his stovepipe hat with one hand and reached for Juliette's hand with the other. He bowed and kissed her knuckle. When he stood erect, his eyes clearly con-veyed, "Please forgive the coarseness of my lips against your delicate skin. You must be repulsed by me."

"I trust your journey was satisfactory?"

"Yes," he stammered. "The private rail car was very comfortable, and the meals served were by far the finest I have ever had."

"I am pleased to hear that," Juliette said, walking past him, causing her skirt to brush against his leg, sending a shiver up his spine.

Lincoln noticed the life-size portrait of Juliette hanging above the fireplace. The only object on the mantel was a flickering black candle cradled in the silver chalice with the inscription on the base, "Dans cette flamme brûle le destin de l'homme". In this flame burns the destiny of man.

"I imagine you must have a million questions," she turned and said in front of the fireplace. Lincoln suddenly remembered he had no idea why he was in New Orleans, this house, or in the presence of arguably the most beautiful woman he had ever seen. *"Only one question,"* he replied apologetically.

"And that is?"

"Why have you and the president summoned me here?"

Juliette knew the moment she laid eyes on Lincoln that he was the right man for the job.

"For one very simple reason, Mr. Lincoln," she responded looking him directly in the eyes. *"I have decided you will be the next President of the United States of America."*

The End

ORDER FORM
URBAN BOOKS, LLC
97 N. 18th Street
Wyandanch, NY 11798

Name (please print):_____

Address:_____

City/State:_____

Zip:_____

QTY	TITLES	PRICE

Shipping and handling-add $3.50 for 1st book, then $1.75 for each additional book.

Please send a check payable to:

Urban Books, LLC

Please allow 4-6 weeks for delivery

OKANGAN REGIONAL LIBRARY
3 3132 03808 3475